THE
MAN
WHO
LOVED
GOD

THE
MAN
WHO
LOVED
GOD

William X. Kienzle

ANDREWS AND McMEEL
A Universal Press Syndicate Company
Kansas City

ISBN 0-8362-2754-9 (hd)

CREDITS
Editor: Donna Martin
Associate Editor: Matt Lombardi

Book Design: Edward D. King
Jacket Design: George Diggs

Printing and Binding: R.R. Donnelley & Sons Co.

FOR JAVAN,
my wife and collaborator

In Memory of Charles Papke Sr.

Acknowledgments

Gratitude for technical advice to:

Louis Betanzos, Chief Financial Officer (retired), NBD Bancorp

John Bradfield, M.D.

Inspector James Grace, Director of Professional Standards, Kalamazoo Department of Public Safety

Sister Bernadelle Grimm, R.S.M., Pastoral Care Department (retired), Mercy Hospital, Detroit

Vicki Hershey, C.R.N.A., Henry Ford Hospital, Detroit

Sharon Lutz, Attorney

Michigan National Bank

    Bonnie Perugino, Branch Sales Manager

    Lynn DeVoll, Financial Service Representative

    Barbara Burrow, Customer Service Supervisor

Colleen Scholes, B.S.N., C.C.R.N., Michigan Heart and Vascular Institute

Andrea Solak, Chief of Special Operations, Wayne County Prosecutor's Office

Werner U. Spitz, M.D., Professor of Forensic Pathology, Wayne State University

Barbara Weide, Inspector, Medical Section, Detroit Police Department

Rabbi Richard Weiss, Therapist in Private Practice

With special thanks for the helpful advice of the late Richard Ridling, Inspector, Homicide Division, Detroit Police Department.

Any technical error is the author's.

THE
MAN
WHO
LOVED
GOD

One

The Past

THIS IS just the way you're built. You'll have to live with it."

Babs's mother was incredulous. In effect, the gynecologist was saying that Barbara was malformed. That couldn't be. Not *Claire Simpson's* daughter.

In every way, Barbara resembled her mother. And Mrs. Simpson was a most attractive woman: she had the spoken and unspoken testimony of her husband and four paramours.

However, Claire Simpson did not need testimonials. She was well aware of and confident in her own striking beauty.

Babs was her daughter. The child's body could not fail her. Babs was young—only twelve. Technically, she was not exactly a virgin. But that was the result of a biking accident. She had not, she attested, been sexually active.

Barbara insisted on a woman—rather than a male—gynecologist. Assured that the girl had not been sexually active, the doctor gave Barbara a routine pelvic examination, then pronounced, "This is just the way you're built. You'll have to live with it."

Claire greeted this diagnosis with deep doubt. She watched her daughter carefully for the next few months. The condition worsened. Barbara complained of pain and pelvic pressure. And her menstrual periods—which had begun only in the past year—had ceased.

Claire took her daughter to her own gynecologist. Once again, Claire explained that her daughter had not had sex.

The doctor was skeptical. He gave her a pregnancy test. It was positive.

*   *   *

There were options.

They could prepare Barbara for the birth, which, if nature ran its course, would take place in four to five weeks. The delivery on this young a female could be tricky. But far greater risks had been taken successfully. And, as the doctor noted, her pelvic structure was excellent.

If delivery proved successful, and if the baby survived, the next option was to keep the child or to place it for adoption.

Or, there was abortion.

Both delivery and "dilation and extraction" held risks. But Barbara was otherwise healthy and stood an excellent chance of surviving either birth or abortion.

All of which led to another question: to tell Barbara the truth—that she was carrying a baby—or to create a fiction?

The decision, in which the physician concurred, was to tell her there was a tumor—a growth—inside her tummy that needed to come out. The doctor would take it out and then everything would be fine.

Barbara was happy. Claire was worried. The doctor was confident.

By no means would every gynecologist have agreed to perform an abortion, particularly at this advanced stage of pregnancy. Even though, at this time, the mid-seventies, it was not against Michigan law.

There was no reason to delay and every reason to complete the procedure as soon as possible. So the operation was scheduled two days hence.

After supper and after Babs had been put to bed, Claire related the day's events to her husband: the doctor's examination, diagnosis, and recommendation. Claire anticipated no opposition or disagreement. Her husband was an absentee partner in their relationship. His business kept him on the road much of the time. However, he did not lack for sexual consolation. Claire had ample evidence of his womanizing. Though this was, in part, a rationale for her own promiscuity, Claire's extramarital behavior was disciplined compared with his. She'd had four—and no more—sexual partners. He, apparently, bedded any female who would accommodate him.

In any case, his reaction to the news was a sort of uneasy silence.

The next day, Claire brought Barbara to a teaching hospital in a far northern suburb of Detroit.

Claire stayed with her daughter through the afternoon and evening. She was there for lunch, dinner, and when they prepped Barbara for the operation. Throughout the day, Claire tried to make light of the impending procedure. "They'll get that tumor out of your tummy and you'll feel good again. Real good."

Babs tried to convince her mother that all this reassurance was doing the trick. But she could sense that something more dire was distressing her mother. Babs was good at sensing the unspoken.

But now Claire was able to at least establish a deeper bond between the two. This was leading to something. After all, Barbara *was* pregnant. Somewhere there had to be a father.

Gentle questioning, backing off, returning to the matter eventually drew out the admission that someone had been doing strange things to her.

Daddy had told her it was all right *because* he was her daddy. But she shouldn't tell Mommy or anyone else what they did when Mommy wasn't home. Barbara doubted that. She had a sixth sense. She was good at sensing things.

Claire quieted her daughter and stayed with the girl until she fell asleep.

Then Claire went home and put an end to her husband.

She ordered him from the house. She vowed a divorce. All this would be done with a minimum of scandal and notoriety—as long as he never again darkened their lives with his presence. There was no room for negotiation: this was unconditional.

His defense was no more than token. He knew it was over. He had known from the moment Claire told him about their daughter's condition.

She didn't know where he would sleep that night. But never again would it be with her or—save the mark—their daughter.

Next morning she arrived at the hospital early and never let go of Barbara's hand till they were parted at the door of the operating room.

Barbara was wheeled into a strange environment of intense light, shiny objects, lots of sheets, several people busy with work they seemed quite used to. They all wore masks. Their work seemed to draw them inexorably to her as filings to a magnet.

She thought the doctor was the same one who had examined her a couple of days ago. When he spoke she was sure; she recognized his voice. She relaxed somewhat when he spoke to her encouragingly. "How are you feeling now, Babs?"

"Okay, Doctor," she murmured. "You aren't going to put me to sleep, are you?" They had talked about this earlier. Terrified of being put to sleep, she feared that she would never again wake.

Behind his mask, the doctor seemed to smile. His eyes crinkled. "No."

They placed her feet in stirrups. An odd position for removing a growth from her stomach. A sheet was draped over her knees.

Wordlessly, they stimulated labor. A saline solution started the movement. Pitocin, to keep labor going, was delivered intravenously. They called it "pit drip." As dilation began the volume was increased.

When dilation approached four centimeters, an epidural anesthetic—Bupivicaine mixed with Sentanyl, a solution more than ten times stronger than morphine—was inserted in the spine, blocking pain from the abdomen down.

From that point on, all went smoothly. The only real problem was the baby's head: It was too large to pass through the birth canal.

The surgical team was ready. If this had been a delivery instead of an abortion, and this anomaly had arisen, at this point they would have performed a cesarean section. As it was, this baby was destined to be destroyed in any case.

So a procedure termed "collapsing the cranium" or "compressing the head" was used.

Once the head was crushed, the rest of the body emerged easily. It was over.

A nurse gathered the small body into her arms and turned to cross to the other side of the room.

In that flickering second, Barbara saw what had come from her body. With that gift that some children have, she was able to identify precisely what she saw. Every detail was etched in her mind and stored in her memory.

Everything was so well formed. The tiny hand with five stubby, perfectly curled fingers. The small, curved shoulders. But most of all, the head. Like a favorite doll that had fallen from the dresser to smash its head against the floor.

But this wasn't a doll. This was a baby who had been living inside her. Now it was dead. She didn't have to ask; the battered little head said it all.

Strange. The doll had fallen while Daddy had been doing things to her. His foot had hit the dresser and the doll had come down. Daddy was responsible for that. Daddy was responsible for this.

Mommy played a part—at least in the deception. Mommy had lied to her. Maybe she was just trying to shield her from this tragedy. But she would never again be able to trust her mother. Never.

Babs felt so alone. More alone than ever before.

Twelve was terribly early to be on one's own. But she felt strong. Extraordinarily strong for one so young. How many girls her age coming from an ostensibly stable home had been pregnant and had an abortion? None that she knew of. And, in effect, raped by her own father?

The doctor, mask dangling from his neck, appeared in her line of vision. "So, how do you feel?"

"Okay." She tried a brave smile, but it was weak. At least she was doing well holding back her tears.

"Everything went well."

She nodded.

"Just rest. We'll take you to the recovery room. Then after a little while, you'll be taken back to your room and you can see your mother. I'll go give her the good news." He left the room.

Good news? What was good about this news? Maybe that she hadn't died—at least not in the sense of physical death. Something had died in this room this morning—something in addition to the baby. Something inside Barbara.

Trust.

No one close to her could be trusted. Not her father. Not her mother. Not the doctor.

Barbara had no way of telling how long she lay in the recovery room. But after some period a cheerful attendant wheeled her to the elevator and took her to her room, where her mother, now beaming, greeted her. "I've talked to the doctor, darling. Everything is going to be fine."

Barbara fixed her eyes on her mother's. This was rare if not unique in their relationship. Claire felt a shiver.

"I *know*," Barbara said.

Claire didn't need to ask.

In that instant, Barbara resolved that, whatever else happened, she would not follow in her mother's path.

The Present

Barbara was only a little more than six weeks overdue. This afternoon, all possible doubt and hope had crumbled in the face of the lab report.

Just a couple of hours ago she'd been sitting in the leather chair in the ob/gyn's office. The doctor half stood, half sat, in front of her, one buttock on his desk, his left toe barely touching the floor. His right leg dangled in a small, lazy circle.

"I don't know whether to sympathize with you, or congratulate you, Barbara." He fiddled with his stethoscope, a habit she found irritating. "Unless you've changed your mind, I know this is not a planned pregnancy."

She stared at him stonily. Her mood grew darker by the minute. "Do I remind you of the Happy Homemaker?" She made no attempt to mask her bitterness. "Of course I didn't change my mind. I was relying on you and the modern miracles of medical science. Some miracle!"

"Now, now. I've told you over and over there aren't any miracles. Not even any sure bets . . . with the exception of total abstinence."

"Do I look like a vestal virgin?"

"That would be a loss. But seriously, we've been all over this. After I worked everything out for you, you decided on a diaphragm—which we fitted. That plus a spermicidal jelly held out the best hope for you.

"But nothing is foolproof. A diaphragm can slip, particularly if you're highly active. Jelly can miss any number of sperm. A condom can tear or perforate, or even overflow. IUDs have been known to coexist with a fetus. And you wouldn't hear of rhythm.

"The most reliable method of birth control—outside of abstinence—is the Pill. But that's contraindicated because of your diabetes.

"Okay, so you took a chance and you lost. You're not the only woman for whom birth control didn't work."

Her mood, already sullen, was deteriorating. "Something tells me that if men were the ones who got pregnant, we'd have long since found the 'miracle' of perfectly dependable birth control."

Silence.

"Barbara," he said finally, "the next logical item of business is what you want to do about this. You're early in the first trimester—"

"What's that supposed to mean?"

"I think you know as well as I . . ." The unfinished sentence hung in the air. He didn't use the "A" word.

"I suppose," she said, "you're suggesting an abortion."

"I'm not suggesting anything. What you do about this is up to you."

She stood and began to pace. "I don't know. . . . I just don't know. . . ."

"That surprises me."

"You thought I'd jump at an abortion."

"It's early enough so there would be comparatively little danger. I doubt that you have any moral or religious reservations about it. And since you haven't changed your mind, I assume you want neither a pregnancy nor a child. So . . ."

"So?"

"Why the hesitation?"

"I've got to think about it. I need more time. I've been thinking about it practically constantly ever since that missed period. But" —she shook her head—"now that I know for sure . . . well, this is a bigger decision for me than you imagine. There are too many complications. I need more time."

"Well, don't take too long. Either we have to end this pregnancy soon, or we begin preparing you to be a mother."

Two

Mother. Mother? Mother! Motherhood!

Barbara Ulrich, to this point in her life, had never associated this concept with herself. Even as a small child playing with dolls, she was not their "mother." They were things her parents had given her. Eventually, she wrecked them, as she did all her toys.

Her mother, even her father, had worried about that. They were concerned that, as an only child, Babs had no sibling to relate to. Dolls were supposed to stand in for the missing siblings.

As time went on and each dismembered doll joined the burial ground of the rest of Babs's toys, her parents acceded to her every request and demand.

They should have worried about denying her nothing.

Now, if things ran their normal course, Barbara would be a mother. Her child could not be flung into a corner and forgotten. Her baby could not be discarded when she tired of it. She could not treat her child as she had her toys.

For one thing, it was against the law.

*   *   *

It was now just a couple of hours since her doctor had dropped the bombshell. Slowly, she was assimilating all the implications of this new possible role fate had flung at her.

Barbara sat before the mirror at her dressing table. Over frilly step-ins she wore a lacy slip. It accentuated rather than obscured her body's perfect lines.

If she allowed this pregnancy to progress, her life would change. Her life would change in ways she had never planned.

She had seen grossly pregnant women. Inwardly she had laughed at their awkward, ungainly attempts at such normally simple acts as walking or sitting down or picking things up.

The alternative: an abortion. But she'd been there, done that. She remembered it all too vividly. She dreamed about it—always that little head, crushed beyond recognition. Never again.

In addition, there was that intriguing question: who was the father?

It certainly wasn't her husband. God knows how long it had been since they'd had sex together.

And yet her husband had no other woman on the side. In all candor, Barbara knew that while she might have an equal somewhere, no one could be *better* in bed than she. No, it was that other bugaboo: work. Al Ulrich had singlemindedly given himself to Adams Bank and Trust. He had risen through the ranks to branch manager.

And beyond that, Thomas A. Adams, president and chief executive officer, was about to open a new branch in one of the most dangerous locations in near northeast Detroit. Al Ulrich had not only applied for the position, he was campaigning for it. He was not playing the sycophant; Al Ulrich genuinely admired—almost worshiped—Thomas Aquinas Adams.

When she'd realized how intertwined her husband and his bank had grown, Barbara had erupted like an uncorked volcano. Her husband's reaction was to cut her out of his life as far as any intimacy was concerned.

Not that she much cared, but, as far as she knew, Al had not been, was not, sexually unfaithful to her. She knew he had near unlimited opportunity. But for whatever reason, he did not cheat.

Having completely suppressed all memory of what little she had known of her mother's affairs, the same could not be said for Babs. Thus the pertinence of the question: who indeed was the father of the child she was carrying?

There were four possible candidates: the bank's president and its three executive vice presidents. That all four worked for the same firm, indeed in the same building, was some sort of tribute to Barbara's sense of brinkmanship. Not only did she chance this volatile juggling in a tight, localized area, she was reasonably sure none of the four was aware of the other three.

Inevitably, someplace down the line, she would begin to show. At which time her husband would explode in righteous indignation. Probably there would be a divorce. Al certainly would not support her or her bastard child. She would have to lean on the real father—whoever he proved to be.

In any case, all four men were quite wealthy. Any of them ought to be able to support her and her child in a manner into which Barbara was eager to ascend.

Thus her hesitation. She didn't want the child, but she would not abort it. And she did want all that the child could extort from its father.

Barbara wasn't facile in math. But it didn't take an expert to figure that in the time frame given by the doctor, two of the four men were the more likely nominees. However, the doctor's estimate of the time of conception was an educated guess, only slightly more reliable than a weather forecast. In that elastic expansion, all four qualified.

Until this moment, Barbara had not gauged the enormity and frequency of her infidelity. To touch base, as it were, with all four suitors, and to have each believe he was her one and only indiscretion, was, she felt, an impressive feat. Not to mention that all four could qualify as father of her unborn child.

As her stream of consciousness progressed, decisions pertaining to her baby gained momentum. Supportive images flooded her mind as fully developed as Orville Redenbacher's popping product. Why stop with one father for her child? Why not try for all four?

It would be the acid test proving or disproving that none of the four knew about the other three. If each candidate thought he had no competitor in his trysts with her, then each would believe he was the father.

And then what?

Each might support the child as his own. And that would come about either voluntarily or through threats.

What was the worst-case scenario?

All of the four would learn of the others' involvement. But . . . what the hell, one of them *was* the father. Of that there was no possible doubt. And whichever one it was, Daddy would be wealthy.

She could not imagine any of them actually being willing to marry her. Fine. She had no inclination to marry any of them. Send money.

There was, of course, one major fly in this pie: Al Ulrich. Her husband would know with certainty that he was not the father. And he was not likely either to keep silent or to accept any responsibility for the child.

He would, in short, be the stumbling block. Somewhere along the way, Al would have to be dealt with. A practical deadline for handling Al would be any time from the present until she began to show.

But first to inform the paternal contenders.

She immediately ruled out use of a computer or any of the other current miracles of technology. This had to be a better-kept secret than those devices could ensure.

Not a letter. Unforeseen, unexpected, and disastrous things came about when the U.S. Postal Service was involved. An envelope could be misdelivered, or opened by the wrong person—a wife, say.

No, it would have to be a note, hand-delivered by her at tonight's party.

To celebrate the opening of the new, perilously located branch, Tom Adams was hosting a dinner party tonight in his posh riverfront apartment. Invited were his three executive vice presidents and their spouses. Also invited were Mr. and Mrs. Al Ulrich and Nancy

Groggins and husband. Either Nancy or Al was to become manager of the controversial new branch of Adams Bank.

Her plan to deliver the message by hand invested new import in the party. Till now, Barbara couldn't have cared less about the gathering. She assumed the party's purpose was to be a final sifting of the two contestants, Al and Nancy—sort of an audition to see how they handled themselves in the spotlight. It would never have occurred to her that Tom Adams might merely want to honor a couple of faithful—even courageous—employees. A statement as it were that their willingness to give of themselves was noted and appreciated.

In actuality, this indeed *was* the purpose of the party.

Hitherto it had made no difference to Barbara which applicant was chosen. Now the realization dawned that, yes, there was an element of jeopardy here. What if Al got the job? What if he were harmed? It was a charged neighborhood, fraught with peril.

What if he were killed?

She shuddered.

But . . . it would go a long way toward solving her problem.

She wondered idly if such a thing could be . . . arranged.

She dismissed the thought. One thing at a time.

There was tonight's party with its newly invested importance. And how to deliver a message to four people among a total of one host and ten guests, with no one being the wiser.

A challenge, no doubt about it. But Barbara thrived on challenges, risk, and living on the edge.

She took from her writing table four sheets of unmarked stationery. Each note would be identical. There would be no addressee, nor any signature. Just a precaution. Each prospective father would know the message came from her; she would make certain of that.

The message would be brief and to the point.

She was in the very earliest stage of pregnancy. The addressee was the father. She was not interested in marriage to the father of her only child, nor in an abortion. But something would have to be worked out. And soon. Oh, and because of the relationship—or lack of it—between Barbara and her husband, as Barbara had explained at the beginning of their affair, Al would know for certain that he was not the baby's father. Something would have to be done about Al.

That should do it.

Now for this evening's ensemble. She would be at her seductive best.

Damn the wives. Full speed ahead!

Three

FATHER ROBERT KOESLER could scarcely believe it. He was going on vacation! It had been several years since he had last indulged himself in what he now looked on as a luxury.

Two considerations contributed to this view. Clearly, one was the priest shortage.

At the start of his forty-three years as a priest, few parishes had only one priest to serve them. Thus when vacation time rolled around, it was simply a matter of filling in, of taking on a few more responsibilities, offering an additional Mass on a weekend. Besides, there were lots of religious order priests, teachers not assigned to a parish, who could fill in.

All that had changed drastically. Not only were one-priest parishes quite common now, parishes were being closed or "clustered."

Granted, it was still possible for priests to carve out some leisure time. It worked if parishioners made do with no-Mass Communion services conducted by a deacon, a nun, or a lay volunteer.

Indeed, Koesler had heard of a recent incident in a suburban Detroit parish. It was the 11 A.M. Sunday Mass with a nearly overflow congregation. The priest didn't show. So a woman who was taking theology and liturgy classes at Orchard Lake's Saints Cyril and Methodius Seminary conducted a satisfying and proper Communion service.

Afterward, one of the male parishioners, congratulating her on her performance, said to her, "They'll probably ordain you now."

"No chance," she replied.

"Why not?"

"I'm overqualified."

Most of the priests who heard this story thought it hilarious.

Koesler's second reason for not taking time off was that finding a substitute for a couple of weeks just wasn't worth the bother. Frankly, he enjoyed what he did as a priest. Leaving his work was like vacationing from a vacation.

But this time off had been handed him on a platter. Out of the blue, a priest had phoned and offered to substitute for Koesler while he got away from it all for two or three weeks.

Koesler had not sought this relief. That the offer was made so spontaneously made it seem like a gift from God. Manna in the wilderness.

With little time to plan, Koesler had selected Georgian Bay in Canada. He'd always wanted to visit that area, rich in missionary lore. Besides, one of his priest friends was stationed in a parish in that vicinity.

The visiting priest who would substitute for him was now upstairs in St. Joseph's rectory. He had arrived this very day and Father Koesler had already given him a tour of the buildings and a briefing on how things were done at old St. Joe's.

That was another new wrinkle. Before so many changes had followed the Second Vatican Council, there was little, if any, diversity in the way Mass was offered or services were conducted from one parish, or even one diocese or country, to the next.

The language was in Latin within the Latin Rite churches throughout the world. Rubrics—instructions—were identical and told the priest what tone of voice to use, what gestures to make, and where to move and when.

That was then. Now there were subtle and some not so subtle nuances from parish to parish within the same diocese.

In the 1950s and earlier, a visiting priest could walk into a sacristy, vest, and go to the altar without even a greeting to or from the pastor. Now the common question before attempting Mass in an unfamiliar parish was, "How do you do it here?"

For Father Koesler the most unusual part of this present improbable arrangement was the identity of the visiting priest. He was a member of the religious order of St. Joseph's Society of the Sacred Heart, or, more popularly, the Josephites.

The Josephites, an order small in number, were dedicated to a parish ministry for African-Americans. Possibly their most famous member was Father Phil Berrigan, who, with his Jesuit brother, Father Dan Berrigan, raised consciousness over the issues of war, injustice, and poverty.

That was the visitor's background. His name was Tully—Father Zachary Tully. And at this moment he came downstairs and stepped into Koesler's office.

"All settled in?" Koesler asked brightly.

"It didn't take long." Tully wore a black suit and clerical collar.

Koesler himself regularly dressed in clericals; he appreciated other priests in uniform. "I notice you didn't bring much with you. I hope our Michigan weather doesn't surprise you too much."

"We're just out of August," the other protested.

"It gets tricky in Michigan. After all, you're up here from Dallas."

Father Tully took a chair opposite Koesler. "That's Texas, and that probably sounds warm to a Northerner or a damnyankee. But we have our winters too. Oh, granted, not like yours," he said, anticipating Koesler's exception. "But we need our warm clothing too." He chuckled. "I remember one Christmas when we had an ice storm in Dallas. Knocked out the electricity and really threw the residents for a loop. Some of the neighborhoods didn't get the power back on for eleven days." He grinned. "Which led to the headline on the front page of one of the Dallas papers: DALLAS OFFICE OF EMERGENCY PREPAREDNESS NOT YET READY."

"Speaking of winter temperatures," Koesler said with a smile, "how about, for medicinal purposes, a drink?"

Father Tully waved the offer away. "No. Thanks much, but I'd better save myself for the party tonight."

"That's right," Koesler recalled, "you're headed for a party, aren't you? Something about a bank?"

"Adams Bank and Trust. That's what got all this going."

"Yes." Koesler warmed to the story. "How was that again?"

"Well, most of us Josephites are at least acquainted with the name Tom Adams. He's been a major league donor to our order. I've always been impressed with his generosity.

"We were set to recognize him and his charity toward us and present him with our annual St. Peter Claver Award. Then we got word that he was going to open a branch of his bank in one of the poorest sections of Detroit. Our Superior General decided to break with tradition and give him the award out of due season as it were. To make it extra special.

"So, don't ask me why, but I was chosen to present the award. That's what I'm going to do at the party tonight.

"We would've preferred a larger ceremony—maybe in the cathedral with your Cardinal Archbishop Boyle. But Mr. Adams preferred a private ceremony with some of his employees and their spouses. And we said—what else?—'Whatever you want, Mr. Adams.'"

"Yes," Koesler urged, "but how did you find out you had a prominent relative here?"

Tully settled into the chair and leaned forward. "Let's see . . . how to put this . . . ? Well, my father died some forty years ago. I was just five then, so I hardly knew or remember him. My mother and her sister raised me. My dad didn't have any religion in his life, so they told me.

"But my mother and my aunt were sort of super-Catholic. So it wasn't very unusual that pretty early on I thought of being a priest."

"That's the way it usually works," Koesler agreed. "Or at least the way it *used* to work."

"Then," Tully continued, "our parish in Baltimore was staffed by a Josephite priest. He sort of took me under his wing. And off I went to the Josephite seminary. About twenty years ago I was ordained and I've spent these years hopping around to various of our parishes. It's been a great life." Tully smiled broadly. "My aunt, when she found out I was going to Detroit—for the first time in my life—told me the story.

"It started with my parents' marriage. It was my father's second marriage, my mother's first. He was supposed to be a widower. Whenever the priest pressed Dad for documentation on his first marriage, he stalled, gave excuses, got nasty. I guess the priest decided life was too short for all this grief. So he ended up taking depositions instead of documents.

"Anyway, they were married. I was their only child. Just after Dad died, his first wife finally found us. I didn't know about all this. Only my mother and my aunt knew. And they chose not to tell me. It was mostly my mother's decision. But Aunt May went along with it.

"Another thing that fits into this picture is that my father was black and my mother, and her family, were white."

Koesler looked at his visitor more intently. Yes, Father Tully could easily pass. "Then, after all that time, why would your aunt suddenly tell you about your father's first marriage?"

"Do you mind if I stretch my legs a bit? Seems I've been sitting a long time."

Koesler smiled and nodded.

Father Tully rose and paced slowly back and forth through the large room. "See," he said finally, "my mother died about ten years ago. And Dad's first wife never told her kids about their father's second marriage—or about me. All my half brothers and sisters know about their father was that he worked in an auto factory and one day he walked out on them.

"Now I was coming back to Detroit, the home of my father. Aunt May did a little probing and found that only one of Dad's kids still lived in Detroit. We had the same name—Tully—and he was a policeman. She didn't want to take a chance on my coming across him without knowing about him—or vice versa."

"So she told you the whole story."

"All she knew. I was fascinated, of course. I couldn't wait to get in touch with my brother. So I phoned him. That was a couple of days ago."

"How did he take it?" Koesler suppressed a grin.

"He didn't believe me at first. Especially when I told him I was a priest. In fact, at that point, he hung up on me."

"And then?"

"I called him back and asked him to hear me out. I told him most of what Aunt May had told me. Some of the details must've caught his attention: he began to take me seriously."

"Did you see him before coming here to St. Joseph's?"

"There wasn't time. I'm supposed to get together with him and his wife for dinner tomorrow evening. I really can hardly wait to meet him . . . and her.

"But you know him, don't you?" He looked expectantly at Koesler. "When I told him I was looking for a parish to stay in while I'm in Detroit, he suggested this . . . St. Joseph's parish. He said it was close to police headquarters and also to their home. He said he knew you. After the way he reacted when I mentioned I was a priest, I was really surprised that he knew any local priest well enough to recommend my stay. And, by the way, once again, I am deeply grateful you invited me."

"Don't mention it. I'm getting a vacation when I'd almost forgotten what that was like." Koesler wasn't sure whether it was his imagination now that he knew the priest was Lieutenant Tully's half brother, but there was a definite resemblance. Evidently the priest had inherited his mother's coloring but some of his father's features. Koesler was sure that when the two brothers met they would be struck by the likeness. "Shouldn't you be getting ready to leave?" the always punctual Koesler asked. "We wouldn't want you to be late."

Father Tully checked his watch. "Just six o'clock. Mr. Adams asked that I not show up until seven. The party starts at eight. He wanted

to get to know me and familiarize me with the guests before they
got there.

"So I've got about an hour. Would you tell me something about
my brother? He said something about your working with him on a
few homicide cases. It didn't seem to make much sense."

"Sure, I'll fill you in. Would you like some coffee while we talk
about it?"

Tully took a moment to weigh the invitation. "That would be
great . . . if it's not too much trouble."

Koesler led the way to the kitchen. He began to heat the water
while Tully sat at the table. Father Tully didn't know what he was
in for.

Four

I DON'T BLAME YOU for being startled when your brother told you he knew me," Koesler said as he sat across the kitchen table from Father Tully. "I suppose you thought the only way Lieutenant Tully would know a priest is if the priest were in trouble with the law."

"No, nothing like that." Tully chuckled. "Just surprised. How *did* it happen?"

"Actually," Koesler explained, "my meeting with your brother took place quite a few years after I first got involved with the Detroit Police. Again"—he smiled—"not as a felon.

"I was," Koesler proceeded, "editor of the *Detroit Catholic*—the diocesan newspaper. So, with that assignment, I was pretty much out of parochial ministry—just helping out.

"I lived at a Detroit parish when there was a series of murders of priests and nuns. I happened to discover the body of the second victim—a nun. I also happened upon the killer's calling card, a plain black rosary."

Tully seemed to recollect. "Yeah . . . I remember that. Didn't the media call it 'The Rosary Murders'? Because the killer left a rosary with each body . . . wrapped around the wrist?"

"That's it. You've got a good memory; that was a long time ago.

"But through that investigation I met some people in the police department. Perhaps the closest connection was an inspector—Walter Koznicki. We've become good friends."

"Is that where my brother came in?"

"No. We didn't meet until much later. See, my contact with the police sort of grew gradually over the years. After that original investigation of the serial murders, I've been involved, to varying degrees, in a few other homicide cases. Sometimes because I happened to be around . . . or because the case involved a parishioner or two. Or just because the case hinged on a knowledge of things Catholic.

"I know," Koesler continued, "that this must sound surreal, but with one thing or another, I've been involved in a homicide investigation just about every year since then."

"You weren't Father Brown in a previous life?" Tully joked, referring to G. K. Chesterton's fictional priest-sleuth.

"Nothing of the kind. It just happened. What can I say?"

Tully glanced at the stove. "The water's boiling."

"So it is." Koesler measured instant coffee into two mugs and added the hot water. He placed the mugs on the table. "Anyway, that's how I met your brother. But it was maybe four or five years ago. And it was just such a case as I was describing: murder with a Catholic twist."

Tully blew across the surface of the coffee and took a sip. He almost shuddered. It must, he thought, be the high degree of heat.

"I think," Koesler said, sipping the coffee with no apparent ill effect, "your brother was the most skeptical of all the officers I've met in the department."

"Skeptical? How so?"

"Skeptical of me," Koesler clarified. "I can understand that any police officer might react negatively when some outsider steps in and tries to out-professional the professionals. I mean, the police are a highly skilled group. I know I'm even less than an amateur when it comes to police procedure. And I never for a moment thought I could do their work. I tried to make it clear that I was at best a resource person. But some of the officers, at least at first, objected to my presence—none more forcefully or wholeheartedly than your brother.

"But, over the years, we've come to a better understanding. I think, by now, your brother even likes to have me around when things Catholic are mucking up an investigation."

Once more Tully tried to cool the coffee with his breath. He sipped, then suppressed a grimace. He focused on the instant coffee container. It was a brand-name product—indeed, a brand he had enjoyed from time to time. Could it be the water? The kettle? The *cup?*

Whatever, this was the worst coffee he could remember. He would have to go easy on the food and drink here until he sampled each serving. "I can understand my brother's reluctance to let you in on a criminal investigation. But I'm still not clear where you fit in. What could be 'Catholic' about a murder case?"

"Hard to say," Koesler admitted. "But maybe I can give you a couple of typical cases.

"Our first go-round is as good an example as any. You mentioned that the media called it 'The Rosary Murders'—"

"And the rosary is almost exclusively a Catholic devotion," Tully interjected.

"Right. But on top of that, maybe only a priest would recognize that particular prayer as part of the penance he might give a penitent to say after confession. And indeed, that was at least part of the clue to solving those murders.

"Then there was another serial murder case where the motto on a papal coat of arms was the clue. And another when the solution depended on knowing the kind of perks a priest might enjoy on vacation. And another when a murderer equated the cards in a poker hand to various officers in the diocese. That sort of thing.

"Any clearer?"

"A little."

Koesler looked at his watch, something he was apt to do many times during the day and perhaps a couple of times through the night. "It's getting close to seven."

"So it is," Tully said as he checked his watch. "Guess I'd better get going."

"Do you have a car? You can borrow mine for the evening. I'll be busy packing."

"Thanks, but I'm renting one. It's on the order." He grinned. "The vow of poverty comes in handy every once in a while.

"Besides," he added, "Mr. Adams said he'd send a car to pick me up tonight." Tully stood and peered through the window overlooking the parking lot. "And here it is now. That is, unless you're driving a Lincoln."

Koesler chuckled. "Not a chance. I'm surprised he didn't send a stretch limo. There's a lot of that going on around here."

"Probably in deference to that vow of poverty," Tully joked.

"I won't be leaving too early tomorrow," Koesler said. "If you have any questions, we can talk about them in the morning. And of course I'll leave you my number at Georgian Bay."

Tully, on his way down the steps, looked back and smiled. "Don't worry, Father, I'll take good care of your baby. And I'll return her to you safe and sound with no heresies flourishing on your return. Trust me. After all, I'm not fresh out of the seminary. Just relax and have a good rest."

Koesler watched Tully's departure until the Town Car turned the corner and disappeared from sight. Even though the car and Tully were gone, Koesler continued to gaze out the window. He wasn't seeing what he was looking at. His mind was miles away.

He was beginning to be . . . what? . . . homesick. And he hadn't even left home yet.

What had he to be concerned about? St. Joseph's parish had existed long before he came into being. It had survived many pastors. It would survive him.

He should be confident in entrusting the parish to Father Tully. For one, Koesler long had had friends among the Josephites. He admired the order.

But Father Tully had asked too few questions when the two had toured the buildings. Then again, as Tully himself had stated, he was not a newly ordained priest, the oil of ordination still moist on his hands. He was a seasoned veteran. Surely he could administer old St. Joe's.

Besides, his brother was Alonzo Tully, a proven professional. Trustworthy and competent.

On the other hand, though the two had a common father, they had different mothers. Raised entirely differently. The priestly Tully could not be measured by his policeman brother. And if he could not be measured by what Koesler knew of his brother, what, indeed, did Koesler know about this visiting priest?

Not much.

Before the phone call, neither Koesler nor the lieutenant had been aware of Father Tully's existence. His call had taken Koesler completely by surprise—a voice volunteering to step in and make it possible for the pastor to enjoy a most rare vacation.

In the final analysis, Father Zachary Tully was a complete stranger. And in the present setup, the visitor would be completely unsupervised.

What if there were some sort of emergency? Could Tully be trusted to call Koesler if he were needed?

But most of all—and this was important—there was this pressing premonition: something was going to happen that would demand the presence of Father Koesler. He *knew* it.

Maybe he could shorten his vacation. One week would give him as much rest as two. In fact, it probably was statistically proven that after such a long hiatus in vacations, brevity in leisure was advisable. Better to get into something like that slowly, gradually.

Doing things cold turkey was not Koesler's style.

But then he laughed at himself. All this rationalization was ridiculous.

In the little time he'd had to get organized, Koesler had prepared pretty thoroughly for Father Tully's short stay at St. Joe's. The most important element of that planning had been to brief Mary O'Connor on the newcomer. Mary, longtime secretary to Father Koesler, could and would see to it that the parish functioned on all cylinders in his absence.

No matter what else happened, Mary would hold the fort.

With a lighter heart, Father Koesler began to pack.

Five

At the outset, Father Tully attempted small talk with his driver. The response was monosyllabic.

The driver's only bow toward a uniform was a pair of leather gloves. Why the hand covering? Father Tully hadn't a clue, but judging from the driver's reaction to other questions, the priest decided not to pursue it.

Riding along Jefferson at this early evening hour, Father Tully was most impressed by the emptiness of the streets.

Downtown Detroit's gigantic buildings—the Renaissance Center, the Millender Center, Cobo Hall, the Pontchartrain Hotel—all of them attested to a vibrant city. But where *was* everybody?

As it happened, they had a very short ride.

Just past Cobo Hall and beyond the Joe Louis Arena stood the Riverfront Apartments, the home of Thomas A. Adams, Father Tully's host for this evening and soon-to-be recipient of the St. Peter Claver Award.

They had to pass through two checkpoints, one to enter the garage and another for the building itself. The security system seemed quite formidable to Father Tully. He had no idea how it would have been viewed by a professional burglar.

They left the elevator at the fourteenth floor and walked a short distance down the hall. The decor, though obviously expensive, was depressing; it seemed dark and confining.

The door to the Adams apartment was opened promptly after the driver rang the doorbell. Father Tully's chauffeur preceded him, peeled off to the right, and disappeared through another doorway.

The priest assumed they would not meet again until it was time to return to the rectory.

Father Tully was ushered into an expansive living room. Off-white walls and ceiling, comfortable leather furniture, here and there a small table, art work tastefully exhibited, and a delightful vista through floor-to-ceiling windows.

The apartment complex was located at the edge of downtown Detroit. At one time, the heart of downtown had been several blocks to the north. But with the Ren Cen, Hart Plaza, and the City-County Building established close to the Detroit River, the city's heart had shifted.

He had no reason to reflect on it, but Father Tully was now at the very place where, in 1701, Antoine de la Mothe Cadillac and companions got out of their canoes and set up camp at the "straits," or in French, *détroit*.

The view from this apartment showcased Windsor, Canada—much industry, some housing, Assumption University, and the University of Windsor—Detroit's Ste. Anne's, the second-oldest parish church in the United States; and of course the dynamic river that connected—via Lake St. Clair and the St. Clair River—two of the Great Lakes: Huron and Erie.

In any case, Father Tully had little time to reflect on the topography. His host had just entered the room. Thomas A. Adams crossed directly to the priest.

Adams's open-arms carriage was amplified by his welcoming smile. Abundant snow-white hair was styled to touch his ears and collar, then graded upward. His handsome face was suntanned and heavily creased, giving it a leathery texture, highlighted by crinkly laugh lines. At several inches under six feet tall, he was about Father Tully's height, though heavier. Noting Adams's dinner jacket, the priest was again reminded that his own clerical clothing fit in anywhere, from a formal affair such as this, to the streets of the barrio.

Evidently, Adams had caught his guest's fascination with the view.

"Really something, isn't it?" he said as he took the priest's outstretched hand.

"Beats anything I've seen in Dallas."

Adams laughed heartily and patted the priest's shoulder.

Several servants bustled about, setting out hors d'oeuvre trays, decanting wine, and performing last-minute cleaning chores on already spotless surfaces. All were liveried, as was the butler who had admitted Tully and his driver to the apartment.

"What would you like to drink, Father?" Adams's gesture encompassed the array of wines as well as the credenza bearing a variety of spirits. "We've got just about everything."

Tully gazed at the display. "Yes, you surely have. Maybe a little white wine."

"Excellent." Adams turned to a waiter who materialized at his elbow, bearing a small tray of filled wineglasses. Father Tully had been unaware of any servants bending an ear in their direction. One must have been assigned to anticipate their desires.

"Would you care to sit down?"

"Mind if we stand by the window? I can't get enough of this view."

"Of course. Good idea." Adams led the way to a jutting corner that accentuated the vista. The rays of the sunset not only made the sky seem incandescent, but lent a magical mystique to the river.

The priest shifted and looked around the room.

"Is there something you want, Father?"

"Uh, not exactly. I was wondering about Mrs. Adams. . . ."

The lines on his host's face sharpened. "There is no Mrs. Adams . . . at least not for about a year now."

"I'm sorry."

"A divorce. I got an annulment."

Tully considered the statement. It wasn't "She got an annulment," or "We got an annulment." Could Tom Adams secure an annulment all on his own? Wouldn't his wife have to at least cooperate in the process? Wouldn't some priest—priests—need to do all the considerable paperwork? What might the stated cause be for the div— uh, annulment? Was this part of a key to Adams's character? He seemed so warm, so open, so congenial. Yet this was a happy occasion; what would the man be like if crossed?

Both men silently gazed out the window. At length, Tully placed his nearly empty glass on a nearby tray.

"Another one, Father?"

"No. Thank you. No more. I'd better stay alert. I'm going to make a presentation, remember: your award." Tully indicated the slender carefully wrapped package in his left hand.

"Oh yes, of course. Harry . . ." Again a servant materialized at Adams's elbow. "Take this package for Father Tully and bring it back just after all the guests arrive . . . at eight o'clock." He turned to Tully. "I think it would be good to have the presentation before dinner and before the liquor has had its effect."

Tully handed the packet over.

Adams smiled wryly. "Mickey would not enjoy seeing me get this award." Noting the priest's puzzled expression, he added, "Mickey's the ex. My works of charity were one of our principal bones of contention. Well," he said with finality, "she made fun of them one too many times.

"But"—he broke into a genuine smile—"she's not here. She'll never again be a part of my life in any way whatever.

"Now, enough of that."

Father Tully was impressed. When this guy cuts you, you're dead.

They were silent again. The sunset was highlighting the city's architecture.

"I was wondering," the priest said finally, "it must be some kind of thrill to have a bank named after you."

"That's up for grabs," Adams said. "Sort of, which came first, the chicken or the egg? In this case, which came first, the family name or a street sign?"

"Please?"

A waiter offered wine from a tray. Adams exchanged his empty glass for a filled one. Father Tully declined the offer.

Adams sipped. "You see, my father started this bank. Its first headquarters had an address on Adams Street in downtown Detroit. Dad probably would have named the bank after himself anyway. Adams Street was the clincher." He shook his head. "Dad's been gone these many years now." Abruptly, he shrugged and lightened. "I've never seen any reason to change the name. Besides, having the bank ostensibly named after my family sort of defines my job—what I do."

Lights were going on in businesses, apartments, and homes as the city prepared for nightfall. Father Tully turned from the window. "You know, I've never actually met a bank president. Would you be insulted if I ask what it is you do? I mean, the question that is guaranteed to drive most priests up the wall is, 'What do you do all day, Father? I mean, after you say Mass?' It shows that the questioner cannot imagine what could possibly occupy a priest after he slips from view at Mass. So, I don't suppose you hit the links every day before or after making an appearance at your office."

Adams chuckled. "Actually that's not far from wrong."

"It isn't?"

"Instead of saying Mass, which I'm sorry I will never be able to do, I review loans. I have to approve a loan if it's in the neighborhood of twenty-five thousand dollars and up for a business or one hundred thousand for a mortgage."

"Wow!"

"No 'wow' necessary." Adams emptied his wineglass. The ubiquitous waiter collected it immediately. Adams indicated he wanted no more.

"What you must remember, Father, is that we're a small bank. Compared with say, Comerica, very small indeed. While I'm checking on a hundred thousand, the big guys are looking at about five million.

"But that's not my main concern. My job, 'after Mass,' if you will, is to be *visible.*

"I knock on doors. Call on the local Firestone dealer. I'm looking for a moderate investment in my bank. I call on as many of the merchants in town as possible. I join the Chamber of Commerce. Lots of civic stuff. I manage to get in the Bloomfield Hills Country Club so I can meet the movers and shakers of our town—to get relatively small accounts.

"I am visible, friendly. I speak before the League of Women Voters. I'm a member of the Lions Club. I do lots of business on the golf course—"

"Excuse me," Tully interrupted, "but isn't the game of tennis where all the movers and shakers move and shake and close deals? Isn't golf too slow and time-consuming?"

"No, tennis has some action, as you suggest. But golf is still supreme.

"But I don't want to give the impression that business is confined to a few specific locations or opportunities. Lots of business is done at breakfast or lunch . . . seldom dinner.

"Why, in the morning at Kingsley Inn or even the Denny's on Telegraph Road there can be half a dozen millionaires discussing investments, loans, mortgages . . . business.

"And my job boils down to a single word: visibility."

"Wow!" Tully breathed, with genuine awe. "I can tell you, that's a busier job description than I could ever come up with. 'After Mass' you're going at warp speed."

Adams smiled and shook his head. "There's much more to it than that. Remember, I said we were a small bank. . . ."

"Yes."

"Well, Satchel Paige is supposed to have said, 'Don't look back; somebody may be gaining on you.' In the banking game, you'd better look back or somebody is going to eat you. Mergers go on all the time. You know that, Father. Comerica, for one of many examples, used to be two moderately large banking institutions. Now it's one gigantic corporation.

"It's called 'cashing out,' Father. Some small bankers get rich by selling out. Others run scared. For instance, I'm an officer in the Independent Bankers Association. We fight the big guys off to remain independent. We fight against interstate banking."

"Well, you must be doing all right. After all, you're opening a new branch. In fact that's at least part of what we're celebrating this evening, isn't it?"

"The new branch?" Adams's lips tightened. "Our mayor is ecstatic. While the banking business in general is cutting its presence in Detroit, here we go opening a new branch right in the heart of one of the roughest sections of the city. And we're getting static from some of our depositors for it. They're worried that we're taking their money on a goofy ride. There's a lot of flak on this—"

"Then . . . why?"

"Why? I suppose this sounds silly, but because it's the right thing to do. It's our chance to show these people that someone cares. Not many think it's a smart idea. . . ."

There was another period of silence. The only sound in the room was the low clatter of silverware and dishes as the staff continued its preparations. Finally, the priest spoke. "Mr. Adams, you are either unique, or very, very rare."

"I know." The statement was made in honest humility, without the slightest trace of boasting.

"I wonder," the priest said, "if there's another businessman who forms company policy on the basis of doing what is right."

"Oh, I'm sure there are lots. You just don't hear about them."

"Maybe. But in your own experience, how many do you know personally?"

"Not many," Adams admitted. "But I'm sure they're around. How could you read Scripture and not be influenced by it?"

"There are a lot of people—the majority, I fear—who listen to it most every Sunday and let it go in one ear and out the other. You really live by the Bible, don't you?"

There was a faint blush to Adams's cheeks. "Let's not go overboard. I try to live close to the Christian ideal. And I often fail. But

I want this to succeed. I want very much to have this branch set an example.

"And, while I think of it, I should tell you about the others here tonight. I've invited my three executive vice presidents and their wives. They all know each other, of course, but for your sake they'll be wearing identification tags. And there'll be two others of special interest. One is Al Ulrich, the other is Nancy Groggins."

"What's so special about them?"

"It's pretty well known throughout our banking family that these two are front-runners for managership of the new branch. Each is already a branch manager. Each is extremely capable. Both would do well in this extremely sensitive position. And, most of all, they both want the position . . . and that's something else: I doubt that management of this new branch is a high priority with many of my employees."

"Fear? Of the neighborhood?"

"To a great degree, I think yes. Some see it as a dead end—though that certainly wouldn't be the case for anyone who does a good job in this spot.

"Anyway," Adams continued, "I would appreciate your reaction and opinion. Al and Nancy are good people, but quite different from each other. See what you think."

"You haven't made up your mind yet? Isn't the opening just around the corner?"

"Later this week. And everybody figures I've already made the selection. But I haven't. I know it's not fair to ask your opinion in this major decision based on one exposure and an observance over just a few hours. But I'll tell you this: I'm leaning toward Nancy. With that in mind, see if you agree or not."

There was a stir in the vestibule as the other guests began to arrive.

"One last thing," Adams said. "I suppose you've been wondering why you were selected to come to Detroit to give me this award."

Father Tully had, indeed, wondered. It couldn't be because his brother was a police officer here; how could Adams know this when the policeman himself hadn't known it?

"I guess," Adams explained, "it would be safe to say the Josephites have been my favorite charity for a good long time."

"I wouldn't argue with that."

Adams smiled. "When I got word that I had been selected for this year's Peter Claver Award, I talked to your superior. We agreed that it would suit both our purposes to link the award with the opening of this very special branch of my bank.

"And I wanted his recommendation for an excellent representative to bestow the award. He nominated you. I checked into your background, your accomplishments, your progress, your present needs. I wholeheartedly backed his choice. And I thank you for taking part in this ceremony."

As it turns out, thought Father Tully, my selection had nothing to do with my brother. Well, that figures. I'm here because my superior suggested me as a Josephite representative and Tom Adams agreed with the selection.

"Now, Father," Adams continued, "I've been informed that you currently are in the process of building on to your church."

Tully nodded enthusiastically. "We outgrew the old building. We're doing all right raising funds. Just slow. Our people don't have much."

"I heard all about it from your superior." Adams reached into his inside jacket pocket and brought out a piece of paper. It was a check, dated, signed, and made out to the Josephite order.

Father Tully took the check, examined it, and looked up at Adams. "This check . . . it's blank."

"I'm aware of that." Adams could not suppress a pleased grin. "You see, in the corner, I've directed that it be used in your building fund."

"But . . . but it's blank! I don't know what you intend. I don't know how much you want to contribute."

"The balance. I want to finish your fund drive."

"I can tell you what that amount is."

"I know how much you need to finish the drive. But there may be incidentals that crop up. The blank check gives you a guarantee that you won't be 'surprised' by any unexpected last-minute expenditures."

Tully shook his head. "Your generosity is almost incredible. I don't know what to say. Except thanks."

"Not at all. I just took a page from the story of the Good Samaritan. I know you're familiar with that."

"Sure. About the Jew who was mugged and left for dead. People who should have helped him passed on by. But a Samaritan, who should have been his enemy, helped the Jew."

"But," Adams interrupted, "it's the next part of the story that I centered on. The Samaritan takes the Jew to an inn and gives the innkeeper some money to take care of the injured man. And the Samaritan promises that on his way back he'll stop and reimburse the innkeeper for any additional expense incurred.

"You see? The Samaritan gave the innkeeper a blank check." Adams smiled at the simplicity of his reaction to one of Jesus's most popular stories.

Father Tully regarded Adams, and thought that unless his former wife was extremely religious and generous, she would have had a decided difficulty understanding him. And so they had split.

It all came down to this: Adams loved God and expected others to do the same.

The priest recalled the simplistic question and answer of the all-but-forgotten *Baltimore Catechism*: *Why did God make you? Answer: God made me to know Him, to love Him and to serve Him in this life and to be happy with Him forever in the next.*

That, basically, appeared to be the way Thomas Aquinas Adams lived.

Six

A COMMOTION at the apartment door signaled the arrival of other guests as well as several photographers—if one could judge by the equipment they carried.

"Ladies and gentlemen," Adams called to the new arrivals, "come in. Thanks for arriving so promptly."

The photographers began checking the room's lighting and their equipment.

Adams turned to Father Tully. "Remember my telling you that my main job is to be visible? This is one of the ways I can do just that. This week our faces—but mostly mine—will appear in the newspapers. Readers may forget that I was given an award. But they'll remember that my picture was in the paper . . . *again.*

"Jack, Lou, Martin . . ." Adams called over his executive vice presidents. "Come on over and get in the photo. Al, Nancy, you come too."

As the members of the group gathered and composed themselves as part of the tableau, they introduced themselves to Father Tully. The priest was grateful for their name tags: they would jump-start his memory if the names failed him during the evening.

"Father Tully . . ." Adams's gesture indicated his three top executives. ". . . it's *mi casa, su casa.* Our homes and our offices are open to you throughout your stay here." The execs murmured assent without much enthusiasm.

There was little jockeying for position. Though everyone knew that the further one stood from the core couple, Adams and the priest, the more likely one was to be trimmed from the published

38

photo, they also knew their place in the scheme of things. The pecking order held.

The plaque was brought to Father Tully, who presented it to Adams as the cameras clicked, whirred, and flashed.

"I know you'll want this to be brief, Mr. Adams," the priest said. "Peter Claver, a Jesuit priest who lived from about 1580 to 1654, gave himself without stint to the service of African slaves. He lived and died their generous servant. In his example, Mr. Adams, you have given your time and interest. Your contribution to our work has been constant, bounteous, and, I think, even extravagant. It is with great pleasure that I present you with this award from your grateful friends, the Josephites."

A beaming Tom Adams accepted the plaque. "Of all the honors and awards I have been given, I assure you I value and prize this"—he raised the plaque slightly—"more than all of them. It shall have an honored place on my wall and in my heart—"

Another commotion at the door. A smiling, somehow feral Mrs. Al Ulrich made her entrance.

The mood was broken. With a frown, Adams quickly concluded. "Please, everyone, make yourselves at home. And on behalf of our banking family, please make our guest, Father Zachary Tully, welcome."

The photographers checked the names of those whose pictures they'd taken. One even bothered to check the spelling of Claver. They shouldered their gear and left.

Adams got the welcome wagon moving by introducing Father Tully to the others in the photo group. The priest read the name tag of each as he or she was introduced.

Actually, he didn't hold too great a hope that he would remember everyone. On the other hand, why would he have to? Outside of getting to know Tom Adams better, as well as going along with anything Adams wanted from the Josephites' representative, the priest planned on spending as much time as possible with his newly discovered family.

But, for now, Father Tully shook hands with each person as introduced. There was Lou Durocher, vice president for mortgage and lending; Jack Fradet, the comptroller, vice president in charge of finance; Martin Whitston, vice president in charge of commercial lending. Then came the two hopefuls: Nancy Groggins with her husband, Joel, and Al Ulrich, whose wife, Barbara, had just finished making a production of having her wrap taken by an attendant.

The only ones now left for Father Tully to meet were the vice presidents' wives, and, of course, the tardy Barbara.

The three vice presidential wives formed a pod. Whether openly or obliquely, they were studying Barbara Ulrich.

"What in the world is she dressed for?" said Pat Durocher. "She looks like she just stepped off Cass Avenue."

"Oh," said Lois Whitston, "let's be more realistic and make her a five-hundred-dollar hooker."

"Well her dress is certainly eye-catching," said Marilyn Fradet, who always tried to say something nice about others. "That black sheath moves every time she does. Sometimes it moves while she's perfectly still—as if it had a life of its own."

"Please, Marilyn," said Pat, "don't use the word 'perfect' in any reference to sweet Babs."

"And," said Lois, "what's with that question about who she's dressed for? She's dressed for our husbands."

"What about her own husband?" asked Marilyn. "He's right here. She couldn't be making a play for anybody else . . . not when her own husband is right here! Could she?"

"She could and she does . . . and she is," said Lois. "Everybody knows they haven't slept together for months—maybe a year or more. But that doesn't mean she's given up 'sleeping'—"

"Our boys are giving us the eye," said Marilyn hastily, glancing surreptitiously at the three VPs. Marilyn was ill at ease with personal gossip. "C'mon, gals, let's play in the appetizers."

Father Tully excused himself and moved toward the VP wives. Conscious that Adams wanted his opinion on whether Ulrich or

Nancy Groggins should become manager of the new branch, the priest aimed to cut through the small talk with the others so he could concentrate on Ulrich and Groggins.

"Mulatto," Martin Whitston said, once Father Tully was out of earshot.

"Mulatto?" Lou Durocher was unsure of the reference.

"The hair," Whitston explained. "Tight to the skin. The lips and nose. Definitely Negroid."

"But with his coloring," Jack Fradet said, "he definitely could pass."

"What are you guys talking about?" Durocher asked insistently.

"The priest," Fradet said. "Father, uh, what was it? . . . Tully? Definitely a mulatto."

"What difference does it make?" Durocher asked.

"It doesn't make a bit of difference," Fradet answered. "He shouldn't be in town for more than a few days. He'll be out of our way in no time.

"But that . . ." He nodded toward Barbara Ulrich, who was making her way toward Tom Adams. "*That* makes a difference. Can either of you guys find a flaw in that fuselage?"

Silence as the three engaged in their study.

"Look at those shoulders," mused Whitston. "That's the one thing I don't like about otherwise knockouts: broad shoulders."

"She'd have to have shoulders that size to keep those hooters up," said Fradet. "And look at them. A bra, any kind of bra, would be superfluous. Anybody think she's wearing a bra?"

Two heads shook simultaneously.

"And the waist! What did they used to call that?" Whitston queried. "Wasp waist—that's it! Look how it highlights the soft curve of her belly. Magnificent!"

"How can you call her belly magnificent when you get a glimmer of those hips? See how they move when she walks. Makes you want to grab! I should say," Fradet observed.

"And legs that don't quit," said Whitston. "Can you see how that dress outlines her thighs? Man, what a package!"

"And we haven't even mentioned her face and her hair," Durocher said. "Those full lips and fun-loving eyes."

"Who gives a damn about her head?" Whitston snorted. "I think I could fool around with the rest of her forever."

"Women's bodies . . ." Durocher waxed philosophical. "Did you ever notice how, like in ice shows—dancers on ice . . . the Olympics, like that—the costumes? The men are always fully clothed, while the women wear just enough not to be naked. But with the cut of what they wear, they might just as well be."

"Time to break this up and join our wives," Whitston said. "You know it's time to break camp when Lou starts in on the heavy stuff. Cover up the men and let the women show what they've got, I say. *Vive la différence!*"

"Yeah," Fradet agreed. "The little ladies are glaring at us. Oh well, an anatomical study of Babs Ulrich is worth whatever we have to suffer now.

"Let's go."

*　　　*　　　*

Father Tully paid his respects to the three VP wives. To a woman, they were far more taken with the hors d'oeuvres than they were with him. So, causing barely a ripple, he raised anchor and moved on.

As he gazed about the room, Father Tully spotted Barbara Ulrich talking with Tom Adams. Just before turning to leave him, she reached up and straightened the white handkerchief in his breast pocket. Was it his imagination, Father Tully wondered, or had she inserted a piece of paper in the pocket?

One message delivered.

As she completed her turn away from Adams, Barbara was face to face with and only a short distance from Father Tully. He held out

his hand. She took his fingers lightly, briefly. They introduced themselves.

"Now, what was it you were supposed to do?"

"Present the award to Mr. Adams."

"Oh yes: the Peter Favor Award."

"Claver."

"Whatever." She thought for a moment. "He gives your group lots
of money, doesn't he?"

"Mr. Adams has been quite generous." Why, he wondered, should
he find that question embarrassing?

She giggled. "I suppose you're the reason his marriage broke up."

"Hardly!" Embarrassment gave way to umbrage.

"Mickey used to give him trouble about all his donations. That's
why he split. He must have given a lot of that money to you. That's
why you gave him the award. So, instead of a wife, he's got another
plaque." She giggled again, gave him a limp wave, and strolled away.

Somehow, for at least a few seconds, Barbara Ulrich had made
Father Tully feel like a home-wrecking leech.

He heard a throat clearing behind him. He turned to face a smiling Nancy Groggins. They had been introduced when the pictures
were being taken, but this was their first opportunity to actually
converse.

"She's something!" Nancy said.

"She certainly is," Father Tully agreed.

"Did you notice her slip something in Mr. Adams's pocket?"

"That was it, eh? I thought she might have been arranging his
handkerchief. All in all, whatever it is, I thought it was a gesture
halfway between wifely and sisterly."

"'Sister' is not a title that fits Babs the way her dress does. None
of the women here would consider her a sister in the feminist con-
text. And the men—in one glance—would know better."

"Why would she do something like that? Such an intimate gesture, I mean?"

"Follow the money trail, Father. Her husband and I are up for the same position: manager of the new branch. It wouldn't be any more money than we're making now. But success at that position in that locality could mean a lot more to whoever gets it—and makes a success of it. And I firmly believe either Al or I could do just that."

"I'm completely in the dark here. What might this position mean for the winner?"

"I—or Al—might displace one of the executive vice presidents. And don't you think for a moment they're not considering that possibility."

"And an executive vice presidency would mean that much more . . . financially?"

Nancy raised her eyes. "Roughly three to four times what we're making now."

Father Tully whistled softly. He never ceased to be amazed at the attraction high money circles held for so many people. It was almost literally a different world from that inhabited by priests and religious who worked with Christ's poor. "That much!"

Nancy nodded. "Of course, financially, I don't need the job as much as Al does. Only because my husband is in construction. He makes about what these VPs make."

"And Mrs. Ulrich?"

"She's not employed. Of course, if she ever wanted to really cash in on what she's good at—never mind; I don't want to go into that with a priest."

"Well . . . what separates you and Al?"

"He's white and I'm black. And it's a black neighborhood. It's a tough 'hood too. Are you going to confront that toughness with a feminine or a masculine personality? There are lots of intangibles. We each have our own style of business, of employer/employee and customer relationships. We're both successful where we are.

"Which of us stands a better chance in this new location? It comes down to a decision based on all these things and anything else the arbiter considers. And it's Mr. Adams's call.

"Now, if you'll excuse me, Father, I really should mingle."

They parted with a handshake.

Father Tully looked about. He had greeted, at least cursorily, nearly everyone. Right now there was no one nearby to meet. Host and guests had visited or were visiting the hors d'oeuvre table.

The three VP wives had clustered, balancing small helpings of appetizers in one hand and a drink in the other. Tom Adams was working the room. In a nice ecumenical move, Nancy Groggins chatted with Al Ulrich. Barbara Ulrich was flitting from one flower to the next. At the moment Father Tully spotted Barbara, she was shaking hands with Lou Durocher. Durocher exhibited only momentary surprise to come away from that greeting with a note in his hand. Which he immediately slipped unread into his pants pocket.

Second message delivered.

Just beginning his trek down the appetizer board was Al Ulrich. Father Tully reflected that he had talked with Nancy, the other candidate. And that Mr. Adams had asked his opinion on the two hopefuls. He joined Ulrich in line.

Ulrich looked up, did a doubletake, and smiled. "I haven't had a chance yet, Father, to thank you and your order for honoring our boss."

"Not at all. If anyone deserved the award, it's certainly Tom Adams."

"You just met him for the first time tonight, is that right?"

"Yes."

"Are you going to be in town for a while?"

"About two weeks. I'm filling in for a local priest so he can go on vacation."

"I hope that doesn't tie you down too much. What I mean is, I hope you'll get a chance to get to know Mr. Adams. He really is a terrific guy—above and beyond his financial contributions."

As Ulrich selected another appetizer, Father Tully looked up to see Barbara Ulrich hand a paper napkin to Jack Fradet. Apparently the napkin contained a note of some sort. Fradet slipped it into his pocket.

Third message delivered.

Father Tully began to wonder about these missives. Did Mrs. Ulrich have one for everybody? Were they like party favors or fortune cookies? Strange.

Returning his attention to the table, there before the priest was a large platter containing an ample supply of deviled eggs, one of his favorite morsels. Would anyone notice if he went overboard? He slipped five onto his plate.

Ulrich chuckled. "Like 'em?"

"Well, yes, now that you mention it."

They moved down the table.

"Speaking of liking," said Father Tully, "it seems pretty clear that you like Tom Adams."

"I've never met anyone like him," Ulrich responded. "I mean, I'm not a particularly religious person. And I tend to be skeptical of people who wear their religion on their sleeve.

"But it's not like that with Mr. Adams. He puts himself and his pocketbook where his mouth is. I think if he could, he'd be the manager of the new branch himself. Of course, that's not possible."

"Speaking of that"—Father Tully, finished at the hors d'oeuvre table, stepped aside with Ulrich—"isn't this some kind of cruel and unusual treatment to keep you and Nancy Groggins on tenterhooks over that job?"

Ulrich reacted as if he himself had been challenged. "Certainly not! This is a difficult decision. There's a lot riding on this new branch. We aren't one of the conglomerate banks. We're taking a big risk opening in that part of town. If we succeed, we're going to be a lot stronger. The city of Detroit needs a lot of this type of financial commitment. It needs a presence like ours."

"And if this move fails?"

Ulrich shook his head. "The biggies will laugh us out of town. They'll pretend that it would take the clout only *they* could deliver to make this work. It would weaken our position in communities where we're already established. It would be a disaster for us. We really can't afford to fail."

"And it makes that much difference . . . who the manager is?"

"The manager sets the tone—or should. The policy of the banking unit. The measure of contact with our customers. That's basically the role of the manager."

"You sure you'd be the better choice?"

Ulrich's smile was slightly twisted. "Nancy is qualified. So am I. I would never claim that Nancy couldn't do the job. I think I could do it better. But Mr. Adams will be the final judge of that."

"You really have confidence in him, don't you?"

"Completely! Whatever he decides, I'll accept."

The priest took a glass of wine from a tray being carried by an ever-present waiter. As he turned, he noticed Barbara dabbing her lips with a lacy handkerchief. As she did, she slipped another of her notes to Martin Whitston.

Fourth message delivered.

What an interesting sideshow, thought Father Tully.

He had no idea how many at this party had been favored with one of Barbara Ulrich's notes. He had seen at least four recipients: Adams, Durocher, Fradet, and Whitston. The president and his three executive vice presidents.

Somehow, Father Tully had a sneaking feeling that he would not be receiving one of Barbara Ulrich's missives. Nor would he even learn what they contained.

The lights dimmed, then brightened.

Dinner was served.

Seven

GUIDED BY THE PLACE CARDS, Father Tully found himself between Barbara Ulrich and Joel Groggins, the only guest the priest had not yet met.

Each guest, upon finding his or her place, remained standing. They knew that Adams dinners always opened with a prayer.

It was expected that Father Tully would lead them. After Adams issued the invitation, the priest complied with the traditional, "Bless us, O Lord, and these thy gifts, which we are about to receive from Thy bounty, through Christ, Our Lord."

And everyone—at least so it seemed—responded with a hearty "Amen." There were no atheists at an Adams banquet.

After seating himself, Father Tully turned to Mrs. Ulrich. But she had already turned away to launch into conversation with Patricia Durocher. That conversation was aided and abetted by Lou Durocher, seated across from Mrs. Ulrich.

Evidently, the priest had been weighed and found wanting as far as Barbara Ulrich's interests were concerned. So, with little regret, Tully turned to his left, where sat a smiling Joel Groggins.

Groggins was African-American—though not nearly as light-skinned as the priest. He was a six-footer, and hefty; his clothes could have been a size larger. "Just in case no one's said it," Groggins said, "welcome to Detroit."

"In point of fact," the priest responded, "no one has. At least a couple of people have made me feel welcome, but no one has said it in so many words. Thanks."

A trolley stopped behind them, offering still more hors d'oeuvres, including something the waiter identified as fresh Petrossian Ossetra Malossol caviar.

"Do you happen to know," the priest asked Groggins, "how much that caviar costs?"

"Forty dollars for a thirty-gram serving."

The priest passed on the caviar, selected a sampling of several other offerings, and the waiter moved on.

"I should mention," Groggins said, "that the price I quoted you was a bit high. I quoted you the price fixed at the Lark, one of our very best dining spots. We'll be going right down a Lark menu, unless I'm very mistaken. Tom Adams could do far, far worse than copy a Lark meal."

"I was talking to your wife earlier. She said you were in construction?"

"That's right. Mostly in Detroit. It's really sad, the kind of image this city's got. It went down on a roller coaster for about thirty years under the previous two or three mayors. But Aker, the present guy, is inspirational. He's got things moving. Of course, we've still got a long way to go. But I'm doin' okay. And lovin' it." His laugh was full-bodied.

"Congratulations. But that brings up the question that's been nagging at me after speaking with your wife, Mr. Groggins—"

"Joe."

"Okay. Joe. Why is she fighting for this position? She is, after all, a bank manager. She didn't mention her salary. . . ."

"Forty-five thousand in round figures."

"And she did say you were pulling down about what the bank's executive vice presidents were making. So why should she compete for the new job and all its headaches?"

Groggins found Father Tully's naïveté surprising in this day and age. "A generation or so ago—and practically forever before that—

it would have been cause for scandal. Women were homemakers. Women—and I know that you know this was the measure of their success, Father—anyway, women stayed home, nurtured their husbands and their kids, went to church and church meetings. Husbands did *important* work and brought home the paycheck.

"But that's history. Women still enter the workforce with a strike or two against them. But they definitely compete.

"And that's what Nancy's doing: She's competing—in this case, against Al Ulrich. It doesn't make any difference how much *I'm* making; she has to score on her own.

"I'm sure you know there's a side issue here, Father. Whoever gets the new job will be Tom Adams's fair-haired child. I mean, Nancy and Al are already favored employees of Adams Bank. But whoever is chosen here will . . . have a chance to go on to greater things."

The seemingly never stationary waiters bestowed pasta as the next course.

"So," Tully said, "there's a lot hinging on Tom Adams's choice."

Groggins nodded enthusiastically. "I'll say! You're about the only one at this entire party who will be unaffected by that choice."

Father Tully thought for a moment. "Me? Myself, alone? What about you? You don't seem to have much riding on this event. How would your lifestyle be involved?"

Groggins shrugged. "If Nancy isn't the choice, we're going to have some instant replays, a lot of recrimination, and not a small amount of resentment and even anger."

"And if she wins this appointment?"

"There'll be some arguments about our enhanced capability. Should we wait for what seems certain to be an executive vice presidency? Should we be upwardly mobile right away? Should we move up even after the appointment? Things like that.

"But let me tell you, Reverend, whatever Nancy and I go through one way or another will be nothing—*nothing*—compared with what the other folks will have to manage."

"All of them?"

Groggins spread his large hands on the table and nodded gravely.

The pasta was followed by a scoop of Italian ices as a palate cleanser. Then came the salad.

Groggins leaned toward the priest confidingly. "Romaine with cashews and hearts of palm and mustard vinaigrette. And, Reverend, it might be a good idea for you to forget how much all this costs. Otherwise you might be sorely tempted to turn down everything like you did the caviar."

Father Tully forked through the salad. It was delicious, as had been everything so far.

As they ate, both the priest and Groggins briefly studied the other diners. There might have been five or six separate conversations going on. No one was paying any attention to the Tully-Groggins tête-à-tête.

Apparently, they were free to talk of anything or anyone they pleased with no repercussion from the other diners, who seemed to have forgotten them.

"God forgive me," the priest said, "but I find this captivating. I mean, I don't have any stake in any of this. I'll probably never see any of you again. So why am I so interested in what's going on?"

Groggins grinned. "Ever watch a soap opera, Reverend?"

"Can't say that I have." A smile spread slowly across the priest's face. "A living, breathing soap opera, is it? Well, God help me, I'm hooked. I never thought such a thing could be. But I am."

The pièce de résistance arrived.

"Steak!" Tully exclaimed.

Groggins was amused. "Black Angus sirloin strip with onions and pinot noir sauce," he clarified. "And vegetable garnish." Noting the priest's somewhat quizzical expression, Groggins grinned again. "Nancy was in on the planning. She told me—in great detail—what we'd be eating tonight."

As they fell to, the priest and Groggins again studied the other diners, who, unimpeded by the food, continued their separate conversations, still uninterested in the only two who were least affected by the intra-company dynamics.

"For one who is only marginally involved in these office politics," Father Tully said, "you seem pretty knowledgeable."

"Nancy and I talk . . . or, rather, Nancy talks. I listen."

"All I know at this point in the soap is that, apparently, either Nancy or Al Ulrich will be the new manager. No chance of a dark horse coming out of nowhere?"

"None that anybody can imagine. If there were any doubt, this party with this cast of characters would not be taking place."

"Okay." The priest sliced a thin portion of steak and swirled it in the sauce. "Forgetting for the moment who gets the appointment, then what?"

"No one knows for certain. But the smart money would be on an inevitable shakeup near the top."

"That I gather. But why?"

"Top priority as this new branch becomes a reality is getting a good start. Becoming a part of that community. Treating customers with respect and understanding. And everything that this entails.

"After that . . ." Groggins shrugged. "This doesn't figure to be a permanent placement. After all, both Nancy and Al would be moving from Bloomfield Hills or Troy to core-city Detroit. It's one thing to pour in everything you've got to insure a successful beginning. It's another thing to subsequently be buried there.

"Everyone expects a major promotion to follow success at the new branch. And where is a manager going to go when he or she steps up?"

"An executive vice presidency?" The priest was the first to finish his steak. The others were as occupied with their conversations as they were with this superb meal. And Groggins had been explaining the terrain.

"Right on."

"A *fourth* vice presidency?"

Groggins shook his head. "From what Nancy tells me, three is the magic number for *executive* vice presidents." Noting the priest's puzzled expression, Groggins made haste to explain. "I didn't mean to confuse you, Reverend. Don't get me wrong: There are plenty of vice presidents in the bank. So moving from branch manager to a vice presidency is not all that significant. That's why the promotion we're talking about would have to be to an *executive* vice presidency. And, as I said, the bank has only three of those positions."

"Then . . . ?"

"One of the three might very well get bounced. Or there is the possibility that a new position might be created between executive vice president and the CEO. But that's as likely as the Lions, Tigers, Pistons, and Red Wings all winning a championship the same season.

"No, the smart money says one of the current VPs will eventually, and in the not-too-distant future, get bounced."

"Then the magic question is . . . who gets the ax?"

"That's the question, okay. But the answer is buried deep in Tom Adams's mind."

"You think he's already decided who it'll be?"

"The way I read it, Adams does not believe in chance or uncertainty. He knows what he's doing—and what he's going to do—long before he has to make a decision."

"So," the priest asked with finality, "who do you think? Or, rather, I guess, what does Nancy think?"

Groggins chuckled softly. "Nancy has her opinion, of course. But I've been thrown together with this group often enough to have my own theory. Suppose I give you a thumbnail rundown on the candidates. Then maybe you can write your own synopsis."

"Fair enough."

"Okay. First of all, there's Martin Whitston. He's in charge of commercial lending."

"Doesn't anyone call him Red?"

"Because he's got red hair?"

"Uh-huh."

"Not that I know of."

"Why not?"

"I guess because he doesn't want to be called Red."

"Just like that?"

"That will tell you something about Martin Whitston. He cares what others call him, as well as what others think of him. He is a very strong character.

"He services existing business. Develops portfolios. He's got to bring in new business and investments. This is a hands-on operation for a bank of this size. He's got two or three people who report directly to him. There's maybe twelve in that whole department."

Groggins's description of this VP position seemed to fit the image projected by Martin Whitston. Whitston wore his hair very tight to the scalp . . . almost the brush cut of old.

He looked to be powerfully built, but not really overweight. Broad in the shoulders; he probably worked out at some gym or health club. Father Tully doubted that he would want to work for Martin Whitston under the best of circumstances.

"My impression of Whitston," Groggins said, "is that he feels like he is confined by the financial limits of the Adams Bank. But, basically, he is satisfied at the moment. And he is supremely confident in what he does."

"Then it sounds as if he'd be crushed if he were the one to be replaced."

"Crushed?" The word was uttered at such a pitch that the others suddenly became aware of him. Immediately, Groggins lowered his voice. "I think if someone attempted to give him notice, he would do the crushing."

Father Tully's now empty plate was removed. What next? he wondered. "What about Mrs. Whitston?"

"Lois? She has her own personality, of course, but I'm not sure exactly what it is. Thing you have to remember, Reverend, is that all three ladies attached to these vice presidents have elected to lose themselves in their husband's careers. Now, look at Lois for a minute."

Father Tully looked. He saw a woman who seemed to be fighting. Fighting to keep her shape when she really wanted to compromise. Fighting to hold on to a youth that had passed maybe twenty or twenty-five years ago. It was a losing battle. But one she engaged in.

"Lois is a joiner. She's a volunteer for the symphony, the art institute, the local PBS fund-raisers. She occupies herself with a lot of busy work. Occasionally, our paths cross at these events. Usually, she's asking me to appear on behalf of one or another of 'em. She's running after something, but I'm not sure what."

The Fountain of Youth, thought the priest.

"Then"—Groggins had almost finished his steak—"there's Jack Fradet, executive vice president for finance—the comptroller. He's high-priced, and worth every penny. His job, mostly, is to forecast the financial climate in the United States. Marketing comes from his area. He audits the bank, complying with state and federal laws. He knows where all the skeletons are buried.

"Look at it this way: The bank is all about money. And Jack Fradet is in direct charge of all the money. Actually, the other two executive VPs report to him."

Father Tully studied Fradet. A smallish man with thick, wire-framed glasses. Although Fradet wore a dinner jacket, the priest sensed he would be much more comfortable in corduroy trousers, a shirt buttoned to the neck, an elastic band holding up either sleeve, and an eyeshade. In short, Bob Cratchet in Dickens's *A Christmas Carol*. Even his fingers seemed in eternal movement—as if he were figuring checks and balances.

"Plain, isn't he?"

The priest nodded slowly.

"So is his wife.

"Marilyn is a stay-at-home. Their three kids are adults now. Once upon a time, they tell me, her entire life revolved around her kids while Jack's life was immersed in his work, the bank. His reputation is impeccable. He's really good at what he does. And he knows he's good. But what he does includes very few people. He's a loner. Among the few that are at all close to him there's a sort of consensus that he considers himself a big fish in a very small pond. But the consensus goes on to hold that he would never make a move to leave Adams. This bank is his life—as far as anyone can tell."

While Groggins finished his steak, Father Tully studied Marilyn Fradet. She was just "there." Martin and Lois Whitston were seated on either side of Marilyn. The couple were talking to each other as if Marilyn were a pillar at Tiger Stadium that embodied the designation "obstructed view."

When husband and wife had finished their dialogue and each began another conversation with others at the table, Marilyn continued to just sit there. She had barely touched her steak. She put Father Tully in mind of Lot's wife immediately after turning back to see Sodom and Gomorrah catch hell from God.

"Regular coffee, gentlemen, or decaffeinated?" A waiter filled their coffee cups.

"She certainly seems to be a million miles from this party," the priest commented.

"Who?"

"Marilyn Fradet."

Groggins glanced at her. "I'm told that's the way it is. Seems like her kids would be doing her a favor to take her in. Talk is Jack has something on the side—if you catch my meaning."

The priest caught it.

"I don't know," Groggins continued, "whether Jack's paramour is a cause or an effect of his relationship with his wife."

The priest shook his head. "Pitiful."

"You said it. One of those relationships that, right at the begin-ning, should have been declared a failure and dissolv—" Groggins caught himself short. "Uh, sorry, Reverend. That's against your re-ligion, isn't it? Divorce, I mean."

The priest smiled. "No, no. The Catholic version of divorce is an-nulment. But before we work on the annulment—which has no standing in civil law—the couple has to get a divorce—which has no standing in Church law."

Groggins's brow furrowed.

"Don't try to make heads or tails of it." The priest chuckled. "Let's just say that divorce has its place in Catholics' lives. And if what you say is so, I guess it should have had a place in Mr. and Mrs. Fradet's life. They certainly do not appear to be happy people."

The waiters removed the last of the dinner plates and filled the remaining coffee cups.

There was a general shifting about in the chairs. Some fresh conversations were begun. Still, no one sought to engage either Fa-ther Tully or Jack Groggins in small or large talk.

"That," the priest said, "leaves one vice presidential couple."

"Lou and Pat Durocher," Groggins identified. "Last and probably least."

"Oh?"

"Lou is vice president in charge of mortgage and individual lend-ing. This is the real meat and potatoes of the banking business. Lou and his staff do things—on Adams's small level—like financ-ing cars for college kids. And they provide mortgage money, of course. They make loans. They establish sales and market plans. This and commercial lending, run by Marty Whitston, are where the banks make money."

"So why your remark that Lou Durocher was the least? The least of the vice presidents? A weak link?"

"A lot of people—Nancy among them—have their doubts about Durocher's judgment. Some of his loans have been highly questionable. Now, whether or not a bank gives a loan is a judgment call. And not all loans work out. But Durocher's batting average is as low as a rookie who's struggling to make it in the majors. And, like it or not, even if it's there by the skin of its teeth, Adams Bank is a major league organization."

The priest measured Durocher in a more searching light.

"Nervous" seemed the appropriate word. He appeared uncertain about his smile. Should he turn it on or off? And the eyes . . . in almost constant movement. As if he felt tardy in comprehending what was going on. As if he had to catch up just to stay even with his conversational partners.

All in all, not the type to whom Father Tully would feel comfortable entrusting something precious, such as money.

Finally, Father Tully considered the other half of the last-and-probably-least team: Patricia Durocher, Lou's wife.

In contrast to her husband, Pat seemed relaxed, enjoying a camaraderie beyond her husband's grasp. And although she was sitting across the table from Lou, she seemed distant from him. She made no effort to include him in her attention or conversation.

Father Tully wondered if this sort of interpersonal behavior marked their less formal relationship at home. Were Lou and Pat also candidates for the divorce mill?

Dessert arrived. Fortunately, after a meal of such elegance, dessert was fresh fruit—strawberries, raspberries, grapes, and melon.

"The Durochers don't seem to fit," Father Tully observed.

"How's that?" Groggins nibbled the succulent fruit.

"They just don't seem compatible. Mr. Durocher looks as if he's trying to catch up with this evening . . . maybe this life! While his wife appears very comfortable handling the chitchat that's going on."

Groggins studied the couple, pausing to spoon fruit. "I guess I just never paid all that much attention. But I think you're right: this was not a union made by computer."

"Well, I'm a bit surprised," the priest said. "What seemed a difficult—if not tortuous—decision, now seems the simplest thing imaginable. If someone were closing in on these vice presidents, and one of the three was going to be replaced by either your wife or Al Ulrich, the obvious choice would seem to be Lou Durocher. I'm amazed that this gentleman ever got as far as he has. You'd think a successful employer like Tom Adams would have long since dismissed Durocher—or at least shunted him aside. I would think Mr. Adams would simply welcome this opportunity to dump dead weight."

Groggins touched napkin to lips. "You hit paydirt with your observation on why a guy like Durocher ever became a vice president. See, Adams likes to think of himself as having a love affair with God. 'The Man Who Loves God.' And he takes the Bible very seriously.

"That's the answer to the question of how Lou Durocher got to be vice president in charge of mortgage lending. Nobody can really figure it out. But it's got to have something to do with the Bible. If you asked Adams, he'd probably come up with some verse to justify putting a virtual incompetent in such a vital position."

The priest pondered that for a moment. "He wouldn't have to look any further than Jesus Himself. Tom Adams might well have thought of the twelve men Jesus picked to be His closest friends, the Apostles. Not one of them was qualified for the job. Most of them were simply fishermen—including the one who would eventually be their leader. One was a despised tax collector. One turned out to be a traitor. But Jesus picked 'em."

"You figure Adams thinks he's Jesus."

The priest smiled broadly. "I only just met the man. But I don't for a minute believe he thinks he's Jesus. Maybe Mr. Adams thinks that Durocher will play over his head if the boss shows some confidence in his ability. The Apostles came to mind because that's ultimately what they did: played way over their heads."

"Yeah." Groggins pushed himself away from the table. "Maybe

you're right. Anyway, that's why this whole business is a crapshoot. If later on, Al or Nancy is up for a promotion to executive vice president, what happens if Adams hasn't finished his experiment with Durocher? Then one of the other two finds his head on the block. And then what happens?"

The priest shrugged. "You tell me. It's like a bomb waiting to explode."

"You betcha!"

The meal wound down. Host and guests milled about. One by one and two by two, the guests approached Tom Adams to congratulate him and admire the award plaque.

Father Tully waited for the others to finish paying their respects to their host. After all, the priest had presented the award and, in his presentation speech, had congratulated Adams; there was no point in doing it again. When his turn inevitably came, Tully would bid his host a heartfelt but simple farewell.

Meanwhile, the priest mulled over all that Joel Groggins had told him during their oddly uninterrupted conversation.

If he hadn't done so already, very shortly Adams would select a manager for the special branch that in a day or so would become a reality.

Probably that manager would be Nancy Groggins. Before the dinner, Adams had told Father Tully that she was his personal favorite for the position. Adams had asked the priest for his opinion. After briefly meeting with both candidates and after all Jack Groggins had said, the priest could not disagree with Adams's choice.

Apparently, that meant that eventually, Nancy Groggins would be up for another advancement. And that was spelled executive vice president. Which meant that one of the three present executive vice presidents would be seeking other employment.

Odds were that the one to be axed would be Lou Durocher, who was named to his present status because . . . well, who knew? Because Adams was trying to follow Scripture in very tangible ways? Because some pop psych cult somehow influenced the move?

In any case, there was practical doubt that the seemingly obvious move would be made.

That meant that one of two very capable employees would be bumped.

How would Jack Fradet react if he turned out to be the sacrificial lamb?

After Tom Adams, Fradet knew the status of the bank better than probably anyone else. What sort of damage would he likely do? Could he do? Father Tully had a gut feeling that the possessor of such intimate and comprehensive knowledge could cause serious, maybe fatal, damage. And to be dismissed from his position while the obvious weak link went blithely on playing hob with mortgage and lending would guarantee an angry and bitter former executive VP.

And if the bumpee turned out to be Marty Whitston?

Father Tully recalled Joel Groggins's response to this possibility. Tully had supposed that Whitston would be "crushed." Whereas Groggins had reversed the verb's voice to predict that Whitston would be the one doing the crushing.

Were Tom Adams to let Lou Durocher go, the CEO would have to admit that his grand experiment in human motivation had failed.

Should he dismiss either Whitston or Fradet, Adams would expose his bank to its possible destruction.

There was no real winner in such a choice.

But never once did it occur to Father Tully that in this vicious circle lurked the possibility of violence—or even murder.

*   *   *

The players in this drama, at least four of them, were not presently contemplating the new branch or its logical consequences. They were much more absorbed with the notes they'd received this evening.

Of the two threats, one engendered by a new branch bank, the other from Barbara Ulrich, the latter was by far the more imminent.

Noting that no one was presently conversing with the host, Father Tully approached Adams, thanked him for a lovely evening, and affirmed Adams's choice of manager: Nancy Groggins was sure to do well.

Adams seemed far too preoccupied to more than abstractedly shake hands and bid the priest farewell.

If Adams had any plans for Father Tully during the remainder of the priest's stay in Detroit, there was no mention of anything of the sort. Nor was there another word said about the choice of manager for the new branch.

Finally, Father Tully realized that he would have to locate his chauffeur on his own or call a cab. Fortunately, the attentive chauffeur found him.

And thus ended an evening filled with unexpected events. It was, as Joel Groggins had implied, a prime time soap opera.

How, Father Tully wondered, would it all end?

Eight

IT WAS a pleasant late afternoon in Detroit.

Waiting for his sister-in-law to pick him up, Father Tully decided a little exercise was in order. Thus, he paced up and down the corner of Jay and Orleans next to St. Joe's rectory.

After last night's award-winning confusion, this had been a pleasant and relaxing day.

Tom Adams had not made any contact. Father Tully had expected a call. He thought that once Adams came to terms with whatever had disturbed and distracted him last night, he would have attended to the visitor. Shown him the sights, given him some sense of the history of this place.

Father Tully had not for a moment expected that the CEO himself would be his guide; some nonessential employee would, he knew, be assigned to conduct the tour.

Nothing. Not a word.

The most eventful occurrence of this day had been trying to get Father Koesler off on his vacation excursion. The way things developed, it fully seemed that Koesler was going to cancel his trip.

He even stayed to concelebrate the noon Mass with Father Tully.

After Mass, Father Tully began carrying Father Koesler's baggage and incidentals down to the car. Reluctantly, the pastor helped stow his things in the trunk and, at long last, left. As Father Koesler's car cleared the parking lot, Father Tully and Mary O'Connor waved good-bye.

It had taken Father Tully and Mary no time to hit it off. He had quickly perceived that Mary played the factotum role with grace and diplomacy. If he got out of her way—which he fully intended to do—everything would run like a finely crafted timepiece.

Mary liked Father Tully immediately. He was a priest, which started him off on the right foot. And his personality seemed much like Father Koesler's. She very much prized Father Koesler.

After peeling Father Koesler away from St. Joe's rectory, Father Tully spent a relaxing afternoon getting acquainted with the buildings and the "feel" of St. Joe's.

Also, it was fun anticipating meeting his brother and sister-in-law—two entities whom, up until just days previously, he hadn't known existed. By the time the late model Ford Escort pulled up to the curb, Father Tully was more than ready to meet his spanking new family.

He was not surprised that the attractive woman driver was alone. Anne Marie, his sister-in-law, had phoned earlier to explain that his brother couldn't get off work until at least five-thirty at the earliest. She would pick up the priest at that time and they would all meet at their home.

As he reached to open the car door, she leaned across the passenger seat and smiled up at him. "Father Tully, I presume."

He thought his ears would crack from the width of his answering grin. "Mrs. Tully, I presume," he replied as he entered the car.

"That title seems so foreign to that last name," Anne Marie said. "I still can't imagine somebody named Tully being a priest. *Father Tully*," she murmured with reverence and amazement.

"If you feel uneasy about the title, how about me? The only Mrs. Tully I've ever known was my mother."

They both laughed as they began the short trip to the Tully condo.

It would be a while before they became sufficiently comfortable to be in each other's company in silence. For now, conversation seemed necessary. Besides, there was lots of ground to cover.

"I don't know everything you and Z—uh, your brother talked about on the phone the other day. But I thought we could clear up some ticklish areas before you two meet in person."

"Sounds good." Father Tully was aware that each time the car stopped, for traffic or a streetlight, Anne Marie turned to study him. Undoubtedly she was searching for a resemblance to his brother. Her husband.

"We're taking a slightly roundabout route to give us a bit more time," she said. "First off, your brother has been married and divorced. And in between that marriage and me, there was a significant other."

"I didn't know."

"The marriage produced five children. They and their mother moved to Chicago when the divorce was final. The girlfriend and your brother parted amicably."

The priest nodded.

"I'm telling you this specifically, Father, because it is important for you to know about your brother and me."

"You don't have to—"

"Yes, I do. It's probably going to make you wonder. See, I'm Catholic. And we were married in the Catholic Church."

"Alonzo got an annulment for his first marriage?"

Anna Marie sighed. "There's the rub. Your brother is not Catholic." *Sometimes,* she thought, *I wonder if he's even religious.* "We went to a priest friend of mine who is pastor of a core-city parish in a very poor neighborhood. Mostly because I wanted it, he tried to find some reason why an annulment might be sought, let alone granted."

"Nothing there?" The priest began to anticipate the outcome of this story.

"The Church does not consider an overwhelming devotion to job and duty a reason to grant an annulment."

"Married to his job, eh? I've known a lot of cops in that fix. By the way, does he—or do you—object to the word 'cop'?"

"Not at all."

"So what happened? When you had to forget the declaration of nullity, I mean?"

"My priest suggested something he called 'a pastoral solution. . . .'"

"You just get married in civil law," Tully completed the explanation, "and look on that as your valid marriage and go from there. Go to Mass. Take Communion. Count on your conscience to lead you."

She glanced at him, surprised that he was familiar with a procedure that she had thought most rare—probably reserved to a few inner-city priests, and maybe only in the Archdiocese of Detroit at that.

He read her thoughts. "Surprised?"

"Yes, frankly."

"Don't be. The procedure's been around a long time. Another spillover from the Second Vatican Council . . . although not specifically conciliar. More a theological development from the *spirit* of Vatican II. It's just an admission that Church law isn't equipped to handle some problems.

"The trouble is, of course, that it isn't canonical. So it can't be applied openly. You called it 'a pastoral solution'—and so it is. But it might just as well be called 'a triumph of conscience.' Because whatever it's called, it recognizes the supremacy of conscience."

"So, you followed your priest's advice."

"No."

"No!"

"I needed something more. Blame whatever, I needed more than my conscience told me."

"You needed . . . a ceremony?"

"Exactly. And that's what my priest gave us. It was a simple ceremony. No Mass. But *in* the church, at the altar, with two witnesses. With that I felt secure."

"One of the problems—maybe the only problem—is that a lot depends on the tone of the diocese. And that's set by the bishop. And bishops come in assorted sizes, shapes, and dispositions. Your bishop, Cardinal Boyle, is reputed to be open. Which, in this case, means merely that he wouldn't take any action against one of his priests who applied the 'pastoral solution.' Not unless his back was against the wall.

"I think your priest, whoever he is, was taking a larger than usual risk."

"Why?" Anne Marie hadn't considered that there could be any risk attached to that quiet ceremony.

"My brother! He's an officer in the Homicide Division, isn't he?" The priest didn't wait for an answer to his rhetorical question. "He's in a position where he can and probably does appear in the media —the papers, radio, TV. It's always possible for someone to learn that Lieutenant Tully got married in a less than strictly orthodox way. If that happens, he gets some coverage. Then, even with a bishop like Cardinal Boyle, a whole bunch of stuff can hit the fan."

"It didn't."

"I'm glad. I'm truly glad. But the priest here really took a chance."

Anne Marie felt an even deeper gratitude to her priest, now that she realized how he had gone out on a limb to satisfy her need for a ceremony.

They were silent for a few moments.

"May I ask you, Father, did you ever counsel anyone in the 'pastoral solution'?"

"Uh-huh."

"Did you ever conduct a wedding service like I had?"

"Yes. But there were times when I was able to convince a couple that it was wiser to stay in the internal forum—just trusting everything to God and a conscience that is not attempting to deceive God."

"Just out of curiosity, Father, why would you counsel against such a ceremony?"

The priest snorted. "Not because anyone I married or counseled was famous or likely to get a picture in the paper. My parishes don't run on that level. We—all the Josephite parishes—aren't moving in the fast lane.

"But, you see, we aren't diocesan priests. We're a religious order. We don't belong to any one diocese. We have parishes in lots of different dioceses. And when we move into such a parish, we fall under the jurisdiction of the local ordinary—the bishop. And, let me assure you, all bishops are not Cardinal Boyle."

"Well," Anne Marie said, "anyway, I wanted you to know. And I wanted to explain our situation to you before the three of us got together. It would be awkward for Zoo. He just went along with everything because he wanted to please me. He didn't know or care about what was going on. From that time on, it was 'What you don't know can't hurt you.'

"That, by the way, was why I suggested to Zoo that I pick you up. So we could have this little talk beforehand."

"It was a good idea. I agree entirely. I'm clear on—wait a minute! What did you call him . . . my brother?"

"What did I . . . ? Oh, you wouldn't know, would you? His nickname . . . he picked it up some time ago. Most people call him 'Zoo' instead of Alonzo."

"But his given name *is* Alonzo. *Zo*, not *Zoo*."

"I know. But that's the way it is. About the only person I know who calls him Alonzo is his boss, Inspector Walt Koznicki. He's kind of old-worldly. He wouldn't think of using a nickname."

Father Tully thought for a minute, then began to chuckle, until the chuckle became a roar of laughter.

"What is it, Father? Something I'm not tuning in on?"

"Know what my first name is?"

"Uh . . . let's see . . . I was geared to just use your title. It's . . . wait: It's Zachary!"

"And my natural nickname?"

"I suppose . . . Zack."

"That's right. Just think: Zoo and Zack. Zack and Zoo."

They both began to laugh until the car almost shook. Fortunately, they had arrived at the Tully home; otherwise, Anne Marie might have caused a traffic accident.

As they drove into the attached garage, Father Tully thought he saw a window curtain move, as if someone were watching from inside. Obviously Zoo had arrived. His car was parked in the garage.

They waited until they got control of themselves. Then they entered the condo. They were still grinning broadly as they walked into the living room where Zoo Tully waited.

The police officer and the priest stood motionless as they looked at each other.

"In all my life," said the priest finally, "I've never known what it's like to have a brother or a sister. And now I'm standing in this room with my brother and my sister."

"In all my life," said the officer, "I've never had a priest relative, let alone a priest brother."

They stood as a tableau for several moments.

On impulse, Anne Marie took each brother by the arm and moved the two of them together as all three embraced. Tears flowed. The two men tried, with little success, to cover their emotion.

After a few moments, Anne Marie moved apart. "You two guys sit down and get acquainted. I'm going to stick some things in the microwave. You'll have to excuse us, Father—oh, nuts, I can't stop using your title. Anyway, what with my teaching and my dear husband catching the bad guys, we don't cook much. Usually it's either prepared food or eating out. We would've gone out tonight, but we thought it was better to be home and get used to each other. It'll just be a little while. Why don't you two figure out what you're going to call each other?"

Father Tully and Anne Marie began laughing again as she went to the kitchen.

"Want something to drink?" the officer asked.

"Gin and tonic would be nice . . . heavy on the tonic."

Zoo made two virtually identical drinks. He handed one to his brother as they sat down in facing chairs. "Now then, what's this about what we're supposed to call each other?"

The priest chuckled. "Anne Marie and I got to talking on the way over. In the course of conversation, she referred to you by your nickname."

"Zoo? Yeah, just about everybody calls me that."

"That's what Anne Marie said. Then I told her my nickname."

"Which is?"

"Not nearly as colorful as yours. It's Zack . . . from Zachary."

Zoo thought about this for a very brief moment. "Zoo and Zack."

"Zack and Zoo. I should get top billing. I'm a priest."

"I'm older."

"You comfortable using our nicknames? People are bound to find it humorous."

"That's their problem."

"Then it's done."

"Done."

"Have you been doing what I've been doing?" the priest asked.

"Checking you out to see if there's any resemblance?"

"There is, isn't there?"

"A bit."

"We sure had different mamas!" Zack observed.

"But the same daddy. I can see him in you . . . and you in me, for that matter."

"I was only five when Dad died. Ma told me some things. But she didn't know him much longer than my five years. What do you remember?"

"Not much more than you. I was just a kid when he left. I don't know what happened. From what my—our—brothers and sisters said, he was a hardworking guy. Worked the assembly line . . . probably what Detroit is best known for. He had plenty of trouble from the rednecks. It was lots different then. Everybody took it for granted that he'd work here and go on supporting his family till he dropped.

"But one day he just up and left. That was it. I hardly knew him, and then he was gone."

"It was my mother's first marriage. . . ." Zack took up the story. "I came along after about a year. And I hardly got to know him. And then he was gone."

Zoo looked at his brother intently. "Your mama must've really been religious . . . I mean you becoming a priest and all."

"Oh, yes, she was. I think it was maybe the happiest day of her life when I was ordained.

"How about you? I gather from Bob Koesler and Anne Marie that you're not exactly a Bible thumper."

"We grew up entirely different. I don't have any religion. If someone really pressed, I'd have to say I'm Baptist. But they'd have to press very, very hard."

"Well, don't worry: I'm not going to try to make a Catholic of you."

"Good. That attitude will eventually make you a happier man."

"Okay, you two." Anne Marie in an apron appeared in the door. "Everything's ready. Father, I hope you like chicken. We're trying to keep your brother off red meat as much as possible."

"Chicken's fine. And it's Zack to my brother, and I hope to my sister too."

Zoo was about to stab a chicken leg when Anne Marie invited their priest brother to offer a prayer, which he did.

All in all, it was an appetizing dinner. In addition to the chicken, there were vegetables and a salad. It could not begin to challenge last night's feast at the Adams suite. Still, this was several levels up from what Zack would have prepared for himself were he back at the rectory.

More important, this meal was punctuated with warm smiles from everyone.

"I'm not exactly in love with my nickname. *Zack*. But, somehow, coming from you two it has a down-home ring."

Zoo smiled. "There's one person you're bound to meet who will never, under any circumstances, use the nickname. In fact, if I'm not proven wrong, he will never call you anything but Father Tully."

"Wait a minute . . ." Zack held up one hand. "Anne Marie mentioned the name . . . I can't think of it right now. Polish?"

"You bet. Inspector Walter Koznicki. My boss—head of our Homicide Division."

"I'm really looking forward to meeting him . . . and your other friends. I can't tell you what a kick this is for me."

"And for us," Anne Marie said.

There was no sense of haste to this meal. They knew they were in for a long evening of getting acquainted. Probably at this table in the kitchen.

"By the way," Zoo said, "before supper, you mentioned Father Koesler. I hope he didn't get the impression he wasn't welcome to come along."

Zack looked puzzled. "Didn't you know? I thought he—or somebody—would tell you. He's gone. A vacation."

"A vacation!" Zoo's reaction seemed out of proportion to the event.

"That's right. I don't know how long it's been since he's had one. I don't think he even knows himself. But if anybody deserves to get away, it's gotta be Bob Koesler."

Zoo seemed stunned. He had stopped eating.

"It's funny with people who don't vacation," Anne Marie said. "They get to resemble big oak trees that are sort of dependable. They're always there."

"That's just it. . . ." Zoo seemed to be coming out of his self-inflicted daze. "He isn't here."

Anne Marie was concerned. "Of course he isn't here, dear. He's on vacation."

"What if we need him?"

"What do you mean, 'What if we need him?' Why would we need him?"

"Hey," Zack said in a joking tone, "what am I, collard greens? I'm a priest! It isn't that you're left with nobody to take care of your spiritual life. Besides, after what you said, I didn't think you'd panic if there wasn't a priest to bring you sacraments!"

"It's not me." Zoo was deadly serious. "What if we come up with one of those cases like the ones that Koesler always helps us with . . . you know, where we've used him as a resource person?"

"What kind of chance would that be, honey? I mean, what are the odds?" Anne Marie said. "It's not as if Father Koesler were on a retainer for the department. Or even that you really expect to use him some more. For all you know, you'll never need his expertise again."

"Still and all, I'd feel better knowing he was here . . . that he was available if we did need him."

"Zoo, he's not that far away," Zack said. "He's just up in Georgian Bay."

"Where's that?" Zoo shot back. "I can't place it off the top of my head."

"It's in Canada."

"Canada's a big country."

"Well, it's in Ontario, that much I know."

"Can you reach him?" Zoo asked.

"It's more a question of will he leave us alone down here," Zack answered. "He left this afternoon, after making sure I knew where all the nooks and crannies are. I didn't think I'd ever get him out of here.

"And then—can you believe it?—who should phone from en route late this afternoon but our reluctant vacationer, Bob Koesler."

"He's really not that far? He's in touch? We can reach him?"

"Zoo . . ." Anne Marie maintained her light tone. "You never seemed so dependent on Father Koesler in the past. Why, I've even heard that there was a time when you resented his involvement in a homicide investigation."

"That was before I got to know him. After I got convinced that his involvement wasn't just because he wanted to meddle in police business. He's not pushy. He just puts himself at our disposal when we invite him to help out.

"I guess I must've grown to depend on him being here."

"Brother," Zack said, "I *am* taking his place. Why don't you lean on me if you come up with some problem that needs help? I had a talk with Father Koesler before he left yesterday. He explained to me, and gave me some examples of how he's helped you over the years.

"All he was doing was leading you through the maze that the Catholic Church is so good at creating. No reason why I can't help you out if, by rare accident, you happen to come up with a 'Koesler situation.'"

"I don't know . . . he's good."

It was all the priest could do to stop himself from laughing out loud. "Well, for what it's worth—and it looks like you don't think it's worth all that much—I offer my services.

"Besides, with Bob Koesler you were dealing with a working pastor. All the while he was helping you, he was supposed to be caring for the day-to-day operation of a—busy, as far as I know—parish. But I'm not going to be weighed down with all that. Bob assured me—and from what I've seen it's true—that the parish secretary can take care of the nuts and bolts of the parish. I'm just there for the ride.

"So: unencumbered with demanding parochial responsibilities, I am yours for the asking. *If* the need arises. And my hunch agrees with Anne Marie that neither Father Koesler nor I will be needed by the Detroit Police Department."

The threesome seemed to be taking turns alternately talking and eating.

"Look at it this way, honey," Anne Marie said. "Supposing that what we don't think will happen does happen. What would you do? You wouldn't call poor Father Koesler in, away from a very well-deserved vacation?"

Zoo looked off in the distance. Of course he would call Koesler. And not just for a phone consultation. Lieutenant Tully would fully expect Father Koesler to come right back and provide whatever help he could. And in fact, the supposition would have it that Father Koesler would want to return and help. It—this dedicated commitment—would be the exact way Lieutenant Tully himself would react.

"I know you," Anne Marie said. "If you're pondering my question that long, you don't think it's all that cut and dried. But your answer would be, Yes, you would certainly call him and expect him to come running home . . . wouldn't you?"

"Well . . . yes, I would. I know what I'm supposed to say. But this is how I feel."

Zack waved a chicken wing lightly. "We're getting sidetracked. I want to get up to date with you folks. And here we are trying to provide for something that has little chance of happening."

"No, Zack. I know the lieutenant."

"I like to be prepared," Zoo explained.

"'Chance favors the prepared mind,'" Anne Marie quoted.

"That's good," Zack said. "Original?"

Anne Marie swallowed and smiled. "No. Louis Pasteur. But it is good, isn't it?"

"I thought if Pasteur said something it would have to be, 'Wash up.'"

"But," Anne Marie said, "it does highlight Zoo's approach to life . . . at least to his work—which is sort of his life."

"That's it," Zoo affirmed. "I want to be ready for anything and everything. I'm in a business of reacting to things I have no control over. I mean, we're sitting here eating and talking while somewhere in this city some guy is getting worked up enough to kill his enemy. Or he got burned in a drug deal. Or he thinks his woman is dissing him. Or his baby is making too much noise.

"And there are hundreds of like scenarios. He's gonna shoot or stab or strangle or run over.

"But I don't know this till we get called to the scene. We look at what he's done. Then we've got to play catch-up. We've got to react to what he's done. Already we're behind. And the longer it takes us to track down the guy who did it and collect enough evidence to take to the prosecutor, the less likely we are to finish our operation successfully.

"So," Zoo concluded, "the more I can depend on sources—like Father Koesler, or technicians, or snitches—the faster I can make progress in wrapping up the case."

"That makes sense," his brother allowed.

"Right. See, I pretty much know by now how Koesler's brain works. You're unknown territory."

"So you want to see beforehand what areas, if any, I could help you in before you need me. I'm maybe one of the ways you can be prepared. If I could be a good resource . . . if I could help you prepare your mind . . . chance or accidental slipups could favor you. Something like that?"

"Something like that."

Father Tully laid his utensils on his plate. He had finished the main course, which had not been preceded by four other courses. "What can I tell you that will help you know whether or not I could be of any assistance to you?"

"I don't know." Zoo finished his meal. "Well . . . okay: Father Koesler keeps mentioning a Church council that changed everything—or at least lots of things—for Catholics. It's nothing that happened ages ago . . . more kind of recent."

"Gotta be Vatican II."

"That's it," Anne Marie affirmed.

"Okay," Zack said.

"I'll get dessert. Everyone for ice cream on your apple pie?"
Two nods favored à la mode.

"Okay. I think I've got what you want to know.

"First off, I'm forty-five—which I used to think was old. But not anymore. Bob Koesler is sixty-nine. Which from where I'm sitting looks pretty old. But Koesler doesn't strike me as being old. Everybody's different, I guess.

"Vatican II ran from 1962 to '65. I was about thirteen when it ended. So, among other things, I was used to segregated rest rooms and drinking fountains, the back of the bus, theater balconies, and lots of other things for 'colored only.'

"Of course we didn't have a parochial school. But I went to catechism regularly—Mama saw to that. And I went with her to Sunday Mass, which was in Latin. And we went to Forty Hours devotions. And benediction Sunday afternoons.

"I learned Latin responses so I could be an altar boy. I learned the fundamentals of my religion out of a little book called The *Baltimore Catechism*. I thought that the only reason so many of my buddies were Baptist was because they weren't smart enough to see that my Catholic Church was 'The One, True Church.'

"And then, as I went through my teen years in the Josephite seminary, I saw all those Catholic things—those things that I was brought up to believe could never change—change.

"Mass and the other sacraments were in English. Soon enough the *Baltimore Catechism* became a collector's item. My Baptist buddies were going to heaven just like that tiny elite minority of Catholics in our neighborhood.

"And eventually, as I grew to manhood, mostly in a seminary, I saw a Protestant minister—of all things—begin to free our people.

"So, Zoo: That's where I am.

"And here's where Father Koesler is: he was ordained in 1954, two years after I was born. He became a priest in a Church where nearly everybody believed—incorrectly—that nothing had ever changed and nothing would ever change. I was ordained in 1977, after everything changed. And everything would continue to change."

Anne Marie brought dessert and coffee.

Zoo flattened the ice cream into a glob, covering the warm surface of his pie. "Then . . . you're sort of a new breed of Catholic clergy?"

"Once upon a time I was."

"Once upon a time! How could that be?" Anne Marie exclaimed.

"There's a wave that came after us," the priest explained. "And, oddly enough, this latest wave pretty much resembles the earlier breed."

"What?" Zoo and Anne Marie chimed.

Father Tully sipped his coffee. Since sampling Father Koesler's brew, every other cup of coffee had been delicious by comparison. It couldn't be the Detroit water. "I hope I can clear this up. Father Koesler is among the last of a long, long line of priests that goes back almost as far as the mind can imagine. He's the kind of dedicated priest who attracted kids like me to follow him.

"I know you've heard about the council, Zoo, 'cause you just got done telling me that Father Koesler had told you about it. It really hit old-time priests hard. Koesler and guys like him landed on their feet. Some others didn't. Some didn't read the documents that came from the council. They didn't understand the changes. They grew to hate and ignore everything conciliar. Most of all, they never grasped the special 'spirit' that came from the council.

"By and large, we, the new breed who matured in the wake of the council, were infected with the council and its spirit. Then a lot of the priests in Koesler's age group and older got fed up. By their actions—and their attitude—they were saying, 'Okay, it's your Church now. It doesn't resemble my Church. So, you can have it.'

"Some of these priests resigned their positions as pastors and marked time until it was okay to retire. And that was another change that happened as a remote result of the council. Before this, priests didn't retire; they died in harness.

"Some of the priests of my group got impatient with Church leaders who were scared by what was happening in all facets of theology, Church law, and, mostly, liturgy. Those leaders wanted to dig in and recapture whatever was salvageable from the past.

"That did two things: It discouraged my crowd; but they were too young to retire, so many of them left the priesthood outright. And it managed to turn seminarians around till they became more like the priests who are now retiring: they're just marking time.

"So, Zoo, that's the long way around answering your question of whether I represent the new wave or new breed. It's a three-layer cake and my gang is the middle.

"Now you've learned something more about me: ask me the time and I'll tell you how to make a clock.

"But it also should indicate that I'm not all that different from Bob Koesler. I wasn't a priest before the council. But I was a Catholic who lived before, during, and after it." He shook his head. "Just listen to me: I'm not asking for an extra job," he explained. "I only thought I could put you at ease during what I'm sure will be a very brief vacation for one of your valued sources, Father Koesler. The way I've run on, anyone could swear that I was interviewing for the job."

Now that dessert was finished they were on coffee refills.

Anne Marie smiled sweetly, leaned forward, and patted the priest's arm. "Zachary, it helped. Believe me it did. I like to think I'm a pretty plugged-in Catholic. But some of what you said was new to me. Besides, it helped us understand what makes you you."

"What about going into the living room? Let's get comfy," Zoo said.

Zachary felt reluctant to leave the intimacy of the kitchen. But, in the long run, it worked. The three newly introduced kinfolk talked far into the evening. They had so much to learn of each other. Anne Marie recounted her life before and since becoming a teacher. She spoke movingly of her first meeting with Zoo . . . how he had rescued her from a purse-snatcher. She counted the incident a product of Divine Providence. The priest found no reason to doubt that.

Zoo, ordinarily not garrulous, spoke sketchily of life in a large family—eight children. All the while his father was with them, they lived in modest lower-middle-class comfort. But after his unexpected departure, life hardened considerably. Now, five of the children had passed on. The remainder, aside from Zoo, lived in distant states. Anne Marie promised to give Father Tully addresses and phone numbers.

Zoo spoke of his life as a police officer and how he'd been "discovered" by Walt Koznicki and how close they'd grown. Koznicki had been Zoo's sponsor in the Homicide Division—then the major league of the department.

Father Tully had already given a bit of a biographical sketch in trying to convince Zoo that there was life before and after Father Koesler. Now, he filled in the gaps.

So absorbed were they no one had thought to turn on any lights. They became aware of this only when it grew so dark they could scarcely see each other.

"Well," Zoo slapped his knees as he stood, "it's getting late. And I've got an early morning. What say I drive you home, Zack?"

"Good idea." The priest felt stiff from sitting so long. "That way I'll be up nice and early to take Father Koesler's first call of the day."

They laughed at the thought of Koesler's lack of total confidence in his parish sitter. He was like a nervous parent phoning home repeatedly to make sure the children were still alive.

As Zachary prepared to leave, Anne Marie hugged him, then kissed his cheek affectionately. That one simple gesture more than anything else this evening made him feel as if he had found his family.

The two men entered Zoo's car for the brief ride to St. Joseph's rectory.

Zoo started the engine, but before he put the car in gear he turned and said, "This is good. I really didn't know how it was going to go. But it was better than I hoped." He extended his hand. "Welcome home."

Zachary took his brother's hand. "It feels almost as if we've grown up together, instead of just discovering each other. Tonight, I'm a happy camper."

"Mind if I catch up on the news?" Zoo said, as he turned on the radio.

The lead story on the eleven o'clock newscast shattered the evening's homey warmth. A police officer had been shot on the Lodge Freeway, not far from where they were now.

A car had apparently stalled on the shoulder of the freeway. A young woman had stood near the rear of the vehicle, in obvious distress.

A lone officer in a blue-and-white had pulled up behind the car. He'd got out and as he'd approached the seemingly empty vehicle, two men had jumped out. The first one had fired a single shot and the officer had gone down.

Several passing cars slowed as they reached the scene. The occupants saw clearly what had happened. With good reason, none of them stopped. But several with cellular phones immediately called 911. Some were so nervous and upset that they were not much help in identifying either what had happened or where. But one caller, who was regularly scolded for watching too much television, relied on what he had seen so often on cops-and-robbers TV. "Officer down," he said tersely. Then he gave a calm description of the location. He answered all the questions asked him by the operator.

Zoo started his flasher and sped down the nearly empty surface street. His police band caught the organized chaos as his fellow officers operated on adrenaline. The police took care of their own in very special ways.

Father Tully volunteered to get out and hail a cab. At the very least, he urged his brother to drop him at the rectory and take off immediately. Zoo took the second option. Seldom had Zachary Tully ever been delivered and dropped so speedily and abruptly.

The priest preferred not to linger on a dark, abandoned street on the fringe of downtown Detroit. He hastened into the rectory, where he turned on the TV news to see if there was any more on the shooting.

Obviously, the shooting had been the lead story on the telecast. Father Tully recalled the TV news maxim: if it bleeds, it leads. Now the newscasters were reporting less momentous and lighter news items. Father Tully hoped they would return to the police shooting before they wrapped things up.

Just before sports and weather the anchorwoman announced that the new and controversial branch of Adams Bank and Trust would be opened for the first time and for the first customers at 9:30 A.M. Friday, the day after tomorrow. And, in a move that surprised many in the banking industry, CEO Thomas A. Adams had named Allan Ulrich as general manager of the new branch.

Until today, the anchor continued, front-runner for this position had been Nancy Groggins, wife of construction entrepreneur Joel Groggins. Mrs. Groggins, who also possessed many of the credentials of Al Ulrich, was African-American and a woman, which prompted some to speculate that she might have related better to the neighborhood.

There followed film of a smiling Nancy Groggins refusing to be baited by reporters and congratulating Al Ulrich.

The next shot featured Ulrich stating that he felt fortunate to be selected by Tom Adams, a man and a business leader respected by his employees and the city at large.

Next there was the mayor with characteristic enthusiasm—so completely absent in his predecessor—marking the launching of this bank branch as turning another corner in the rebuilding of Detroit.

Next, weather and sports. While a happy sportscaster and weather forecaster interplayed with happy anchors, Father Tully pondered.

This made no sense. Just last night, Tom Adams had explained the choice of bank manager, asked Tully's impression of the two candidates, and given the impression he would name the candidate the priest favored.

Trying to be conscientious in this modest commission, Father Tully had made a determined effort to talk with and learn about both candidates. He understood, especially after his conversation with Joel Groggins, what would be expected of the new manager. Father Tully sensed how well matched these competitors were. Where one was slightly stronger in one category, the other was correspondingly strong in another. And vice versa.

Nonetheless, Father Tully had duly reported his choice to an oddly distracted Tom Adams. The priest was in agreement with Adams that Nancy Groggins should be the new manager in this pressurized position. Indeed, he had—at least until this moment—taken her accession as a fait accompli.

What could have happened in less than a day to change Adams's mind? Whatever it was, it must have been significant.

One more indication, thought Father Tully, of how little I understand big business. *Hi diddlydee, the priestly life for me!*

At this point in his rumination, the news program was all but completed. Before signing off, the anchor directed a return to the exterior of Detroit's Receiving Hospital, where a TV reporter was doing a standup summation on the police officer who'd been shot.

Tully's attention returned to the set.

"Carmen," the sober-faced reporter said, "we're told the condition of Officer Marcantonio is listed as serious. As we speak he has been taken to the operating room and surgery is under way. The doctors and other officers we spoke with were very guarded. As further details develop, we'll keep you informed."

Carmen Harlan's face filled the screen. "Thank you, John. We're running out of time. But before we go, here's Dennis at the crime scene."

"Thank you, Carmen. I have with me Lieutenant Alonzo Tully,

who is the senior officer on the scene. Can you tell us, Lieutenant, what we have here?"

Father Tully leaned forward. He was so immensely proud of his brother.

Lieutenant Tully was occupied with something out of camera range. He appeared to be paying minimum attention to the reporter's question. "It looks like one of those Good Samaritan set-ups."

"Can you tell our viewers just what that is?"

Both Tullys regarded the reporter as if he might be slightly retarded. Who would not know the original Bible story and/or its modern-day application in crime annals?

"It's a scam," Lieutenant Tully explained, returning his attention to what was occupying him off-camera, "where two or more people pretend they've got car trouble. They pull off the road onto a shoulder—usually, like tonight, on a freeway shoulder.

"A female stands by the car. She seems helpless and scared. Her accomplice, or accomplices, hide, usually in the car, but sometimes behind nearby shrubbery.

"They wait for some good-hearted person to pull off the road and—like a Good Samaritan—offer assistance. Then, when the would-be benefactor gets close enough, the accomplices jump out of hiding. They rob, maybe mug, maybe even kill the innocent motorist. Then they take off in his car—and theirs too if it's not a klunker they may have swiped.

"Tonight they had bad luck. The one who stopped to give aid was a cop. So there went their scam. And they shot him."

"Lieutenant Tully, do the police have anything to go on?"

Tully looked directly into the camera as if he were addressing those responsible for this attack. "Yeah, we've got a pretty good description of the vehicle they're driving, as well as of the perpetrators themselves." With emphasis, he concluded, "Their bad luck has just begun."

Back to the studio for a speedy signoff, followed by a voice-over promising the "Tonight Show" "after these announcements."

Father Tully would not wade through countless commercials. He turned off the set and headed for bed.

How silly it had been for him to even consider seriously helping his brother. There was nothing "Catholic" or "religious" about a Good Samaritan crime except the designation. Father Tully could take solace in the fact that even the redoubtable Father Koesler would be of no service to Lieutenant Tully in this case.

The priest decided right then and there that he was going to relax and enjoy this visit to Detroit and his prized contact with his newly discovered family.

Lieutenant Tully would just have to muddle through on his own.

But before he retired for the night, the priest prayed for the wounded officer, and for the surgeons who, as this prayer was being offered, stood between this brave man and death.

Nine

THEY WERE to meet at Carl's, a venerable chophouse on Grand River near downtown Detroit. Anne Marie, on her lunch break from school, picked up her brother-in-law.

Only within the past hour was Lieutenant Tully certain he would be able to join them. At nearly 11 A.M., the Good Samaritan suspects had been arrested and booked.

It was Friday. Virtually all of Lieutenant Tully's Thursday had been spent on the Good Samaritan shooting. Meanwhile Father Tully, escorted by one of Tom Adams's PR people, had been taken on an all-day tour of Detroit and environs.

Anne Marie and Father Tully arrived first. They were seated at once at a table for four. There were no tables for three. Anne Marie explained that the relatively small crowd for lunch was a sign of the times. Twenty or so years ago, noontime would have found a crowd in the lobby awaiting tables. However, under a new administration, it appeared that the downtown area was on its way back up and, hopefully, would soon return to its former vitality.

Father Tully scanned the ample menu. He concluded this was basically a meat, fish, and potato restaurant. Anne Marie confirmed this, but assured him that what they did here they did well.

At this point Zoo arrived. Father Tully noted him nod to several of the patrons as he approached the table.

Obviously his brother was well known and, seemingly, well liked. This pleased the priest.

They greeted each other, Zoo kissing Anne Marie and patting his brother's shoulder.

They passed on alcohol, ordering coffee instead. Zoo and Anne Marie were frequent patrons and knew what they wanted: ground round for him; salad for her. Father Tully settled for a tuna sandwich.

"I know I shouldn't feel this way," said the priest, "but I can't help but think I've been a slacker. Yesterday you were working so hard on the Good Samaritan shooting that we couldn't get together even for a minute."

Zoo's smile was sardonic. "Feel you should've been out there helping me catch the bad guys?"

The priest laughed. "No . . . no. We've been over that. I just felt as if I could or should be able to do something."

"Cheer up, little brother. You've got some time left. And in my business you never know what's gonna turn up next."

"It all worked out well," Anne Marie assured Father Tully. "Yesterday was your day on the town, courtesy of Thomas Adams. How was it?"

"A grand tour." The priest broke a bread stick, and nibbled. "My guide knew his history of this city extremely well. I could almost see Cadillac's landing party. And the construction of Ste. Anne's. And the cholera epidemic. The street cars. Hudson's. The place where Ty Cobb and Charlie Gehringer played. And—a real pity—the riot area." He looked at them seriously. "You should really be proud of this city."

"We are," Anne Marie said. "Or, at least, we will be again."

The coffee arrived. Zoo immediately took several appreciative sips.

"I hope," the priest said to his brother, "we're not keeping you from your job."

Both Zoo and Anne Marie laughed.

"If you're keeping me from anything, brother, it's sleep. But sleep can be fitted into the cracks of life." It was obvious that, for Zoo, coffee was replacing sleep.

"He's been on the shooting case two nights and a day," Anne Marie said. "He's not kidding about sleep; all he's had over the past roughly thirty-six hours are catnaps."

"And," Zoo added, "fortunately for our luncheon date, most of those catnaps came earlier this morning."

Conversation halted as their order was served.

Zoo cut into one of the largest circles of ground round Father Tully had ever seen. Anne Marie's salad was huge. And the priest's tuna, fighting to escape its layers of bread, was nearly buried in chips.

"We made the arrests pretty quickly even for us," Zoo said, picking up the conversation. "We collared the girl and her driver just hours after the shooting. The second guy was a little harder to find. But we got him early this morning.

"We went slow. We went by the book and made sure to touch all the bases."

Father Tully decided to use knife and fork in eating his sandwich, rather than disgrace himself by squirting everyone with squeezed tuna. "What I don't understand is why *you* stayed on the case. After all, it wasn't a murder . . . thank God."

Zoo shrugged. "It was a cop. And only a fluke kept it from being homicide. But"—he smiled at his brother—"I guess you wouldn't buy the fluke bit, would you?"

The priest returned the smile. "Oh, we're not quick to claim miracles. The fact that the bullet hit the Bible in the officer's shirt pocket could, I'd be the first to admit, qualify as a fluke."

"I'll bet his family doesn't think it's a fluke," Anne Marie said.

"Not for a second," Zoo said. "And I really can't blame them. There's no way of tellin' where a bullet's gonna go once it enters a body. Take the Kennedy bullet: went through him and maybe Governor Connally. I don't know whether that really happened, but it could've."

"So what really happened here, Zoo?" asked Anne Marie.

The lieutenant paused to swallow. "Deflected. It went through the pocket Bible and coursed downward. . . ." He gestured to show the invisible path the bullet took. "Lodged in his abdomen. Still and all, it was a tricky operation . . . a lot of internal bleeding. But it looks like he'll make it."

"Thank God," the priest intoned.

"Maybe . . . maybe. Maybe 'Thank God.' If it hadn't been for that bulky little book, the slug definitely would've taken some other direction. No one could know which way. But it easily could've killed our guy. So at the time of the shooting through the time of the operation, it could've been a homicide." Zoo looked somber.

"I know Sergeant Marcantonio. Met his wife and kids. A good cop. Besides, I started the investigation . . . see?" He addressed his brother. "There were lots of reasons I followed this thing through to the end."

The priest nodded. "Ordinarily I'm against capital punishment. But if there had to be one crime that carried that penalty, I'd vote for the Good Samaritan offense. In addition to being cowardly and terrorizing and deadly, it definitely discourages well-meaning people from coming to the aid of someone who really does need help. So I'm doubly glad you caught them."

Anne Marie caught the waitress's eye and asked for a doggie bag for the remainder of her salad, which was substantial.

"I'm sorry I have to leave," she said. "If I don't get back to school, my kids—good as they are—will be plotting the destruction of our building."

Zoo looked up, suppressing a smile. "I suppose you're going to stick me with the check."

Straightfaced, she replied, "As a taxpayer, I pay your salary. It's the least you can do." She scooped up the doggie bag and left.

"You two have a lot of fun, don't you?" said Father Tully.

"You noticed."

"It's obvious. This is better than anything that went before?"

Zoo looked sharply at his brother. "You want to know about my personal life before Anne Marie?"

The priest shook his head. "Anne Marie brought me up to speed when we first met. When she picked me up and drove me to your home. She thought it would be easier on everyone."

Zoo was finishing his lunch, as was the priest. Both, for far different reasons, were fast eaters.

"She's right," Zoo said. "As usual, she's right. She undoubtedly told you: it's the job. My being a cop was what challenged the other two relationships. With my first wife, I didn't know there was going to be this competition. But it grew. Both of us fought it. We fought it until there wasn't any strength left. So we called it quits.

"I was alone for a long time after that. Then a real neat lady entered my life. This time, I knew about the job and how it would complicate my life with somebody—anybody—else. I was straight with Alice. We thought we could lick it as long as we were aware of the problem. Turned out we couldn't.

"Then Anne Marie came along. We were together a long time before we thought seriously about marriage. We talked and planned. Honest, I was the one who fought getting married. Early on, Anne Marie was convinced we could do it. And so far"—he rapped the table—"so good."

The waitress, taking Zoo's gesture as a summons, popped up at their side. "More coffee?" Zoo shook his head and presented a credit card.

"Oddly," Father Tully said, returning to the subject at hand, "I think I'm best able to understand what you're saying."

Zoo looked surprised. "You're not married!"

The priest chuckled. "No. And my experience with women is more like that of a spectator. But it's coming."

"What's coming?"

"A Roman Catholic clergy that freely chooses to be married or celibate. It's just around the corner. There's hardly anybody in the seminary studying to be a priest. The time is fast approaching when there won't be enough priests left to serve the Catholic population. Catholicism is a sacramental religion. And to make sacraments you gotta have priests. When the supply of priests dwindles down to a precious few, the Pope and the bishops will undoubtedly be forced to accept what just about everybody seems to think is the ultimate solution to the priest shortage: a married priesthood.

"Personally, I don't think this is the answer. I think the Church has to open up interiorly, fearlessly—like it did back in the days of Pope John XXIII.

"But the first step will be an optional married clergy. And that's when we meet problems like yours: which comes first, my priesthood or my marriage?"

The waitress returned. Zoo added a tip and signed the chit. As he tucked his wallet in his pocket, Zoo, one eyebrow arched, said, "Would you get married . . . I mean if the Church let you?"

"I don't really know. I may never get the chance to know. When I say the move to optional celibacy is just around the corner, I mean the Church's distance to the corner. The Church thinks in hundreds of years. And, while I doubt this change will wait for a hundred years, I also doubt it'll take place tomorrow.

"As for there being problems for priests and their wives, I don't mean it would be an epidemic. I'm sure that cops who experience marital problems are in the minority. Not everybody, by any means, is as dedicated to police work as you are. And not all priests would experience similar problems. But I think the average for priests would be higher—at least in the beginning.

"I could be wrong, but I think that among priests the sense of total dedication and availability is more common than among police."

"Interesting," Zoo said, whether or not he agreed.

The two rose and headed for the exit.

"Say," Zoo said, "when Anne Marie was giving you a little history on me, did she mention anything about our wedding?"

"How do you mean?"

"Well, I was married before. But at no time during the process of getting married did that come up. We did have a few meetings with her priest. I kind of anticipated we'd have to get into that. From some of the things I picked up working with Father Koesler, I know your Church requires more than a civil divorce before another marriage. It's called an annulment, no?"

Father Tully nodded. He desperately wanted to change the subject. Nothing came to mind.

"It was like waiting for the second shoe to fall. The subject just never came up. I didn't push it. I was happy it was apparently going so smoothly. I was sure if the priest insisted on getting this annulment there would be lots of paperwork and long delays."

Father Tully made no comment.

"Well, that was *her* priest." Zoo smiled indulgently on his brother. "Now I've got *my* priest. So, how about it: Do you have any idea what went on?"

Zoo's beeper sounded.

"'Scuse me, I've got to get this." Zoo headed for a phone.

Father Tully breathed a sigh of relief. He knew perfectly well what had been done and not done in the marriage of his brother and sister-in-law. He had, on occasion, done something similar for couples. Resulting in a valid and real marriage in civil law as well as sincere consciences. But being invalid and carrying no weight in Church law.

Father Tully had every reason to believe that the consciences of both partners to his brother's marriage were at ease. Asked if they were married, neither one would have responded, "a little bit" or "partially." Their consciences were at peace and Father Tully was not about to upset this package.

Zoo returned from the phone transformed. Where a few moments ago, he had been relaxed and mildly inquisitive, he was now all business. "There's been a murder. That new branch of Adams Bank and Trust—somebody was killed."

Excitement almost snatched Father Tully's breath away. "Who was it? Do you know who was killed?"

"The manager." Zoo was walking so rapidly that his brother found it hard to keep up.

Zoo was parked around the corner on Grand River so they didn't have to wait for Carl's parking attendant. As they entered the car, Zoo said, "I'll drop you off at St. Joe's."

Was this a pattern? It was beginning to seem that when it was time for Zoo to drive his brother home, some emergency intervened. Father Tully was definitely ready for a change of routine. "If you don't mind . . . I'd really like to go with you."

Zoo, starting the car, glanced at his brother. "This is not a field trip."

"I know. And I'm very well coached that you do not suffer non-professionals gladly. I know all that. And I won't get in anybody's way. But I'd like to go with you. I just may have something to contribute . . . and I'm not playing Father Koesler."

Zoo said nothing as he drove toward St. Joe's. Suddenly, he veered away from the parish and headed out Jefferson. "Okay. But stay right where I tell you. Why do you want to come on this run, anyhow?"

"That award party I was at the other night: I met the full cast of characters who run this bank. I met the new manager, Al Ulrich. Mr. Adams asked me to give him my impression of Ulrich and Nancy Groggins as to which would make the better manager for the new branch.

"As a matter of fact, before I had a chance to meet either contestant, Adams confided that he favored Nancy. And, after meeting both of them, I agreed with Adams and I told him as much before leaving.

"That's why I was so surprised when Adams announced that he had selected Ulrich for the job.

"Now Ulrich is dead.

"I just have a very strong feeling that I should be there. I can't tell you why. The whole idea is new to me. It's almost like Providence wants it that way."

"Okay," Zoo said. "But just stay put and observe."

Ten

As THEY approached the crime scene, Father Tully surveyed the territory. It was a mixed bag.

The housing ran from neatly kept bungalows to empty flats without panes or doors. Once, years ago, this had undoubtedly been a working, middle-class neighborhood. One whose front porches had held gliders. In spring, summer, and fall, neighbors had gathered to talk, to listen, to learn, and to live. Neighbors who had never heard of the phrase "drive-by shooting."

But that was a time whose return no one could hope to anticipate.

Tully's car, flasher blinking, pulled up to the new bank building.

"What's happened to this neighborhood?" Father Tully asked. Yesterday's tour had featured nothing like this.

"Gangs. Drugs and might make right."

An extensive area was cordoned off by bright yellow ribbon signifying a crime scene. All unauthorized people were to observe the restriction and stay out.

"Remember: you're a spectator."

Father Tully followed Zoo, stepping over the tape.

Several detectives from the lieutenant's Homicide Squad were on the scene. Two of them, Sergeants Phil Mangiapane and Angie Moore, walked toward the newcomers. They hesitated when they saw a man in clerical clothing accompanying their leader. Angie Moore was the first to note a resemblance—albeit slight—between the two men.

Moore and Mangiapane had intended to bring the lieutenant

up to date on what they had learned. The completely unexpected presence of a strange clergyman gave them pause.

The lieutenant perceived this. "Sergeants Mangiapane and Moore, meet Father Zachary Tully."

The name stopped them in their tracks.

Mangiapane was the first to extend his hand. "*Father* Tully? You couldn't be . . . no you couldn't—"

"I'll betcha I could," said the priest.

Mangiapane's hand stayed extended even after the priest had shaken it.

Angie Moore, perhaps because she'd had a bit more time to adjust to this incredible event, seemed entirely composed. "Glad to meet you," she said as she shook Zack's hand.

With a note of pride in his voice, Zoo said, "Father Tully is my half brother. We have the same father. Until a couple of days ago each of us didn't know the other existed. My brother's a priest . . . a Catholic priest. He belongs to the . . . uh . . ."

"Josephite order," the priest supplied.

"And," Zoo said, "he's gonna be here for maybe a couple of weeks."

By now, Mangiapane was able to close his mouth. "A Catholic priest! Who could . . . ? Is this for real?"

"It's for real, Manj. Now: what've we got?"

Angie Moore was by far the more self-possessed. "It looks like robbery armed and murder."

"It was the bank manager?"

"Yeah," Moore said. "This was supposed to be opening day. Sort of letting the neighborhood welcome the bank and the bank making itself at home here."

"Opening day," mused Zoo. "Okay, give me what you got."

"This is a new branch of Adams Bank and Trust," Mangiapane said.

"That I know."

"Well," Mangiapane, undaunted, proceeded, "the general staff have been working with each other for a while. They were specially trained for this neighborhood. The manager," he consulted his notes, "Allan Ulrich, was named only a couple of days ago. Yesterday he met with his staff for the first time . . . to give them a rundown of procedures and stuff like that."

"He—Ulrich, that is," said Moore, "decided he would be the person to open up in the morning, Monday through Friday. He was supposed to arrive at 8 A.M.—and, according to the cameras, he did."

"Cameras going all night?"

"Yes," Moore said.

"Go on." Zoo looked at Mangiapane.

"The staff put up the decorations"—he motioned toward the bunting on the walls and the helium balloons lightly grazing the ceiling—"late yesterday afternoon. Everything was ready for opening day. Like Angie said, Ulrich was here right on the button at eight.

"A little while after that, the film shows that he went to the door. That's just out of camera range, so you can't immediately see who came in. But then you see Ulrich backtracking into the lobby. He's got both hands raised. Then the perp fires—one shot. Hits Ulrich in the forehead, between the eyes. His knees buckle and he hits the floor.

"Then the perp moves in. It's either blind luck, or the guy knew where the cameras were aimed. 'Cause he pretty well stayed out of the picture. Just some shots of a shoulder, his back. But then he got into the control room and killed the power: the cameras go off then."

Moore offered some backgrounding. "They had a signal set up. Ulrich planned on coming in an hour before the other employees. He would be here at eight. The rest were supposed to arrive at nine. And the bank would open for business at nine-thirty.

"When Ulrich had gotten everything set up, he was to raise the blind in his office. That was the signal: The employees would know it was safe to enter. When the first of them got here this morning, Ulrich's car was in the lot, but the blind was still down.

"They phoned the bank. There wasn't any answer. So they called the police. But the police were already on the way: the monitoring system that protects bank security had caught noises that sounded like someone trying to break into the safe.

"A couple of patrolmen got here and checked things out. The perp was gone. Impossible to know exactly when he left, but it had to be before the employees got here. And the employees were here five or ten minutes before the cops got here.

"Of course they found the body. And some marks on the vault. Looks like the idiot thought he could get into the vault by hammering the lock open.

"As soon as they found the body the patrolman called us. And . . . we responded. You weren't summoned because you were tying up the Marcantonio shooting.

"And that's pretty much where we are, Zoo."

"One more thing," said Mangiapane. "Just before the perp shot Ulrich, the manager seemed to lunge at the perp. Maybe he was trying to be a hero."

"It wasn't a good moment to become a hero," Moore added.

"You'd think he'd know better," Zoo commented. "Money isn't worth a life. Those are words to live by in this day and age. If you got something somebody wants, and the somebody is waving a gun, give him what he wants real quick. We might be able to get the thing back. But we can't bring a guy back to life." The statement was made for the benefit of his brother, but when he looked over his shoulder, there was no sign of Zack.

"Okay . . ." Zoo looked about. What was his brother up to? "The body's been picked up?"

"Yeah," Mangiapane said. "Doc Moellmann himself is doing the autopsy."

"Okay. What's going on now?"

"Rughurst's over there," Mangiapane inclined his head to where the FBI was on the job, as was usual in similar cases involving banks.

Zoo smiled. "We know S. A. Rughurst, don't we?"

Mangiapane and Moore nodded.

"Our guys," Moore said, "are interrogating the employees. And over there in the corner is . . ." She looked at her notes. "Nancy Groggins. Married to Joel Groggins, the construction guy."

"Yeah," Zoo said. "What's she doing here?" And, under his breath, "And what is my brother doing talking to her?" This definitely was not what was meant by being a spectator. "Make sure that our guys get around the neighborhood. See if anybody saw or heard anything."

"Right, Zoo." Both Mangiapane and Moore headed out to do that very thing.

Lieutenant Tully strode toward Nancy Groggins—and his brother.

The employees, to a person, were visibly affected by what had happened. Some fought back tears. Others wept openly. Nancy Groggins dabbed at her eyes with a small lacy handkerchief. She looked up, blinking, as Lieutenant Tully approached.

"I was just trying to console Mrs. Groggins," Father Tully explained.

"Are you an employee here, ma'am?" Tully asked.

"I . . . well . . . I guess I am now."

"How's that?"

"She was the other person who was being considered as manager of this branch," Father Tully explained. "I mentioned her earlier, didn't I?"

Zoo directed a pained look at his brother. It seemed to say, I don't tell you how to say Mass, do I? The priest backed away slightly.

"Yes, ma'am," Tully said. "How is it that you may be an employee here?"

"Mr. Adams phoned me just a little while ago. He asked if I would consider taking Al's position—at least on a temporary basis . . . until things settle down."

"And you told him . . . ?"

"I said of course I would. For as long as Mr. Adams wants me to stay."

"Aren't you a little nervous about that decision? After all, the bank hasn't even officially opened and already there's been a murder."

Nancy nodded and, without looking up to meet Tully's eyes, said, "We all knew this was a dangerous section of the city. That Al's death belabors the fact doesn't change things. I volunteered for this assignment and I'm as ready now as I was before.

"Besides"—she raised her head—"Mr. Adams said he would provide security guards—at least until the neighborhood gets used to us. And maybe longer, if that's what it takes. I don't think anyone—even Mr. Adams—knows what the future holds now."

"You seem to have an awful lot of faith in Adams."

"You don't know the man." Her tone made it a question.

Zoo shook his head. "I know who he is. But not that much about him."

"A wonderful man," Nancy attested. "Wonderful man. You know, I was talking with Al just last night—" She halted, noting confusion on the lieutenant's face. "I'm sorry: Al is the man who . . . the man who was shot." She dabbed at her eyes again with her handkerchief. "He was so enthused about opening this branch. It *is* a thrill. You put your own stamp on the operation. It's something like having a baby.

"Anyway, while we were talking, Al said that even as late as yesterday, Mr. Adams was trying to help Al and his wife with their marriage . . . get them to a marriage counselor."

"Oh?"

Nancy Groggins instantly realized that Lieutenant Tully's one-word question was not an idle one; the information she had just given Tully—that the Ulrichs had marital trouble—could be considered a motive for murder. Her eyes widened. "I didn't mean . . . it's not that . . ." She halted, in some confusion.

"Yes?" Lieutenant Tully prodded gently.

"Well, what I meant was, that just shows how concerned and involved Mr. Adams was with his employees. Even with an opening as important as this, he had time to try to help his people personally," she concluded lamely, but loyally.

Lieutenant Tully gave no indication that he had already made a mental note to check out the widow as a possible suspect in this death. He merely asked, "So, what happens now?"

"There's been a press conference called at the bank's headquarters later this afternoon. My appointment will be announced. Mr. Adams will handle that, of course.

"Pretty much the rest of today we'll try to adjust to what's happened. We have counselors coming in to talk with our people. Mr. Adams's idea, as usual.

"Then, tomorrow and Sunday, we'll come together, get acclimated, map our strategy, and get ready to open on Monday.

"The mayor was supposed to be here Monday for the official grand opening. We'll just combine what should have happened today along with what was planned for Monday. That's about it."

"Okay," Tully said. "Thank you very much, Mrs. Groggins. And," he added, "lots of luck."

As the lieutenant turned, he motioned with his head for his brother to follow him. Almost out of the side of his mouth, Zoo said, "Zachary, stay close to me. We can't have you wandering about in a crime scene. And don't volunteer any questions or opinions. *I* don't have any problem with you. Right now you've arrived out of left field. You're the lieutenant's brother, so you're tolerated."

"Gotcha." Father Tully fell into step behind his brother. Like a faithful, humble wife, he thought.

The lieutenant crossed the floor to greet the FBI agent.

Rughurst's grin was sardonic. "Is the Detroit Police Department supplying priests for criminal investigations? So now you'll have a prayer?"

Tully smiled. "Special Agent Harold Rughurst, meet Father Zachary Tully."

"Tully?"

"My brother."

"This is a long way from Halloween."

"My long-lost brother."

"How come we've never heard of you, Father? Where've you been hiding?"

Responding to a question directed to him personally couldn't violate his brother's admonition of noninvolvement, thought Father Tully. "I'm a Josephite priest. Currently, I'm stationed at a small parish in Dallas. We—the lieutenant and I—just discovered each other a short time ago. Because I'll be here in Detroit only a little while, I'm trying to get as much of my brother as I can. That's why I'm here with him now."

"Well," Rughurst said. "Welcome to Detroit, Father. I guess this pretty much convinces you that Detroit comes to its reputation honestly as the country's murder capital."

"Coming from Dallas, actually, I don't find this so extraordinarily different."

The agent returned his attention to Lieutenant Tully. "Nice work on that freeway shooting."

"Thanks."

"How's the officer . . . Marcantonio . . . how's he doing?"

"Pretty good. He's a lucky guy. If it hadn't been for that Bible in his pocket . . ."

"Yeah, I read about that." Rughurst glanced at the priest. "Maybe prayer is helping after all."

"It couldn't hurt." Zoo was eager to get back to this case. "You here from the beginning of this one, Rug?"

"Practically. I got here while the techs were working. Your guys have the tapes—at least up to where the perp cut the power. They don't look like they'll be much help. But you never know what the experts can squeeze out of them."

"How's it look to you, Rug?"

"It looks like the price you pay for opening a bank in this god-forsaken neighborhood. Like opening a candy shop in a building filled with chocoholics."

"The mayor liked it."

"Sure, it looks good for the city. Return, renaissance, whatever the hell. But this is still a trouble spot. How come there wasn't any police presence?"

Tully shrugged. "They didn't want it. Adams's idea. Thought it would create the impression that the bank people were afraid . . . like they expected trouble."

"They'd have to be nuts if they didn't expect trouble."

Quixotic is the word they're looking for, thought Father Tully. But I'm not going to give it to them.

"You saw the tapes, Rug: whaddya think? The perp look like a local?"

Rughurst massaged his chin, which was cleanly shaven. "Yes. Looked like he was wearing an old sweater and maybe jeans. Couldn't see much of him from the waist down. And a cap covering his ears and pulled down low over his eyes. What I can't figure is why Ulrich opened the door for him."

"Maybe he had his piece out and Ulrich decided he'd stand a better chance with the perp inside where he might be able to wrestle the piece away. I mean, if the guy's holding a gun on you and all that's between you is plate glass, you can be pretty sure if you don't open the door he can waste you from outside."

"Yeah, could be, I guess. In fact," Rughurst added, "the tape does show Ulrich making a move on the perp. That's when he bought it."

"It makes sense all right," the lieutenant agreed. "But the way this scenario is playing out, Ulrich could've opened the door because he didn't want to be inhospitable to one of the neighbors."

Rughurst burst out laughing, but stopped quickly when a few of the grief-stricken employees looked at him sharply. "If it was a neighbor, his feet weren't touching the floor."

"Spaced out, you think?"

The agent nodded definitively. "Whoever heard of taking a bank vault with a hammer?"

"That what he used?"

"That's what it looks like. He must've had a sawed-off sledge. He bashed the vault pretty good. But all he did was make dents. He must've been pretty high. Probably still is."

I know the answer. They don't know about the threatened executives. But how am I ever going to get them to listen? This playing detective was fun, actually, but in this situation very frustrating. Father Tully made a mental note to ask Bob Koesler about it—either on his return or during one of his inevitable phone calls.

"Well," Zoo said, "we'd better get on with this. The media will be breathing down our neck."

"Can you blame them?"

"Not this time, I guess. This is made to order for them—all this prepublicity and all."

The two officers, agreeing to keep each other posted, parted with a handshake, Rughurst nodding a pro forma good-bye to the priest.

Zoo and his faithful shadow crossed to Sergeant Moore, who had just ended an interview with one of the employees. "How's it going, Angie?"

"We're making good time, Zoo . . . but we're not coming up with anything significant."

"Anybody remember someone hanging around this building over the past couple of days?"

Moore frowned. "Yeah. Trouble is there's been a lot of that. The locals were fascinated with this new toy on the block. Not very many are gainfully employed, so watching the comings and goings here was almost better than TV . . . at least it was live entertainment."

"Nobody even a little extra suspicious?"

"Oh, a couple. We're following up on them. A lot of our people are on the street, so we'll probably come up with something soon. It's just frustrating for now. Whoever did this was so dumb—"

"Or high."

"Or high," Moore agreed. "If he was on drugs, even if he's down by this time, he's probably still up emotionally. In any case, it shouldn't be that hard to collar him. That's what's frustrating. We are so close and still so far."

"Hang in there," Zoo encouraged. "I'm going back to headquarters. Let me know if anything breaks."

"Right, Zoo." Sergeant Moore nodded. "Glad to meet you, Father."

"Same here," the priest responded.

Eleven

Lieutenant Tully and his brother were in the car, heading back toward downtown Detroit. They drove in silence. Mostly because Father Tully was reluctant to speak.

"So," Zoo said finally, "how do you feel about your first homicide?"

"It's hardly my first. I've been at the scene of more of them than I want to remember. It's my first experience in the investigative side of a killing. And that is fascinating."

Zoo smiled. "It gets to be routine. The thrill is in the chase. This one won't be very thrilling. Just dogged investigative work: keep asking questions until you find someone with the right answer. It'll happen; it just takes time."

Silence for a few more minutes.

"Did I tell you much about that party I attended night before last?" the priest asked.

"The one at Adams's place? No, not much, as I recall."

The priest turned slightly so he could measure his brother's reaction to his words. "I managed to meet everyone at the party. Outside of Tom Adams, I can't say anybody else there wanted to meet me."

Tully snorted. "*That* kind of party, eh?"

"I guess."

"What was the lineup?"

"There was Adams. Then there were the three executive vice presidents and their wives. And the two candidates for the new branch. As the party developed, there was a double of odd man out—Joel

Groggins and me. The rest of 'em had no trouble relating to each other. Groggins and I were left hanging . . . so we hung out together—"

"Wait a minute. What about Mrs. Ulrich? She wasn't in that tight inner circle."

A good sign. He's listening to me carefully. "No, she's not," said the priest. "But that didn't seem to bother her any. She made a late entrance and sort of took over . . . maybe not as the life of the party, but as a significant guest."

"Okay. So you and Groggins—he's the construction guy?"

"Yeah."

"Okay. So you and Groggins were sort of walled off."

"Yes."

"And his wife is the Nancy we just spoke to in the bank."

"Yes."

"So?"

"So, while nobody else seemed to want to make conversation with us, he and I talked all through the meal."

"I don't want to rush you, but I'm going to be dropping you off at the rectory. Does this story have a point?"

"The point is Groggins gave me a brief sketch of each of the main characters and their interactions. There was an air of tension in that room and Groggins's accounts made the friction pretty clear.

"Alonzo, it boils down to this: The vice presidents—and necessarily their wives—felt threatened by the real possibility of being fired."

"Fired! Why? What for?"

"It all stemmed from the creation of this position of manager of the new branch. The two final contestants both volunteered for the job. The thinking was that Adams would want to reward whoever made a success of the job. The only feasible reward would be an executive vice presidency. And that meant that one of the present executive VPs would be elbowed out.

"Hmmmm."

"You could feel something in that room. Fear—fear that could lead to violence."

"I think . . ." Zoo began cautiously. "I think I know where you're going."

"Is it too much to presume? In the light of what happened this morning, I mean? Is it too farfetched to think that someone at that party was responsible for the death of Al Ulrich?"

After several moments, Tully sighed deeply. "You know, Father Koesler's help and advice concerned religious matters. He didn't really get involved with police work."

"I was sure you were going to say that. For this moment, I'd like to escape from Bob Koesler's shadow. I've asked myself the question over and over. And as far as Father Koesler is concerned, I'm sure that if he'd been in my shoes the other night—heard what I heard, seen what I saw—he'd be telling you exactly what I've just told you."

The lieutenant thought this over. "I'm sorry, brother. I was out of line. I guess it all stems from your taking Koesler's place. Then all that talk about how you want to help me like he has.

"Well, let me tell you, I may just go the rest of my life without needing the help or expertise of any religious person. Maybe yes, maybe no. And I gotta admit that I've been a little jumpy about you thinking you've got to help me. But I shouldn't have overreacted.

"Just keep one thing in mind, Zachary: police tend to follow the most obvious solution in a criminal investigation. Right now we're working on the assumption that this attempted robbery/murder was committed by a guy who was stupid or drugged enough to think he could break into a bank vault with a sledgehammer. We assume he's still in the neighborhood. Or, if he's running, if we ask the right questions often enough, we'll still pick him up.

"But what you learned at last night's party could be significant. If our first lead dries up, we might have to look at that party. In that case, you're saving us a lot of time by giving me a rundown now. So, go ahead, brother: Tell me about Mr. Groggins and his insights and his gossip."

Now that he knew he had his brother's undivided attention, Father Tully swiveled to face forward, forgot about the traffic, and concentrated on his story.

"The way Groggins told it, each of these executive VPs is very nervous and equally determined that he will not be the sacrificial lamb. But if each thinks the new manager has a chance to unseat a current VP, that could be a motive to murder whoever was chosen . . . couldn't it?"

Lieutenant Tully made a hmmmm sound, which segued into what could have been taken for "Maybe."

"But," he countered, "what good would it do to waste a bank manager if there are other candidates in the wings eager and willing to step in? Case in point: Nancy Groggins. She's the runner-up to Ulrich, no?"

"Yes."

"And there she is right now, taking over for Ulrich. Seems to me she might just as well have been the first choice."

"But," said Father Tully, "our story has just begun. Who knows what comes next? Maybe Mr. Adams will have second thoughts about keeping this hazardous branch open. Maybe this buys time for whoever planned Ulrich's murder. Maybe—please God no— Nancy Groggins is the next planned target.

"And," the priest continued, "if one of the VPs *is* responsible for this, obviously he isn't the person caught by the bank's camera. That would have to have been someone paid to commit the murder.

"And, if this is true, then no robbery was intended. The killer was paid to commit murder. And the ludicrous attempt to hammer the vault open was—what do they call it in mystery novels?—a red herring. Whoever set this all up wants the police to be looking for someone stupid enough or drugged enough to think he could open a heavy vault with a hammer. Whereas his goal was accomplished as soon as he shot and killed Allan Ulrich. The rest of it was just to throw you off the track."

Zoo was happy his brother hadn't said "throw *us* off the track." At least he wasn't including himself in the investigation process. "Okay, if we pretend—'cause that's all we're doing with your scenario just now, pretending—if we pretend that one of the executive VPs stands to be dumped by rewarding Ulrich, which VP is most vulnerable? Does anybody know who Adams's prime target would be?"

Father Tully pondered. Initially, he had not dared hope that his brother might agree to consider this hypothesis to its natural conclusion. "Well," he said finally, "Groggins did provide me with a brief sketch of each VP. None of them is a leadpipe cinch to be expendable. But the way I understand it, this is the lineup:

"There's Martin Whitston, in charge of commercial lending. He's a no-nonsense manager. He knows what he wants and he gets it. He even looks the part: if you asked central casting for a powerful character brimming with self-confidence, they could send you Martin Whitston without benefit of makeup.

"Then there's Jack Fradet, the comptroller. A bean counter. But essential to the organization. He's got what's frequently referred to as 'the overall view.' He can tell whether the bank as a whole is developing, declining, or holding steady. He looks bookish. Out of everyone at the party"—he turned and grinned— "outside of Groggins and me, that is—Jack Fradet seemed the most out of place. He shouldn't be at a party; he should be at the office on a tall stool at a tall desk, his feet not touching the floor, posting numbers in a ledger.

"I was told that Jack Fradet is highly trusted. In effect, he knows where all the skeletons are buried. Adams Bank and Trust has been almost his only employment. I think he has every intention of being buried in one of the bank's vaults.

"Finally, there's Lou Durocher. He's Tom Adams's prime protégé.

It seems as if Adams decided something along the lines of Henry Higgins. Just as Professor Higgins takes a woman of no social grace off the street and transforms her into a lady—a 'princess'—just so, Tom Adams took Lou Durocher, a man with very little self-confidence, and tried to build a new backbone. So far, I guess, it— the experiment—hasn't worked out all that well.

"Basically, Mr. Durocher is in charge of mortgage and lending, and isn't accomplishing what he needs to. He's prone to make mistakes—mistakes that are awfully easy for even his subordinates to see.

"Nor can he hide his defects behind any sort of false front. His gestures are sort of tentative. He's a bit shifty-eyed.

"Alone among the wives, Mrs. Durocher—Pat—is the only one who is the antithesis of her husband. Lois Whitston is a go-getter. Marilyn—Mrs. Fradet—kind of disappears, like a shadow of her husband. Whereas Pat Durocher is sort of aggressive. Very outgoing, and seems to have a lot of self-confidence.

"And"—Father Tully turned back to his brother—"that's about it."

Zoo smiled. "You were very busy at that party. I don't think a trained spectator—even a cop—could've done better."

The priest shrugged. "It wasn't that difficult. Practically nobody paid any attention to me. Outside of Joel Groggins, no one at the table said one word to me. So Groggins kept busy—since no one was talking to him either—by giving me thumbnail sketches of the guests. While he was doing that, I was free to sort of study them and the way they related to one another.

"Once Groggins started talking about the reward that was practically set apart for the new bank manager, it was just natural to try to guess who would be axed to make room for the new kid on the block.

"Now, with Al Ulrich dead, I can't help but wonder which one of these VPs would be the logical suspect. It would have to be the one who was most certain that he was going to get the ax . . . no?"

"What's your guess?"

"That's the rub . . . Adams's corporation seems to be doing quite well—for its size, that is. Moving someone out of a top management position simply to reward a faithful employee doesn't sound like good business to me. Why would you bust up a winning combination?

"Of the three, two VPs are doing exceptionally well. But it's conceivable that Al Ulrich—or, now, Nancy Groggins—could replace either Martin Whitston or Jack Fradet very nicely.

"To me, the weak link is Lou Durocher. He's not living up to the demands of his position. I think an objective spectator would necessarily put the finger on Durocher.

"But that would mean that Tom Adams would have to abandon his experiment. It might even go against his concept of his religion. And that, I am positive, Adams would be most reluctant to do.

"Finally, the bottom line is that this is Tom Adams's call. And after the flipflop he pulled in going from his selection of Nancy as new manager to an overnight switch to Ulrich, I haven't a clue as to how his mind works."

"Maybe," Zoo said as they pulled up in front of St. Joe's rectory, "somebody knows exactly how Tom Adams's mind works."

"Somebody? Who?"

"If your theory is correct, the person responsible for Al Ulrich's death."

Twelve

BARBARA ULRICH perched on the edge of a straight-back chair. Appropriately, she wore black.

All was quiet at McGovern and Sons Funeral Home on North Woodward in Royal Oak. The establishment's appointments, down to the deep pile carpets, were chosen for the absorption and muffling of sound. Further, besides Mr. McGovern, no one was visible but Babs and Marilyn Fradet.

Good old Marilyn. Married to a bank comptroller who probably thought of his wife in terms of her chemical net worth of some ninety-two cents.

Marilyn alone, of all the bank's hierarchy and wives, had come to Barbara's side when news of Al Ulrich's tragic death was broadcast.

Of course life went on. Nancy Groggins, as Al's successor—temporary or otherwise—was undoubtedly up to her ears in the grand opening. And the others: Lou, Martin and Jack, plus Tom Adams of course, were being questioned by the police and interviewed by the media.

But here it was, late afternoon on a beautiful spring day, and none of them had so much as called to offer condolences.

On the other hand, all of the above were well aware of the fractured state of the Ulrich marriage. Maybe it was foolish to expect a call.

It was nice of Marilyn to come along—even if she was precious little company.

The two women were seated across the desk from Charles Mc-

Govern. They had just settled on the wording of Al's death notice.

Death notices are far more expensive than people realize. As at so many other times in life when businesses have one at their mercy, the papers overcharge for this "service." Al Ulrich's death notice would run in Sunday's combined edition of the *Free Press* and *News* on a one-time-only basis. Actually, as a prominent banker whose name had become far more familiar through his appointment as first manager of a controversial branch, he would merit an expanded and complimentary write-up on the obituary page. Finally, since this prominent banker had been murdered, he was front-page news, his death the leading story on TV and radio newscasts.

By and large, Al Ulrich's death was well noted.

How did Barbara feel? A new definition of mixed emotions.

In direct antithesis to her mother, Babs had wanted a husband who would not so much as look at another woman with lust in his heart. She'd found one who didn't even look at *her* with lust in his heart.

That hadn't always been true.

Al and Barbara had had a months-long torrid affair that might have been called an engagement. They called it a torrid affair.

He was climbing the corporate ladder at Adams Bank and Trust. She was in public relations. They met at a cocktail party hosted by her company.

He was dark, hirsute, well built, with a dangerous, erotic look in his eyes. She was—well, physically perfect.

Gradually, as the minutes went by, they shut out everyone else. It seemed so natural for them to end the evening at her place.

They sensed this was not a one-nighter. Both were sexually experienced. They took their time. No more alcohol. They kissed lingeringly, deeply. The trail of discarded clothing was like an arrow pointing to the bedroom.

That night set a pattern for months to come.

Then, one Saturday in June, they were married. He was Mr. Virility in his black tux. In her white gown she put Elizabeth Taylor, that once and future bride, to shame.

Early in their honeymoon she made it clear there would be no children. Not under any circumstances.

He was bewildered.

Why hadn't this literally vital consideration been thrashed out before they married? Why are so many serious matters overlooked in nearly every engagement?

People are in love. Prone to dismiss serious details, confident that a love so strong can solve any emerging problem. No need to bring up anything that might prove troublesome. Love conquers all.

U.S. divorce statistics argue against love's omnipotence.

With the Ulrichs, children, or the absence of same, became the bone of contention. It proved formidable.

He refused to make love at the whim of a calendar. Nor would he interrupt the progression of sex to slip on a protective sheath. Let alone endure a medical procedure that would sterilize him. Barbara, for her part, was as adamant in refusing to consider standard methods of birth control.

As time passed, their respective decisions solidified and a transformation occurred.

Al Ulrich had always been devoted to his job. He now became completely dedicated to both his job and his employer. Barbara, for him, had become an extremely attractive ornament clinging to his arm at important social functions.

Barbara did not fancy becoming an object.

Again, there were options. Divorce was the simplest. But Ulrich's attachment to the bank and to Tom Adams was intensifying. This dedication was such an obsession that it became his entire life. It would not have mattered who his wife was. She would be his badge of respectability. If his spouse were Barbara or someone—anyone—else, it made no difference.

Barbara had found if not the philanderer she had sworn to avoid, nor a mate dedicated to her, at least a consort who was going places.

He was a rocket that would catapult her into a society where she would feel right at home.

So, if not a divorce, then an unchanging continuation of the status quo.

Barbara collected her lovers one at a time with no particular plan. One led to another. Only in retrospect did she realize that she had the complete collection of Al's superiors as paramours. She never adverted to the fact that she was duplicating, at least numerically, her mother's track record.

How did she feel now that her peculiar version of a husband was dead—murdered?

Mixed emotions.

It was at very least odd to terribly tragic for any comparatively young person to be snatched from life. And whatever else might be said, Al's death had been a profound shock.

There was one certainty: when her child was born, Al would not be around to deny paternity.

This opened another field of speculation. At the recent award dinner, she'd revealed her pregnant state to the four candidates. The notes she had delivered had intimated that Al could be a problem. Was it possible? Could one of them . . . ?

It was time, Mr. McGovern suggested gently, to select a casket.

Barbara shook her head. "Casket? He's going to be cremated."

McGovern nodded. "But for the viewing—and before the service . . . ?"

"I forgot about that. I don't know what kind of service we can have. We don't have any religious affiliation. . . ."

McGovern smiled. "We've found that a service helps all the mourners through a difficult time. We can arrange something non-denominational that will be quite nice. Of course whether you want the body present is entirely up to you."

Marilyn Fradet cleared her throat. If she hadn't made an occasional sound the other two might well have forgotten her presence.

"Babs, don't you think it would be sort of expected? I mean, to have a service and have the body present? I'm sure Tom Adams will be there. Everyone knows he's very religious. And he and Al were so close. . . ."

Were they ever! "You're right, of course, Marilyn." Barbara turned toward McGovern. "Okay, let's take a look."

"Certainly." He led the two women into an adjoining room.

McGovern had had years of experience with the bereaved. They came in every variety from truly emotional wrecks to the casually untouched. This widow was just to the left of the untouched. Either that or she was holding herself together heroically. His trained senses told him that Barbara Ulrich might have mourned for a matter of minutes. But all that nonsense was over now; she would play the role. The untrained onlooker will believe she is crushed and is bravely standing fast. But he would know the truth. And so, undoubtedly, would the clergyman. Experience and a practiced eye, that's all it took.

The room was filled with caskets. Most gleamed either from polished metal or stained wood surfaces. There were soft linen or silk interiors with pillows. Someone with a macabre sense of humor might have mistaken this for the scene of a terminal slumber party.

Barbara's gaze fixed on a box that seemed out of sync with the rest. It looked as if it were made of reinforced cardboard. Perfect for burning, she thought, and undoubtedly inexpensive, or relatively so.

But if there was going to be visitation and if the body was there for viewing, she knew she couldn't get away with such a practical casket. Spare me, she thought, from the Cadillac of the industry.

Semidistractedly, she heard McGovern quoting prices and extolling the strengths of the various boxes. As far as she could tell, he didn't even mention the cardboard casket.

"This one seems good," Marilyn said to her.

Fortunately, she had indicated one of the mid-range caskets.

Barbara approved.

All that was left to settle was the time of the funeral and the visiting hours. The funeral would be three days hence at ten in the morning. Visitation from three to five and seven to nine the day before the funeral. Any other details, such as the service and the clergyman, McGovern would handle.

Barbara thanked Marilyn. She hadn't done much, but she was the only one who'd bothered to call, let alone show up to help.

Barbara drove toward their—no, scratch that—*her* downtown condo apartment.

She'd have to get used to being single again. Now that she considered it, she thought it might be fun. With the car in gear, her mind shifted into neutral. In an abstract state, Barbara once again fixated on those notes she'd so cleverly slipped to the four potential fathers.

Besides revealing her pregnant condition and the charge of responsibility to each, she'd mentioned Al. What she'd meant by that was vague, even in her own mind.

What if Al hadn't been killed?

She would have had her baby. That was a given. Outside of a spontaneous miscarriage, there was no way in the world she would have an abortion. Never again would she gaze at a destroyed baby that she had carried.

Well, then, what?

Al would have done everything short of hiring a skywriter to tell the world—or that part of the world that might be concerned—that he was not, could not be, the father of this child.

Then what? Somewhere, the baby had to have a father. Not four.

Tom, Jack, Lou, and Martin—each individually knew full well that he could be the missing piece. If she had been successful in her careful scheme, none of them knew about the other three.

At that point, she might have selected one and named him as father. The other three would think Christmas had come early.

And which one would she pick?

That didn't require much thought. She certainly would have selected Tom Adams. Not only was he by far the wealthiest, he was also single—and with a very demanding conscience.

She could have divorced Al. Or have let him divorce her. It made little difference.

On top of that, although she wasn't entirely clear on this, there was something in Catholic Church law about annulments. As she understood it, this was Catholicism's version of civil divorce. The big thing about it was that it cleared the way for a Catholic to marry again in the Church.

She knew that Tom Adams had gotten not only a divorce from that bitch he'd married, he also had gotten an annulment. Which freed him.

What about her?

If memory served, she thought Tom Adams had said something about the various reasons one could be granted an annulment. Yes, she thought, parenthetically, the lesson had been delivered one time by Tom as postcoital pillow talk. And one of those reasons had to do with children: something about if one married partner refuses to let the other have a child . . . that, or something very much like that, is grounds for the declaration of nullity.

And that would certainly have applied to her and Al.

That meant that she would have been free in Church law as well as civil law to marry again. The way would have been clear for her marriage to Tom Adams. And wouldn't that have been sweet!

Yes, had Al lived, that would have been the scenario.

But Al was gone.

Now what?

She hoped she wasn't getting greedy, but . . .

Al was gone. Evidently it would take time to get used to that. But it wasn't painful.

So now, when her baby came, Al would not be around to wash his hands of the child.

However, each of the four had been told he was the father: Her notes had delivered the glad tidings.

With Al out of the way, Barbara could—with four important

exceptions—let the world believe that the late dearly departed Allan Ulrich did not live to see his son or daughter. Sad.

But a happy momma.

Why not? With four wealthy men supporting one sorry widow and one lonely child.

She was smiling. She'd have to be careful of that. She was, after all, a devastated young woman whose mate had been taken from her. His death was terribly premature and she would miss him more than a person could bear.

It would be difficult to project this pitiful state. It called for an award-winning performance. Because once she carried it off Barbara was in a win/win situation.

There was no way she could lose.

Thirteen

FATHER TULLY looked forward to a pleasant evening.

He would walk the few blocks from St. Joseph's rectory to police headquarters, where at four-thirty this afternoon he was to meet his brother's superior officer, Inspector Walter Koznicki.

The inspector was to give the priest a tour of headquarters, during which they would get to know each other. Then at about six, they would be joined by Alonzo and Anne Marie Tully and they would all dine at a downtown restaurant.

From what he'd seen of downtown Detroit at the end of the business day, Father Tully felt justified in being a bit apprehensive. His consolation was that two of their party would be wearing guns.

Actually, an abnormal fear of the city was really uncalled for. It was merely his way of entertaining himself as he walked.

The priest was not afraid of Detroit—day or night—though he preferred not to hang around alone on a dark corner of the city. And he would have been happier if no one carried a gun.

Headquarters—1300 Beaubien—was an impressive structure. A sizable block of brick and marble, its statement was that it had been here a while and it would stand for the foreseeable future.

He climbed the steps to the lobby and entered an anthill of uniformed police and others whose casual familiarity with the place and each other indicated they were plainclothes officers.

He received many cordial nods as he made his way to the elevator. This he attributed to his clerical collar. So far in Detroit, he had worn clericals more often in a few days than he would in his

Dallas parish in a month. But the man for whom he was pinch-hitting seemed to favor the uniform. It was far easier, he admitted, to follow suit . . . an unintentional pun.

The elevator introduced him to the fifth floor; signs directed him to the Homicide Division, where a helpful officer ushered him to the inspector's office.

He could tell that Inspector Koznicki's smile of welcome was genuine. The priest had volumes of experience with plastic smiles. This was not one of them. Koznicki was sincerely happy to welcome the brother of his favorite officer. The happiness was multiplied since the visitor was a priest. Inspector Koznicki was very much a practicing Catholic.

They sat across the desk from each other.

The setting put Father Tully in mind of *Gulliver's Travels.*

It was an ordinary office with ordinary furnishings. But the man whose office it was seemed many times too big for it.

Koznicki was not huge in a freakish way. He was—in the same sense as John Wayne—larger than life. And, at least in these circumstances, as friendly as a St. Bernard.

After opening pleasantries, the priest detailed his relationship to his newfound relative. The inspector was impressed with their unusual discovery of each other after so many years. And how vastly different were their backgrounds, given each had the same father.

The inspector explained that since several matters demanded his immediate attention he would have one of his officers show Father Tully around.

The priest marveled at how he was attracting "B" level guides. First a bank officer had been detailed by Tom Adams to show him the city. Now Inspector Koznicki was about to deputize someone to show him the department.

But first, Koznicki wondered, was there any word from his friend Father Koesler?

It seemed to Father Tully that the Detroit Police Department—at least in the persons of Inspector Koznicki and Lieutenant Tully—missed Father Koesler as much as Father Koesler missed Detroit.

Father Tully recounted this afternoon's call from the once and future pastor. "Father Koesler is staying with a priest classmate in Collingwood. I gather that Leo Rammer will do anything to keep from playing golf, which pleases Bob. . . . I guess his game has gone to rust."

"I think," Koznicki said, "he never was very serious about the game. Lately he has played most infrequently, if at all." He chuckled. "Listen to me. 'Lately'! It has been years." He smiled again. "It is funny how the time seems to compress as the years pile up on one. I am surprised Father even took his clubs with him."

"A mistake, I think. Each thought the other had kept at it. I think they're both glad neither wants to hit the links."

"Besides not playing golf, what else is Father doing?"

"Sightseeing, it seems. Yesterday they took in a boat cruise in the Muskoka-Georgian Bay area. He says—well, I guess Canada claims—there are thirty thousand islands in that bay. Says it's the largest concentration of islands in the world. I didn't ask if he'd counted them."

Koznicki smiled broadly.

"While they were in the neighborhood, they took a look at something the locals claim is unique. It's called Big Chute. I'm not too clear on what it does, but I gather it substitutes for locks that move boats from one waterway to another. Seems they ran out of money at that point to build a conventional lock. So some engineering geniuses devised this mechanical lift that moves both back and forth. It's based on some sort of cable or pulley technique.

"Anyway, I think the main purpose of Bob's call was to find out if I was keeping his parish in the condition to which it is accustomed."

The inspector nodded. "Did you tell him about that sorry business at the bank? Your being in Detroit does have something to do with the Adams Bank, does it not?"

"That's right. I came here to present the St. Peter Claver Award to Mr. Adams. I did tell Bob about the murder of the branch manager. Of course Bob knew about the branch opening. And he knew of Tom Adams, although they'd never met. And even if he hadn't gone on vacation, he wouldn't have known any of the principals in that tragedy. It was just an accident that I'd met all those people.

"But I'll tell you this: I am very impressed with Tom Adams. He puts his money where his ethics are—"

Koznicki answered the phone before it could ring a second time. One thick eyebrow raised. He handed the phone to the priest. "For you, Father."

"Hello, Father Tully here."

"Fred Margan here, Father."

The voice wasn't familiar, but he recalled the name. It was the guide Adams had appointed to show the priest the city. "I remember you."

"It was my pleasure, Father. You certainly have heard of the tragic death of our man, Allan Ulrich?"

"Yes. I am sorry."

"Thanks. Father, I'm calling for Mr. Adams. This has really hit him hard. He would have made this call, but he is just laid low."

"I am so sorry to hear that. Is there anything I can do?"

"Well, yes, as a matter of fact, there is. Mr. Adams wondered if you could say a few words at the funeral. Neither Al nor his wife had any real religious affiliation. So the widow has no one to call on. And since Al and Mr. Adams were so close in life, Mr. Adams is doing all he can to help. And he wondered . . . if it isn't too much to ask . . ."

"No, I'll do it, of course. I don't know where or when the funeral's scheduled—"

"It's Monday morning at ten, from the funeral home. I'll pick you up at your rectory at nine-thirty if that's all right with you."

"See you then. In the meantime, my condolences to Mr. Adams—and to the widow, if you see her."

"Sure. And thanks."

Father Tully returned the phone to the inspector. As he explained the call, Koznicki nodded in understanding and agreement.

"Well," the inspector said, as he stood, "I guess it is about time for your tour. I hope it will not be boring."

"Hardly!"

As the inspector reached for the phone to summon the priest's guide, there was a staccato knock at the door. Before Koznicki could acknowledge it, the door opened and a detective leaned in. "Sorry to interrupt, Inspector, but I thought you'd want to know: some guys from narcotics have nailed the guy we think pulled off that bank job this morning."

"Where is he?"

"Holed up in a house on the east side—Newport. He's armed and he's got a hostage."

"There are officers on the scene?"

"More by the minute."

"We will go." The inspector grabbed his jacket.

"May I go with you?" Father Tully spoke on the spur of the moment.

Koznicki hesitated.

"I'll stay out of your way. But I would like to follow this through."

"Very well, Father. But you must stay out of harm's way."

As they left the police garage, the inspector half turned toward Father Tully. "If you listen carefully to the radio you will know what is going on at the scene. It will be somewhat garbled and there's some static, but listen and you will understand."

True to his words, the air was filled with voices, some agitated, some calm and authoritative. Without doubt, the situation had to be filled with tension and danger.

They arrived at the scene in minutes. The neighborhood had

turned out as if this were a traveling circus performing live now for the spectators' entertainment. The police had cordoned off an ample area around a nondescript two-story house, and were directing onlookers even farther away from the action. The area was ringed by uniformed officers, as well as members of the Special Response Team.

Before joining his troops, Inspector Koznicki again warned Father Tully not to leave the car.

There was no reason for the priest to leave the car. It was parked close enough, although within an area of safety, that the priest could follow much of the action without peril.

He spotted his brother half kneeling behind a police car. Someone was with him, someone familiar. It was the FBI agent—what had Zoo called him?—Rug . . . Harold Rughurst.

Seeing the two together reminded Father Tully of the differing theories about this crime. His brother and Rughurst had pretty much agreed that the perpetrator was someone off the streets and probably on drugs. He had shot Ulrich in much the same manner a hunter might casually kill an in-season animal. And as an indication that this was indeed the case, the poor fool had tried to break into a bank vault with a sledgehammer.

Father Tully's scenario was considerably more complicated. In his scheme, one of the bank's executive vice presidents, for self-protection, wanted Al Ulrich dead. He did not or could not do the deed himself. So he hired someone to do it and to make it look as if the motive had been robbery, when what actually was intended was murder.

Whichever theory might be valid, the answer lay with the young man in that house. Soon, if this confrontation ended peacefully and successfully, everyone would know that answer.

Father Tully scrutinized the crowd. Some seemed highly agitated, as if wondering, How could something this violent be happening in my neighborhood? Some were quite unconcerned, as if they were watching an unexciting television program. Some seemed to be celebrating the action. They were laughing and joking. Father Tully could picture them betting on the outcome.

He jumped, startled when the driver's side door opened and someone slid into the car. He relaxed when he saw it was a uniformed Detroit policeman.

The priest offered his hand. The officer, eyes on the outside action, didn't notice the gesture. The priest cleared his throat.

"Oh . . . hi, Father. I'm Patrolman Teasly, Bob Teasly. Inspector Koznicki sent me.

"I wasn't going to leave the car," the priest said defensively.

"Nothin' said about leaving the car, Father. I'm just s'posed to make sure nothing happens to you. That was the inspector's idea. He thought maybe I could tell you exactly what's goin' on."

"Okay . . . uh, Bob?"

"Yeah, Bob is okay."

"So, what's going on?"

"You really Zoo's brother?"

"Yes."

"You sure don't look it. And nobody can get over Zoo havin' a priest for a brother."

"Put your last buck on it."

"My, my. Wow."

"So, what's going on?"

"Well, Father, it all started this mornin' when that bank was broken into and the manager killed. Some of the narc guys called in some markers and got a name. They put out an all-points. The kid's name is Lamar Burt. "Then a 911 came in: wife abuse. Turns out the lady's a live-in, they ain't married, but her man is Lamar Burt. Our precinct crew responded before we matched the two, but the dispatcher reached our guys before they got here, and told 'em the murder suspect and the abuser were the same guy. Lucky he got 'em in time or we coulda had a couple of officers down.

"The first crew kept the place under surveillance while they called for backup—plenty of backup 'cause once Lamar got the idea of what was goin' down outside, he opened up—uh, started shooting."

"Anyone hurt?"

"Luckily, no—not yet, anyway. What's goin' on right now is bargaining. We got a phone connection and our negotiator is trying to talk sense into the suspect. There's no out for him: we got him one way or the other. We're just tryin' to find some things to concede that'll get him to come out peaceably."

"Right now, I think we're tryin' to get him to let his lady go. He's holding her hostage."

"What's that . . . over there?" The priest indicated a mobile trailer parked on the lawn not far from them.

"That? Oh, that's SRT."

"What's that?"

The patrolman smiled. "Special Response Team—that's the department's version of SWAT. Anytime we get a barricaded gunman, this team is called in."

They watched in silence. After a few minutes, the patrolman started whistling softly. "Pretty impressive, eh, Father?"

"Yeah. Looks like they're wearing enough body armor to go to the lists."

"The what?"

"The lists. You know, in the olden days, the knights would put on their armor, be lifted onto their horses—which also had armor—and accelerate headlong toward each other with huge lances. The object was to unseat the other horseman. It was a tilting tournament—you know: jousting."

"Yeah, I've seen it in the movies. Like in *Camelot.*"

"Right. And Sir Lancelot not only unseated one of his opponents, he killed him and then brought him back to life."

The patrolman shook his head. "I sure hope it doesn't come to that now."

"What?"

"If the shooting starts again, somebody's gonna be dead . . . but I don't think anybody's gonna bring 'em back."

"You think this is going to end violently?"

"I sure hope not. As long as they're talkin' most likely nobody'll start shooting."

Even as they spoke, the police negotiator shrugged, shook his head, and put down the phone. The priest and the patrolman looked at each other. "What now?" Father Tully asked.

"We'll have to wait. I've seen 'em come out like babies, cryin' and rollin' around on the ground. And I've seen 'em come out like Butch Cassidy and the Sundance Kid."

Fourteen

THE QUIET before the storm.

No one could predict a storm, but it surely was quiet. Everyone—police and spectators—stood or crouched motionless. Everyone either knew or sensed that communications had broken down. And everyone knew that the breakdown was not on the part of the police.

The next move had to come from within the house. There wasn't a sound.

Suddenly, the front door slammed open. The frail body of a young woman was flung out the door. She tumbled down the stairs and lay motionless on the ground. She could have been dead, or she could have been paralyzed with fear.

Silence again.

A young man leaped through the doorway. He had a wild look about him—and a gun in each hand. He squeezed about two rounds from each gun before an SRT volley cut him down.

Father Tulley saw none of this. Just as Lamar Burt appeared at the door, Patrolman Teasly pushed the priest down and covered Tully's body with his own.

It was over in seconds. Teasly helped the priest up. "Well, it was Butch and Sundance."

"Wow!" Father Tully studied the scene. All was pretty much as it had been before the shooting. Except that officers began to move. Members of the SRT came forward cautiously. It was unlikely that the suspect—or anyone—could have survived their enormous firepower. But they took no chances.

When they reached the body, an officer knelt and felt for a heartbeat. He looked to the officers on either side and shook his head. It was over.

Officers swarmed into the house. Others tended to the young woman.

"It's okay to go out now," Teasly said to the priest. "But stay back by the car here. The techs have a lot of work ahead."

"Thanks." The priest brushed off his black suit, and exited the car.

Everyone had been frozen in place by the gunfire. Now that the climax was behind them, life began again—for everyone but Lamar Burt.

The police began what for them was routine work. Members of the media were casting like fly fishermen for comments and the inside story. Some bystanders were clearly distressed. One elderly man was vomiting. Some, bored after the excitement was over, wandered back to their homes. Others appreciated the show almost to the point of applauding. A few paid off or collected on quickly transacted bets.

Lieutenant Tully turned and, for the first time, spotted his brother. Approaching, he said, "What are you doing here?" Then he saw Koznicki. "Don't tell me, you're here with him," he said to his brother.

Koznicki, Tully, and Rughurst met at the car. Father Tully, because he was already there, made a fourth.

"You okay?" Zoo asked his brother.

"Fine. I just gave that poor man conditional absolution."

"You what?" Zoo was more amused than surprised.

Even Inspector Koznicki found some humor in the priest's remark. "I fear there were multiple conditions in your forgiveness, Father."

"What is it, this conditional whatever?" Zoo inquired.

"I don't know what he's done," the priest explained. "I don't know if he's sorry for whatever wrong he did. And I don't know whether he's still alive. But with all those questions hanging in midair, I gave him absolution."

"If it worked, I'm godda—uh, sure he needed it," Rughurst added.

One by one, a series of officers made their way to what amounted to a command center, with a special agent of the FBI, an inspector and a lieutenant, both of the DPD's Homicide Division.

"This Lamar Burt," the first officer reported, "he's got a full house rap sheet. Everything from loitering when he was a kid, to robbery, robbery armed, carjacking, attempted murder. He's been inside better than half his life. He is—was—twenty-seven." The report ended, the officer departed, to be shortly replaced by another officer.

"We found a stash in the house . . . looks to be better than seven or eight G's. We're talking to the woman. She's been with him off and on for about five years. They're both crackheads. Sometimes it gets a little hairy. Like today, he was bouncing her off the wall. She thought he was going to kill her. That's when she called 911. She didn't know he was wanted—not till we showed up and he started shooting."

"Was he with her this morning?" Koznicki asked.

"No. He left real early this morning. She said he'd been casing some place . . . he wouldn't tell her what or where. He got back here midmorning. He was really pissed. Whatever he'd tried to pull off evidently hadn't worked. He was furious. He snorted some coke and then started on her."

"She got any idea where the cash came from?" Rughurst asked.

"No, sir. She never knows how much he has in there or where it comes from. It's really like a bank to him. He withdraws and invests. She tried to get hold of it once, just to see how much he had. He nearly broke her arm. We told her about the nearly eight thousand dollars in the beanbag now. She wasn't impressed . . . she's sure it's held more, but seldom less."

"No way of telling whether there was a recent big deposit?" Rughurst asked. "Maybe five grand? Maybe for a hit? Somebody took out a contract? Anything like that?"

The officer thought for a moment. "I don't think anybody asked her that specifically. I'll check that out and get right back to you."

A third officer approached. "No surprise, he's got an arsenal in there. But one of the guns he was firing when he jumped out of the house just now was a nine millimeter—same caliber used in the bank killing this morning. It's on its way to ballistics."

"Great."

The second officer returned. "I asked her. She thinks he'd of told her if he had a contract. Far as she knows, he's never had a contract. But she was kinda spacey. I think she's talkin' now because she's scared shitless. She'd tell you anything she thought you wanted to hear whether she knew the answer or not."

The three officers looked at each other. "Well," Rughurst said to Koznicki, "what d'ya think?"

The inspector glanced at Zoo. "There are no witnesses to the shooting in the bank this morning. We do have film showing a portion of the perpetrator's body. We will check that. I would not be surprised if Lamar Burt is still wearing the same clothing he wore this morning."

"We got solid leads that name Burt as the perp," Zoo said. "He didn't open up on us just because his woman called 911.

"I think," Tully added, "it comes down to the gun. If we can match any of Burt's weapons with the bullet that killed Ulrich, I think we got our guy."

"What about the possibility that Burt was hired—that there was a contract on Ulrich?" Rughurst said.

"There is no suggestion of that in any part of our investigation," Koznicki responded. "There is a considerable amount of money in the house—but no indication where it came from. His woman states that, to her knowledge, Burt has never been offered a contract. She thinks that if he had been, he would have told her."

"So, then, what d'ya say? Does this wrap it up?" Rughurst didn't want to hang around.

Koznicki looked at Lieutenant Tully. Tully nodded.

"Subject to all of our hypotheses proving true," the inspector said, "we are satisfied. This should close the case."

Rughurst compressed his lips and nodded curtly. "Done!" He headed out.

Lieutenant Tully turned to his brother. "Listen, I'm sorry about dinner tonight. I can't possibly make it. You can go along with the others. There're just a lot of loose ends here that have to be tied up."

Koznicki studied his watch and murmured, "It is getting late. However . . ."

The ball appeared to be in Father Tully's court. Obviously the only reason any of them would meet for dinner would be for his benefit.

"You're right: It *is* getting late," the priest said. "We didn't count on all this when we made our plans. On top of which, tomorrow's Saturday and I should be planning the weekend liturgy. Tonight would be the best time to do that."

"Listen," Zoo said brightly, "why don't we plan to get together tomorrow morning, say about nine for brunch. Anne Marie should be free. How 'bout you, Walt?"

"That would suit me perfectly, as far as I can tell now. Would you be free then, Father? Would you be done with your liturgical planning?"

"I'd better be. Or the ghost of Father Koesler will haunt me. Besides, the Saturday Mass is late afternoon."

"Then it's a date," Zoo said. ". . . or at least as far as a homicide detective can promise."

Koznicki turned to Father Tully. "Your brother has much to do here, Father. If it is agreeable with you, I will drive you back to the rectory."

"I'd be grateful."

As Koznicki and Father Tully began their drive, the priest was acutely aware of the modulation of his adrenal glands. Headed to the scene of today's confrontation, Father Tully had been in his own personal fast lane—hyperconscious of his surroundings, the neighborhoods they had whizzed through, the traffic lights they ran.

Now, everything had eased up into normal time passage. His breath came at a much more relaxed rate.

Out of the blue Koznicki chuckled. "These past few days have been a rather intense welcome to Detroit, have they not, Father? This is not the manner in which we welcome all our guests, especially clergymen."

"I know that, Inspector. This was supposed to be a sort of vacation for me. Somewhat different from the more traditional vacation your friend Father Koesler is enjoying—or enduring, as the case may be.

"I was sent here by my religious superior to present an award and, also, to meet my family for the first time. That was all I was looking forward to. There was so much catching up to do I thought there'd be no time for anything else. I wasn't counting on the freeway shooting of a police officer. And I certainly had no thought that I'd witness a barricaded gunman actually get killed."

Koznicki grew solemn. "No one wanted to see that confrontation end the way it did. Our officers are very carefully trained and selected for the chief virtue they must exhibit in such situations."

"Patience?"

"Exactly. The temptation when dealing with desperate and frightened people is to run out of that precise virtue. Our patience must outlast their impatience.

"Today's experience was a good example of that dynamic in reality. Mr. Burt was the one who broke the line of communication. That young man started down the road to a fatality when he hung up the phone. Tragic!" Koznicki's tone softened. "But tell me, Father, did you really absolve the young man?"

"Yes. It was almost a reflex response. I recall well the priest who taught us moral theology. He was a Navy chaplain in World War II. He was stationed on an aircraft carrier in the Pacific. He told us that once, during the last phase of the war, a kamikaze dove for his ship. And—in my teacher's own well-chosen words—'I gave conditional absolution to the sonuvabitch before he hit the deck.'"

Koznicki laughed aloud.

"I've got to say," the priest continued, "I've never heard a more generous act of forgiveness. I mean, when someone is trying to sink your ship and kill you . . . to pick that time to pray for forgiveness for him . . . well, I thought that was darn near heroic.

"But I did gain some insight today. That response of forgiveness does become a bit of a reflex action. He wasn't as focused as a kamikaze pilot, but that young man could have killed someone in his wild shooting. I guess a priest's training as well as his daily experience places the soul over the body in importance. That's just the way it goes."

The inspector entered the parish parking lot and stopped at the side door of the rectory. The priest was about to leave when he sensed that Koznicki had something more to say.

"Father, I have no idea what your previous experience with the police has been. And I certainly do not wish to give you the impression that everyday police work is as demanding as today's episode with a barricaded gunman."

"I know that, Inspector."

"The point I want to make, Father, is that even if such bizarre behavior is blessedly unusual and comparatively infrequent, still, a policeman's time is not his own. Engagements and appointments are made to be broken."

The priest looked puzzled. The inspector was preaching to the converted. Long before he'd come to Detroit, Father Tully had had plenty of contact with police departments in many U.S. cities. These departments differed from one another in sometimes subtle, sometimes evident ways. But in general, cops were busy people. Father Tully was more than willing to concede the inspector's point.

"Even though police work literally never ends, some are more dedicated to it than others." The inspector paused, seeming to weigh his next words. "Father, I do not know how much you know about your brother's divorce. But I assume, as a priest, you must wonder—"

"Inspector . . ." Father Tully reclosed the car door and turned to face the officer. "I didn't have the vaguest idea what I'd find in Detroit. All I knew was that my brother was here and that he was on the police force. I didn't know where he lived, whether he was married, if he had children—or even what he looked like.

"Since I've come, Anne Marie sort of brought me up to date on things, including his first marriage and this present one as well. My brother shared a bit of history with me. So I think I know. But I'm grateful to you for volunteering to clue me in."

"Yet," Koznicki persisted, "there is one condition that you may not know of, but is very pertinent."

The priest leaned back with an encouraging smile.

"While it is true that police work is never-ending, not all individuals are equally dedicated. I, perhaps, know that better than Anne Marie and even than Alonzo. He does his work in what, to him, is a very ordinary, run-of-the-mill fashion. He expects his fellow officers to equal his dedication. In that expectation he is almost always disappointed. His dedication is more complete and more compelling than that of any other officer I have ever known.

"I may be wrong, but I think that people who enter his life in special ways—in everything from police work to marriage—cannot comprehend what it is they are getting into.

"Let me repeat: he expects his fellow officers to be as single-minded as he. That seldom happens. But it does explain why his squad completes more investigations and has a higher conviction rate than any of the other six squads in homicide. He expects anyone who wants to share his life, in marriage or not, to grasp how total, how complete, is his dedication.

"No one, yet, has been able to do that. So far, Anne Marie is coping marvelously.

"In this regard—Alonzo's intense fidelity to his work—I know him better even than a wife could.

"And you must know this also: if you are going to stand close to him as the brother you are, you must realize, as his wife must, that his work comes first in his life—even ahead of his wife and children." He looked at the priest meaningfully. "Even ahead of you."

They sat in silence. Finally the priest spoke. "You've given me a lot to think about, Inspector. And it's something I must think through. I thank you most sincerely."

Koznicki smiled as he nodded. He watched as the priest left the car and entered the rectory. When he was safely inside, the inspector drove away.

Maybe tomorrow there would be brunch.

Maybe.

*   *   *

Father Tully checked the answering service. Four calls for Father Koesler, none of them urgent. A few calls regarding the time of weekend services. No emergencies, thank God.

He dug out the sacramentary wherein he found the Scripture readings for this weekend's Mass. With a notepad and pen and readings, he was sure to come up with some thoughts for a homily. He always did.

Settling into a comfortable chair, he reflected on Inspector Koznicki's parting words—the part about the total involvement of a police officer in his work . . . being constantly on call.

Earlier, when his brother had made practically the same statement, Father Tully had compared police work to the priesthood. Now, on second thought, he saw differences.

Back in Father Koesler's heyday, there had been a similar totality of time and service.

It was a different world then—at least a different Catholic world. Pre-Vatican II priests were the deputed "holy men" of parochial life. In addition to administering sacraments, which priests of Tully's time continued to do, Koesler's priests heard endless confessions, forgave countless sins.

Today, few people die at home. They tend to expire in nursing homes, hospices, and hospitals. Places where institutional chaplains have anointed them—at the first sign of illness—not with the dreaded extreme unction, but with the more encouraging sacrament of the sick. Offering one answer to the question: what's in a name?

No longer was there the sense of urgency that had accompanied a 3 A.M. call to the rectory, and the dash of the race with death.

Those two sacraments alone, confessions that would not quit, plus the summons of unschedulable death, had yesterday's priests on a par with police and with an open-ended call to service at any time, day or night.

Additionally, pre-Vatican II priests had had all the answers to all the obvious questions. Which kept parishioners calling on the phone or in person. Most parishes could guarantee the presence and availability of a priest anytime one was needed for anything.

Today's shrinking numbers made the rectory priest an endangered species.

But not Father Zachary Tully. The parishes he served were so poor that no one was standing in line to take a departing pastor's place.

Strange what problems most of today's Catholics could solve on their own. And strange what poverty can create in terms of dependency.

But this was not getting the required homily thought out. He would have to get some serious work done. One never knew what might interrupt—and brunch would be served in just a few more hours.

Fifteen

BARBARA ULRICH, a bit numb from all that had happened today, sat in her living room. The blinds were closed. She wore only a half slip and a bra.

Frequently she wore nothing at home. It was part of a peculiar game she and her late husband had played. She would try to tempt him and he would resist temptation.

God! Now that she looked back on it, how sick they had been. The more Al lived in and for the bank, the more she had pulled their relationship apart.

Was he really gone? She had to keep reminding herself that he would not be coming home—ever again. The games were over.

The sound of the phone seemed unreal. Who would call her at a time like this? Telemarketing, probably. She reached over the arm of the couch and picked up the receiver. "Hello?" she said absently.

"Barbara, this is Marilyn . . . Marilyn Fradet."

For a second, it didn't register. "Oh . . . yes, Marilyn. What is it?"

"Did you hear the news? Do you have your radio or TV on?"

"No. What news?"

"They got Al's killer!"

"What? What are you talking about?"

"Turn on your TV. Channel Four. No, wait; it was a bulletin. It's over now."

"I can't focus, Marilyn. What is this all about?"

Marilyn forced herself to speak calmly. "Babs, evidently the police got some leads and followed them. They led to a young man— I didn't get the name—I was so surprised.

"Anyway, he was barricaded in a house on the east side. I guess he decided to shoot it out. It was more like suicide. The police had their sharpshooters there. They killed him. They think he must've been on drugs."

Barbara made not a sound.

After a few moments of silence, Marilyn said, "I'm sorry if I bothered you with this call. I just thought you'd want to—that you ought to—know."

Slowly, Barbara comprehended what Marilyn had said. The facts settled in her consciousness. "No. No, I'm not putting reality together very well just now. Was there anything else? I mean, was anyone else involved? Just one kid? No idea that he might've been hired to kill Al?"

The question puzzled Marilyn. "No, Babs . . . not that I heard. And I think I caught the entire bulletin."

"Can you remember anything else at all? Anything more than you've told me?"

A hesitation. "Well . . . the pictures. They had film showing the guy charging out of this house. He looked crazy . . . wild. He had guns in both hands. He was firing, firing. And then he was shot, killed—dead. It was godawful. They shouldn't show things like that. It was more violent than some of the movies. You'd think—"

"That was it? Nothing more?"

"Well, um . . . the news reporter—Mike Wendland, I think—was interviewing a policeman. The name was familiar. I couldn't place ever meeting him. But he was the only one I saw being interviewed. He seemed to know everything that had gone on."

"You can't remember his name?"

"He was a lieutenant. A homicide detective. He was black. His name . . . his name was . . . Tully, I think. Yes, I'm sure that was it: Lieutenant Tully."

"That's it?"

"That's all I can think of, Babs. I'm sure they'll repeat the news at eleven."

"Yes. Well, thanks, Marilyn. It was good of you to call. I really appreciate it."

"You sound so tired, dear. I think you ought to unplug the phone. Everybody and his brother will be calling you."

"Good idea."

As soon as they hung up, Barbara followed Marilyn's advice and pulled the plug.

But she did not rest.

This was not playing out the way she had expected. Her version of Al's death was that one of the VPs had contracted for the killing to keep Al from replacing him in the bank's hierarchy. The only question was which VP.

The information that Marilyn had reported simply made no sense. Some punk kid? Acting on his own? Stoned senseless? That was what had ended Al's life? A bank robbery that had no hope of success? One shot at point-blank range?

That was not the way anyone, especially Al, should exit this life.

She had to have more information! But where could it come from? Not from the police. They would be polite once they knew they were talking to the widow, but they wouldn't open up. And you couldn't trust the media; they would have little more than she herself could glean.

That name . . . the one that Marilyn had finally remembered. *Lieutenant Tully.* It had a familiar ring. Why? Why would the name be familiar?

Tully. Tully. Tull—of course! The priest she'd met at the award dinner. The one who Fred Margan had told her would be presiding at Al's wake.

Yes, that was it: Father Tully!

Was this a coincidence? Could they be related? In either case, definitely a coincidence.

She plugged the phone back in. A few calls, several blind alleys, and then bull's-eye. St. Joseph's parish, downtown. Taking some other priest's place for a week or two. Lots of other interesting things to tell, but no time. She had to place another call immediately.

*   *   *

Father Tully was in the final phase of developing an idea for his homily. For a moment, he considered letting the answering device take the call.

Then he asked himself, "Would good old Father Koesler answer his phone?" Tully didn't even know Father Koesler well enough to give an educated guess at the answer. But from the brief time they'd spent together, plus all that he'd heard, he knew what his absentee pastor would do. Slowly he lifted the receiver. "St. Joseph's."

"I want to speak with a Father Tully." There was eagerness in Barbara's voice. "Is he in?"

"This is he." Tully was taken aback. Outside of his local relatives and the occasional connection from Koesler hardly anyone had called for him.

"This is Barbara Ulrich. We met the other evening . . . you know, when you presented that award to Tom Adams. Do you remember me?"

Did he ever!

"Yes, I remember," he said, instantly collected. "Please accept my sincere condolences."

Why would the widow call him? Well, Adams, through a spokesman, *had* asked him to say a few words at the funeral. Probably Adams had mentioned it to the widow and . . .

"Thanks," she replied dispassionately. "What I'm calling about, Father, is what happened, I guess sometime this afternoon. The police caught—and killed—the kid who shot my husband. I know this is a long way from firsthand knowledge. But a friend called me a little while ago and said she'd seen a bulletin on TV. She said the person being interviewed was named Tully—Lieutenant Tully. Any relation?"

He smiled. He was so pleased to claim that relationship. "Yes. That was my brother."

So far so good, thought Barbara. "By any chance did you talk to him about what happened?"

"Better than that. I was there."

She felt that she'd hit the jackpot—or, more to the point, that she held all but one number to win the lottery. "Can you talk to me about it?" She hesitated, but her voice gave every indication that she intended to continue. "What I mean, Father, is that my husband left home this morning headed on a new direction in his life. And then —just to become another statistic. I'm finding it so hard to adjust to it all. Tell me I'm wrong in thinking there must be more to it than this."

Father Tully didn't quite know what to make of it. Every indication, everything he heard, all that he'd observed about the relationship between Al and Barbara Ulrich contradicted the concern she suddenly showed toward a husband with whom she had not gotten along—to say the very least.

Was it idle speculation? Genuine concern?

He felt uneasy. Shouldn't she be calling the police? Shouldn't she be talking to his brother? By her questions and her statements, she seemed to indicate she was not satisfied with the "official" findings in the case. She couldn't bring herself to believe that one young crook could have caused all that damage. Well, in truth, he didn't believe it either. And, bottom line, she *was* the widow, and thus deserving of special treatment.

In any case, she'd asked a direct question and, he thought, deserved an honest answer. "Mrs. Ulrich, I don't know exactly what to tell you." He pushed the books and notepad off his lap, stood and, holding the phone in one hand, began to pace. He frequently did that during lengthy and/or demanding phone conversations.

"I happened to be with Inspector Koznicki at police headquarters when he got notice that a man, who was suspected of being your husband's killer, had barricaded himself in a house with a hostage.

"I went with the inspector—he's the head of homicide—to the scene. There was indeed a young man holed up there. He had a woman hostage. The police negotiated as long as the young man let them. Then he came out shooting. The police had no choice."

"And they think this kid did it all by himself?"

"They retrieved a gun the young man had used. It was the same caliber as the one that killed your husband.

"When I left my brother there—at the scene—it looked as if they had lots more work to do . . . things to check. But they seemed certain that this was the man who killed your husband."

Silence.

Father Tully could think of nothing more to say. She had asked a direct question. He had answered it to the best of his limited knowledge.

She wasn't sure where to go from here. "Look, Father, the other night at the dinner, if I remember correctly, you were sitting next to Joe—you know, Joel Groggins, Nancy's husband? Well . . . I don't know how to put this politely, but Joe has a habit of talking about things."

Somehow she made it seem there was a character defect in Joel Groggins because he had talked all evening to the priest. Whereas Father Tully had been grateful for the conversation. If there were a character flaw on anyone's part at the dinner, it surely belonged to her, one among others who had shut him out that evening. She had sat next to him through the dinner and never once even looked at him. This, the priest thought, was a small insight into her character.

"Joe pretty much knows where all the skeletons are buried in our little bank. Being married to Nancy, he'd have to."

She must be aware that Groggins had undoubtedly painted a rather lurid outline of her by no means housewifely personal life. But she couldn't afford to be concerned about that right now. "What I'm interested in, Father, is whether Joe filled you in on our executive VPs—with regard to the spot they'd be in depending on who was chosen as the new bank manager."

The priest almost replied in an uncontested affirmative. Groggins most assuredly had suggested that at least one VP had plenty to fear from whoever was named new manager. Tom Adams's gratitude was going to cost *some*body his job.

But Father Tully pulled up short. Mrs. Ulrich had used the word "depending." That a VP would be displaced "depending" on which of the two candidates was selected.

"Well, I was given to understand that, yes, one of the VPs would have to be displaced after a successful branch bank management. But I thought that was the case whether the selection was your husband or Nancy Groggins. You just said that the VPs need fear only one contestant."

"My husband, of course." Her tone was one of genuine surprise. "Don't tell me Joe is so far outside the loop that he thought his wife could be named an executive vice president! Or, what's even harder to conceive, that Nancy didn't know the score."

"Are you sure, Mrs. Ulrich? It made sense to me the other night when Joel Groggins revealed this pecking order.

"This new branch of Adams Bank was a practical testimonial to the city of Detroit—an act of faith in a city that's trying to get its act together. To emphasize this commitment, the branch is located in one of the toughest areas in a tough city. This act of faith would have to be duplicated by anyone named manager.

"I take it there were few applicants. But, of those who applied, top contenders were Nancy and your husband.

"Then the thinking was, again if I'm not mistaken, that once the branch was functioning nicely, whoever made a success of it as manager would be rewarded. The reward would be a step up. And that would be next to the top—an executive vice presidency.

"But since there are only three such positions, one present VP would have to go. And I don't mind telling you, Mrs. Ulrich"—in his pique he released information that otherwise he probably wouldn't have—"the front-runner, at least at the beginning of that award dinner, was not your husband."

"Tom told you that?" Her tone was almost playful.

"Yes, he did. He asked that I give him my evaluation after the evening was over. And, to be frank, I agreed that Nancy was the more appropriate choice."

"Well, she's got it now. And the VPs are happy now. For the most part," she added, almost meditatively.

"But why should there be any difference in the way Tom Adams would treat Al and Nancy?"

"As the French say, *Vive la différence*. The overlooked difference is due to Tom's appreciation of men and women. Leaders are men, not women. Top movers and shakers are men, not women. Executive vice presidents are men, not women. At least according to Tom Adams's Bible."

"You're saying . . ."

"I'm saying," Barbara insisted, "that if Al had been named manager—which, in the end, he was—yes, someplace down the line he, not one of the bean counter vice presidents, would've been named an executive VP. And one of the sitting execs would probably have been eased out with a golden parachute.

"Now that Nancy's manager of the new branch, she can look for a reward if she makes a go of it. I hope she doesn't think it's going to be the executive spot. Remember, Father: executive vice presidents are men, not women. That's the Gospel—at least according to Tom Adams."

"Then, Nancy . . . what?"

"Likely one of the run-of-the-mill vice presidencies. Or, perhaps her pick of any branch she wants to manage. Maybe a significant financial bonus. But not—I repeat, *not* a job reserved for men only."

"You're sure," Father Tully persisted.

Barbara nodded decisively. "I'm sure," she voiced. "Anybody who thought Tom Adams saw some sort of equality between Al and Nancy simply didn't know the man's machismo philosophy."

Silence.

"This sheds a slightly different light on my thinking," Father Tully admitted finally.

"How so?" Barbara very much wanted to explore his thoughts on her husband's death. She thought she detected some parallel in their thinking.

The priest hesitated. Had he said too much? Then in a self-mocking tone, he said, "During that party, with all that Joel Groggins was telling me, I thought—no, this is silly . . ."

"No, it isn't. Go on."

"I thought . . . this situation has got to put an awful lot of pressure on the three men whose livelihood is threatened." Again he hesitated.

"Did it occur to you," she prompted, "that they—or one of them —might do . . . something to prevent this from happening?"

He chuckled self-consciously. "Yeah. It did. I think I must be reading too many mystery novels. These are fine upstanding citizens—"

"Upper class . . . above this sort of thing; it wouldn't even enter their heads. Like that?"

"Yes. Exactly."

"Don't bet on it, Padre. They're human like everyone else. If anything, they've got more of a stake in their future than most other people. They're at a level in society that is very demanding. It's tough to retain what they've achieved through their position—executive vice president—and through their income. A solid threat to their status would definitely not make them happy campers. So what do you think now, Father?"

A pause.

"I meant that the idea sort of occurred to me," the priest said slowly. "It just popped in and out of my mind. You really think it could have happened? That would mean . . ." He hesitated again.

Was he going too far? ". . . that one of those men would have paid
Lamar Burt to kill your husband. I find that almost unimaginable."

"It could have been more than one."

"I beg your pardon?"

"I mean, what if two of the VPs—or even all three—got together and put up the money for a contract on Al. That would be a
conspiracy, wouldn't it?"

"To my mind, that would be incredible to the second or third
power."

"It's just a thought." Actually, Barbara was counting on there
being no conspiracy across the board. No, those men would go their
separate ways without consulting each other on delicate matters
such as murder . . . and adultery. "Just something to keep in mind.
And, as for murder being a practiced option for these guys, remember that they're playing for the highest stakes they can imagine."

"I suppose," the priest agreed reluctantly. What was this woman
doing? Where was this conversation leading?

"Now that we've gotten beyond the possibility that at least one of
them might have been involved in my husband's death, can you
think of anything that was peculiar about the shooting of that kid
this afternoon?"

"Peculiar?" He racked his brain. "N . . . no. Everything seemed to
proceed in an ordinary way—given the fact that it was an extraordinary event. The young man was, in effect, trapped. He chose to
possibly imitate God knows who in a movie, and go out with guns
blazing. That was about the size of i—wait!" Father Tully suddenly
recalled something.

"What is it?"

"Something I do remember. After the shooting this afternoon—
when the police were tying up loose ends—one of the officers
mentioned that they'd found a sum of cash—a stash, I believe he
called it."

"How much?" Her voice was eager.

"Almost eight thousand dollars."

"Any one of the three—Jack, Lou, or Marty—could have afforded that without any pain. I'm sure that's more than enough for a murder contract. What did the police say?"

"They said it probably represented money for or from dope dealing."

"The police didn't know about our three guys and their very solid motive."

Father Tully's pacing intensified. "Well, I guess they did. I informed my brother—"

"And he said . . . ?"

"That I should stay out of police business."

"And that was it!"

"That was it. And, as far as I was concerned, that really *was* it. You and I have talked about it just now. But this is the first time I've seriously thought of it since my brother's warning."

"They're not even going to consider it?"

"I think the way my brother put it, police procedure follows the obvious line of investigation and doesn't run off after bizarre leads." Father Tully realized that this entire conversation was not only fraught but possibly problematic.

"Mrs. Ulrich, I think you and I see the possibility of a contract killing. But I have to admit, there isn't a shred of proof for this theory. I, for one, am convinced that the police definitely are not going to investigate this killing further unless some pretty strong evidence comes up."

"Huh, huh, huh," she almost grunted. Then, half to herself, "Maybe standard police procedure discourages going further with this investigation. But it doesn't stop me."

"Uh . . ." Father Tully hesitated, then shrugged. "It probably isn't my place to say this, but don't you think that what you're proposing is sort of dangerous? What if you're right? What if one of these men is responsible for your husband's death? And what if you flush him out? You said it yourself: there are very high stakes here. Nobody wants to see another . . . act of violence." He stopped short of using the word "murder."

"Don't worry about me." It sounded as if she was almost laughing. "This is one cookie who can take care of herself."

Father Tully stopped pacing and sat on the arm of his chair. "Mrs. Ulrich, really now, I understand that these executive VPs would be protective of their position—and conceivably fearful of losing it. But for me, this was just idle speculation—and I've discarded that notion now that the police have dropped the investigation. Look: without any prejudice, I think we're dealing with exceptional officers in an excellent police department." He paused, but she made no comment.

"In the brief time I've gotten to know my brother," he continued after a moment, "all I've been able to observe, all I've heard about him, tells me I can be proud of him and confident in his ability. He heard me out when I suggested that one of the VPs could be responsible for your husband's death. He listened to me with an open mind—of that I'm sure. And he dismissed the idea." He paused again. Still no response from Mrs. Ulrich.

"To be honest," he said reflectively, "I haven't completely abandoned the theory. It keeps popping into my head from time to time. Especially since each of those VPs—or maybe just one of them—could have a very credible motive. But for all practical purposes, I no longer consider it seriously. My brother said it: leave police work to the police—and in this instance, I think he's absolutely right.

"Look at it this way, Mrs. Ulrich: If you try to get involved in this thing, what can you accomplish? If you—if we—are wrong, you could make some powerful enemies. If you're right, you could be exposing yourself to great danger: you'd be dealing with someone who has already paid for one killing and could do it again.

"So I urge you, Mrs. Ulrich: leave it alone. Leave it to the police." She could have terminated this call some minutes ago. She certainly didn't need his peroration urging her to give up her quest for the perpetrator of her husband's murder. But it was easier just to let him go on while she pondered her next step. It would probably be good to let the priest think he had talked her out of it. "Okay. Thanks for all your information and advice. I promise I'll think this over very carefully. I won't do anything foolish. Promise."

Father Tully took the lightness of her tone to mean that she would let the matter lie. Buoyed by all the good he had just accomplished, he bade farewell and hung up.

He gathered the books and papers that had hit the floor at the start of his pacing. He began putting them in order. He had been so close to a concept for his homily. But then his intense involvement in the conversation with Mrs. Ulrich had all but completely derailed his earlier train of thought.

As he organized his references, he gave a final consideration to the death of Al Ulrich.

In his experience as a priest serving in one poor parish after another, Father Tully had known more than a few individuals who would have casually accepted a contract killing. He had met only a very few who could have or would have hired someone to do the job.

Had he just met three of the latter type?

Best he himself take to heart his brother's admonition: leave police work to the police.

At last he was comfy again, his papers and notes gathered close. Except that now he was having a difficult time concentrating on the sermon he was trying to put together.

Damn! If only she hadn't called. Their conversation had insinuated a seemingly permanent distraction in his mind. Now he was trying to rid his consciousness of the vague bothersome thoughts. At last he pinpointed the shadowy misgiving: it was Barbara's seeming conviction that no harm would come to Nancy Groggins in her position as manager of that new branch.

That conviction was predicated at the outset on the hypothesis that Al Ulrich had been killed by a hired gun . . . and that one of the VPs had done the hiring. Finally—and Barbara seemed alone in this—on the assertion that none of the VPs need any longer worry about being ousted from his position for the simple reason that Tom Adams would never raise a woman to his bank's hierarchy.

If all this were true, then there would not be another killing. Nancy Groggins, while ineligible for a top executive position, would not be in any danger—other than from the street threats that everyone faced.

Father Tully dug into his homily, vowing to at least try to erase all else from his mind.

* * *

Barbara had repaired to her tub for a long, leisurely soak.

From the moment the suspicion of murder by contract had occurred to her, she had bought it without reservation. Now she felt confirmed because someone else shared the same suspicion.

The fact that that someone—Father Tully—had done his utmost to discourage her from, in effect, carrying out her own private investigation, did not deter her. She knew that in his heart the priest believed as she did. And that was more than enough for her.

Gently, she marshaled the bubbles that skimmed the surface of her bath.

Jack, Lou, and Martin: as long as they needn't get their hands dirty or bloody, any one of them could easily afford to pay someone else to do it. The kid had had eight grand. It hadn't taken the cops long to find it.

Until now Barbara had given no serious thought to Tom Adams's being a suspect. But why not? He'd have as much if not more to fear from a public scandal when Al loudly disavowed paternity.

She had informed all of them—Jack, Lou, Martin, *and* Tom—

that she was pregnant. Her husband was not the father. But he had to be dealt with.

Now it was quite possible that she could get more than abundant support for herself and her child from all four men. At first blush that might appear impossible to carry off. But hadn't she structured affairs with all four while none of them was aware of the others?

Another idea had come to her during the conversation with Father Tully. These guys had been playing fast and loose as far as any sort of ethical behavior was concerned. Adultery with the wife of one of their co-workers. And now at least one of them, she was certain, was responsible for that co-worker's death.

Could one—or all of them—be guilty of more?

The CEO and his executive officers were subject to few checks and balances. Might there be any other skeletons in their closets? If there were, mightn't there be a basis for additional blackmail? For blackmail surely was what she actually planned.

In any case, her immediate plans were clear: one by one she would lead each of four men to conclude that he was the father of her unborn child. Failing their initial belief, she would convince each of them that he was the father.

That should result in a more than comfortable income for her. Actually, she would do well financially if even only one were convinced—especially if that one were Tom Adams. What, indeed, had she to fear? After all, one of them *was* the father. She couldn't miss.

On top of that, she might very well uncover more dirt. Based on the track record of each of her lovers, with the possible exception of Tom Adams, they easily might be as dishonest in their business lives as they were in their private lives. Discreet yet determined questioning might uncover secrets they desperately wanted to keep hidden. This was new territory; she would have to proceed with caution.

It would require research and investigation. Fortunately, Al had been open with her, at least concerning the bank's business operations. Based on that information and knowledge, she ought to be able to open up some cans of misconduct that could cause one or more of her paramours to squirm. She would start digging. This was a win/win situation; she couldn't lose.

She completely disregarded Father Tully's admonition.

Sixteen

SATURDAY AND SUNDAY had been what all the Tullys hoped for
during Father Zachary's visit: a peaceful time to grow in the knowledge and love of one another. The Koznickis were with them for Saturday brunch. For the remainder of the weekend, outside of the
Masses presided over by Father Tully, it was family time.

Now it was Monday and the priest had a eulogy to deliver.

*   *   *

Father Tully took a seat at the rear of the chapel, an excellent van-
tage for people watching.

He had arrived at McGovern Funeral Home some twenty minutes before the service for Al Ulrich was scheduled to begin. He
would have been earlier still but for the phone call from the pastor
of St. Joe's. Father Koesler had been away from his parish almost one
whole week. He could not quite let go.

Ostensibly this morning's call was to relate yesterday's adventures
in the good company of Father Koesler's priest classmate in Ontario.
In actuality, the call was about St. Joseph's parish in Detroit. But Father Koesler didn't want to appear so openly possessive as to make
it obvious that he missed his parish and was checking on how things
were going.

But back to the adventure. Yesterday—Sunday—Father Koesler
and his priest buddy had toured the rebuilt stockade of Ste. Marie
Among the Hurons.

The Jesuit mission, established in 1639, had lasted a mere ten years—during which time some Indians were converted to Catholicism and some Jesuits were martyred. Many of these martyrs were famous among parochial school students—among whom was Robert Koesler when he was a lad and people got away with calling him Bobby.

It had been an evident thrill for Koesler to visit the martyrs' shrine, as well as the fort, which had been burned to the ground when the Jesuits retreated, and much later rebuilt according to the original specifications.

To be honest, Father Tully was more than a little vague about the North American martyrs. Koesler gave a brief rundown featuring Isaac Jogues—the most famous of them all—and Fathers Brebeuf, Lalemant, Garnier, and Chabanal; as well as two laymen, René Goupil and Jean de la Lande.

Koesler omitted any detail of the terminal agonies of these dedicated saints. Although he did mention a humorous prayerful invocation found in a book titled *St. Fidgeta and Other Parodies*. The invocation, logically inserted in the Litany of the Saints, prayed, "From the Sisters who tell us precisely what the Indians did to Saint Isaac Jogues and his companions; good Lord, deliver us."

Actually, schoolboys lapped up the macabre details of the torture and slaughter of these saintly priests. However, once the lads matured to become students in the seminary, where the martyrology was read to them immediately after lunch, the effect could be a bit nauseating.

During their visit to the old fort, Fathers Koesler and Rammer spent much of their time in the chapel, a long, narrow building constructed principally of logs. A plain wooden table served as the altar. Ornate vestments, complete with the old fiddleback chasubles, ready to be donned, hung on nearby hooks. On the altar sat a chalice that appeared to have barely survived a couple of wars.

Also on the altar lay prayer cards—two small, one large. These supplied the Latin prayers when the celebrant found it inconvenient to read the missal.

Regular Mass had not been offered in that chapel for almost 350 years. Yet all was in readiness to begin again.

Koesler was most impressed with the realization that these vestments, implements, missal, and prayer cards had been in use a century or so before this present crude chapel was built. They were the exact same paraphernalia and trappings that had been in use in the era of his own ordination. They had remained in common use until a few years after the Second Vatican Council. Now, occasionally, with special permission, they were still used.

For Fathers Koesler and Rammer, the visit to the chapel in Huronia was a refreshing occasion for nostalgia. This was obvious from the warmth in Koesler's voice as he concluded his account of that visit.

At that point, the conversation took an expected turn. "How are things in Detroit?" Both men knew what specific section of Detroit Koesler referred to.

"Goin' good. Just like you said, I get out of the way and Mary O'Connor keeps things running."

"Great! How'd the weekend liturgies go?"

"Nobody walked out till I was all done with Mass."

"Sorry. Silly question."

"That's okay. I know how you feel. As I told you before, the only out-of-the-ordinary thing that's come up is the shooting of Al Ulrich."

"Al . . . Ulrich?" Koesler couldn't place the unfamiliar name.

"He's *not* one of your parishioners. I told you about him: the one who was slated to be manager of that new branch of Adams Bank?"

"Oh yes. Tom Adams—the one you gave the award to—his bank. That's too bad. Poor man." Koesler had no reason to know Ulrich and, indeed, had never met him.

"I'm supposed to give a eulogy for him at ten this morning."

"Hey, I'd better get off the line and let you get going."

"That's okay. We've got some time." Better now rather than having Koesler call back later in the day with some newly remembered detail. "Wasn't there anything about the murder in the Canadian media? It was big here. . . ."

"No, not a word. I've been through that before though. Lots of times when we think we have a major story, the foreign press doesn't give it any coverage at all. But you were involved in this one, as I recall."

"I thought I was. I met Ulrich at that award dinner party. The rest of the cast of characters were there too. And I got to meet them."

"The rest of the cast of characters? What characters?"

"The upper echelon of Adams Bank. Especially the three executive vice presidents who stand to gain from Ulrich's death."

Koesler started to chuckle. "'Stand to gain'? Are you developing a list of suspects? You really don't have to play cop just 'cause you're at St. Joseph's, you know. It doesn't come with the territory."

Tully bristled, partly because he had already been made to feel an intruder in this investigation. And now Koesler seemed to be making fun of him. "I know. I know. I know. I've been through all this with my brother. I've backed off and I intend to stay backed off. Besides, the thought of being of service to the Detroit Police Department never would've occurred to me if it hadn't been for you."

"Me?! What did I have to do with it?"

"Just that when my brother learned that not only was I on the scene, but that you were gone . . . far, far away in a distant land"— Tully made Koesler's vacation spot sound like the prelude to an episode of *Star Wars*—well, I was only trying to reassure the lieutenant that we belong to the same outfit, you and I . . . that he shouldn't consider suicide simply because you had left town for a little while."

"Well, I am surprised," Koesler said. "I didn't realize I'd had that sort of impact on your brother. I've just helped out a little from time to time—usually when there was some Catholic ingredient in an investigation. But you and I went over that when we first met—"

"I know. But as soon as my brother learned you'd gone, it was as if Detroit's only doctor had left the city and an epidemic of some sort was about to strike.

"Believe me, Bob . . . please, please believe me: I am not now, nor do I expect to be an expert religious resource for the police department—in this or any other city."

"Good. That's a good resolution."

"But"—Tully's tone was impish—"I do have a solution for this murder case that is completely outside the police investigation."

"You're incorrigible!" Koesler laughed and hung up.

*　　　*　　　*

Sitting in the chapel of McGovern Funeral Home, Tully smiled as he recalled the conversation. Immediately he composed himself and reverted to a serious mien as he returned to his people watching.

A good-sized crowd was gathering. As he expected, he knew almost none in the group. Then a tall, slender black man, bald, with neatly trimmed facial hair, swept down the aisle, trailing a couple of men who had to be bodyguards. It was a safe guess that this was Donald Aker, mayor of Detroit.

Father Tully experienced a momentary flush of pride in being of the same race as this dynamic leader who believed so completely in his once-beleaguered city.

The mayor paced himself expertly as he moved toward the bier and the widow. He greeted those within reach. He smiled, but a restrained smile befitting the gravity of the moment. Pound for pound, thought Tully, this was as skillful a working of a room as he'd ever witnessed.

It seemed as if the mayor spent considerable time comforting the widow. In reality he was in and out in no more than a very few minutes.

He and his entourage exited the same way they'd entered— the mayor continuing to work the room as he moved out. Undoubtedly he was headed toward the bank that, but for a gun, would have been opened by the now deceased. Today was the official opening. Within minutes, Mayor Aker would be working a crowd at the newest branch of Adams Bank and Trust, where a minute of silence would be observed in memory of its martyred manager.

Then, as if in a rite of pageantry, a procession entered at the chapel's rear. All were stylishly attired in dark mourning garb.

First came Joel Groggins, unaccompanied. He shook hands with the widow, who, even if not dressed as expensively as the others, easily was the most attractive of the many attractive women present. Groggins touched Mrs. Ulrich's arm as he spoke with her.

Father Tully guessed Groggins was needlessly explaining his wife's absence. Naturally, Nancy's presence was required at the bank she'd inherited from Al Ulrich.

Next came Lou and Pat Durocher. Pat's face was shadowed behind the black mesh of a semi-veil. She and Barbara turned their faces at an angle from each other and kissed air.

While Pat paused to view the body in the open casket, Lou said something to Barbara, in response to which she nodded vigorously. Tully couldn't know or even guess what had been said. But he noted that Lou Durocher seemed somehow rumpled without actually being rumpled. Could he be nursing a hangover?

Then came Jack and Marilyn Fradet. Marilyn, considerably more at home with the widow than Pat had been, put both hands on Barbara's shoulders, and they stood facing each other. Whatever Marilyn said caused Barbara to smile.

Marilyn viewed the body briefly, then moved to a reserved chair.

Jack, again evidently uncomfortable out of working attire, seemed awkward as he stooped to whisper something. It had to be only a whisper because he leaned almost against Barbara's ear while speaking. Barbara turned her head in his direction and whispered something in return. Jack then seated himself next to his wife. He made no effort to view the body.

Next, Martin and Lois Whitston took their turn.

Lois gave Barbara a reserved hug, patted her shoulder, said something briefly, glanced hastily at the body, and went to her chair.

Martin addressed Barbara vigorously. His voice was clearly more audible than his predecessors'. Tully could see some of those seated nearby lean forward as if trying to listen in.

Barbara hastily grabbed Martin's arm, cutting off any further speech. Quietly she said a few words. He nodded, left her side, and moved to the casket. He appeared to be praying. Maybe he was, thought Father Tully. Just because the priest assumed Whitston had no religious affiliation didn't mean Whitston couldn't pray—or even that he had no religious affiliation.

Finished, Whitston seated himself.

Last came Tom Adams. Of everyone here, Adams seemed most moved by this death. He was the antithesis of the robust host of his award dinner. Then he'd been very much in command; now he seemed somewhat lost.

As Whitston left Barbara, Adams made no immediate move to come forward. It was several seconds before he finally stepped up to her.

Now it looked as if the widow was consoling the mourner rather than vice versa. Adams's shoulders shook. He appeared to be fighting back tears. It was most affecting.

A memory stirred in Father Tully. The award dinner: Tully recalled watching Barbara Ulrich slip some sort of missive to each of the men in this hierarchy. Jack, the comptroller; Lou, the mortgage man; Martin, in commercial lending; and Tom, the CEO.

Now the same cast had shared something with Mrs. Ulrich.

Tully wondered about that. Especially since Barbara suspected that one of them had arranged for her husband's death—a suspicion she'd shared with the priest. He had advised her to follow his brother's admonition: to let the police do the police work. He fervently hoped that she would take his advice.

What must be going through her mind? What passed between her and her suspects just now? Did it have something to do with the notes she'd given to them at the dinner?

He glanced at his watch. A few minutes after ten. Mr. McGovern closed the doors, a signal that the service, such as it was, would begin.

Father Tully stepped up to the bier. He looked briefly at the corpse. Traditionally, those who attend viewings make comments that run from a simple, "My condolences," to the least common denominator, "He looks so natural," to the ridiculous, "He never looked better."

As far as Tully was concerned, the American Indians, among other peoples who lived with nature, had the best method of dealing with human remains: wrap them in a hammock, suspend it from two tall trees, and allow the birds and other animals to fold the deceased back into nature.

That method was not likely to become popular in today's society.

Personally, Tully thought the mortician had done a workmanlike job on Al Ulrich. He looked, in slumber of course, just as he had when the priest had met him for the first and final time last week.

Father Tully anticipated no problem in delivering this eulogy. Once he had introduced himself, a priest only lately arrived from Dallas, everyone would accept that he'd had little opportunity to know Al Ulrich other than fleetingly. It was easy to be credible while speaking vaguely about a deceased whom one had known only in passing.

He would make no apologies for being a Catholic priest who had been invited to deliver this eulogy. At the same time he did not want to exclude those in this gathering who were not Catholics—Protestants, Jews, or even merely unaffiliated theists.

He would point out that Jesus, for many the most important person who ever lived, sought the company of those whom polite society avoided. He was there for those who needed Him no matter who these needy happened to be.

When the self-righteous dragged before Jesus a woman taken in the act of adultery, he prevented the mob from executing her. His closest companions were the blue-collar workers of that day: fishermen, a tax collector.

There was no class consciousness in His life in any sense. He could be found at table with anyone from the very wealthy to the poorest of the poor.

The next point needed to be presented cautiously. Tom Adams was not Jesus Christ. But it was his decision that was putting a financial facility at the service of those who tended to be forgotten, overlooked, ignored.

Nor was Al Ulrich a messiah. But he *had* volunteered to lead this effort. He *sought* the position.

While neither Adams nor Ulrich was any place close to divinity, nonetheless what they tried to do and what they did was good by nearly anyone's standard.

That was Father Tully's outline.

He turned to the assembled group. They were looking at him expectantly, attentively.

All except Barbara Ulrich. She seemed lost in thought.

"Good morning. My name is Father Zachary Tully. I am a Josephite priest from Dallas, Texas. I was asked to say a few words this morning.

"I did not know Al Ulrich well. We met but once. And that was last week. However, I am very well aware of what Al Ulrich and"—he inclined his head slightly in the CEO's direction—"Tom Adams were attempting to accomplish in the midst of Detroit's inner city.

"Their enterprise was not unlike at least part of the mission of Jesus Christ."

To this point, Barbara Ulrich heard Father Tully. Then his image grew faint and her attention began to lapse.

It was all coming back to her.

Seventeen

AL ULRICH could have been her ticket to the promised land.

Barbara Ulrich gazed past Father Tully and contemplated her late husband.

How had she come from there to here?

It had all started with Daddy. Daddy and his damnable "love games." Then the change she'd felt inside her. The mistaken diagnosis, partly due to her reluctance to reveal what she instinctively sensed to be her shame.

Mother prying the details from her in the hospital.

That sight! She would never, could never, forget the tiniest detail. The broken "doll" they had taken from her, its head crushed and shattered.

For a long while after the abortion, she couldn't return to the normal world. There were dreams—nightmares. It was a mercy she never saw her father again, though his absence contributed heavily to the unnaturalness of her home life. Between that and the unconventional atmosphere it all added up to a deeply dysfunctional household.

Mother had a lovely home sans husband. So she no longer needed entertain her boyfriends in cars and motels. Barbara had to make room for "Uncle" Peter and "Uncle" Roy and "Uncle" Lloyd. And, as time passed, other similarly premised relations.

To give the devil his due, mother Claire made certain that none of her suitors ever got familiar with Babs.

It had not taken Barbara long to identify the sounds coming from her mother's bedroom. Schoolmates were liberal in providing details of sex, adult style. Some of the information was imaginative fiction. Barbara's experience with Daddy provided cold facts to straighten out in her mind the actual process of "lovemaking."

She was a high school teenager. She was gorgeous. She would have nothing to do with boys. The boys, hormones raging, were all over Barbara—sometimes literally. She fought them off.

Claire Simpson was spared one of the curses of mothering a teenage girl. She never had to worry that Babs was being led down a primrose path to perdition. If anything, Mother was concerned that her spectacularly beautiful daughter was headed toward a cloistered convent without the benefit of organized religion.

Claire sent Barbara to a psychologist—a woman.

There was an immediate at-oneness between Babs and Dr. Hunter —or Joyce, as the doctor promptly permitted.

During therapy, Barbara was able to vent all her repressed hostility toward her father, and even her mother. As a direct result of therapy, Barbara became a far more well-adjusted teen. She attended mixed parties. Eventually, she even went on dates. Her one major fear was pregnancy. She knew that should she become pregnant and there was no miscarriage, the child would be carried to term and be born.

This led to a dilemma. In no way did Barbara want a child. A child was not part of any plan she could envision for the short or long term. Yet her memory of her involuntary abortion was so powerful she could never repeat that. If she became pregnant, she would have the baby she didn't want. She strongly doubted that she could give up a child for adoption. So the master plan was: *don't get pregnant.*

This decision placed a considerable burden on both her and her dates. After all, the hormones were raging.

However, none of her dates could claim that he was unaware of the ground rules. If, driven by tormented testosterone, an attempt at intercourse was made, in effect it could only be labeled rape.

It was no surprise then that, among many of the boys in her graduating class, Barbara was known as the Virgin Queen.

However, she was making progress. After all, she was attending parties and going on dates. And that was more, much more, than she could have attempted before becoming the patient of Dr. Joyce Hunter.

In college she was able to relax some of her rigid rules of dating. She attended Western Michigan University in Kalamazoo.

One eternally popular song, "I've Got a Gal in Kalamazoo," was written about this quaint city. It was sometimes known as Mall City, with the claim that it had preceded even Minneapolis with a downtown traffic-free shopping mall. If Mary Tyler Moore had launched her cap in Kalamazoo, things might have been very different.

As it is, Kalamazoo boasts a couple of colleges, a university, some hospitals, and lots of medical specialists. It is also the hometown of noted author and poet, James Kavanaugh.

The highly intellectual level of life in the Mall City prompted Barbara to reevaluate her own coed life. Was she shriveling her personality by not mixing more freely with her fellow students? She determined to wade a bit more deeply into the mainstream of campus life.

Which did not, in any way, mean that all barriers were lowered. She insisted on plenty of protection for her partners, as well as taking stringent precautions herself.

Had she been even a tad less glamorous and attractive, she would never have been able to enforce her prophylactic paradise. But even with all her caveats, her dance card was always full.

Still, she couldn't see the point of it all.

Rarely did any of her partners seem at all concerned about her pleasure. Foreplay was fun. But the cataclysmic climax was for the gentleman. She could not dismiss the thought: there must be more to this than that.

Then one evening, she entertained a classmate in her on-campus dorm room. Gretchen was attending WMU on a basketball scholarship. They had helped each other on occasion. Barbara tutored

Gretchen in her liberal arts courses; Gretchen helped Barbara create a regimen of exercise for herself.

This was an unusually peaceful time in the building. Gretchen and Barbara were among the few students not attending any of the many campus events scheduled for this evening.

When they finished working on Gretchen's English composition assignment, they, more from boredom than anything else, started playing word games. To neither's surprise, Barbara won consistently.

In feigned frustration, Gretchen started to roughhouse. Which led to tickling. Both young women grew aroused. As they rolled on the bed, Gretchen's touches became more intimate. At first Barbara tried to break clear. When she could not, a transformation occurred. For the first time, she could let down her guard. Suddenly she arched, her body rigid. It was almost as if tetany had occurred. Just when she thought she was about to break asunder, her body began to undulate. The orgasm exploded within her. She threw her arms around Gretchen and kissed her deeply over and over.

Before she allowed herself to relax, she brought Gretchen to what was for her a more knowing, practiced climax.

Then both young women lay quietly on the bed utterly quiescent and physically at ease and calm.

But shortly, confusion clouded Barbara's afterglow.

What had happened here? Clearly, this was what it was all about. *But with another woman?*

Gretchen began the preliminaries again. Barbara couldn't repeat. Not now. She was too confused. It became almost a rape situation. The scuffle bordered on cruelty. Gretchen angrily left.

As soon as Dr. Hunter had an opening, Barbara made an appointment. With Joyce of course there were no secrets. What a caring mother was supposed to be, Joyce was.

They had been over the dating situation before. Barbara had set the guidelines for lovemaking. Joyce had created the emotional space for Babs to do this. Now Babs wondered if she had been wrong in, perhaps, being too careful.

Maybe the problem was just that she hadn't yet found the right man. That could be it.

These were young men . . . boys, really; what did they know about lovemaking? They were self-centered, just taking care of Number One. Once she got out on her own, once she got out of college, once it became appropriate for her to date older, more experienced men, everything would straighten itself out.

Then why had she nearly exploded with Gretchen? Was it just all that pent-up energy inside her seeking an outlet?

Barbara's eyes met Joyce's silent gaze. Under that penetrating look, Barbara spoke more and more slowly until she fell silent. "I . . . I'm . . . a lesbian, aren't I?"

Joyce nodded. And smiled.

"And . . ." Barbara hesitated, fearing that she was about to be dead wrong and, at the same time, apprehensive that she was correct. ". . . and so are you!"

Joyce's smile took on a melancholy tinge. Again she nodded.

"But you can't be!"

"Why not?"

"You're married! You've got a child!"

"It's time to talk about this," Joyce said.

"Time? Now? You mean you've known about this right along and you never brought it up? And 'now' is the time to face it? Is that what you mean?" Barbara's tone became angry.

"Yes, now is the time," Joyce stated flatly. "Not long after we met, I was pretty sure you were gay."

"But . . . how? I like boys. I always have."

"That's not the point, Babs. Boys who are homosexual don't hate girls. They're just not physically, sexually attracted to them. Girls who are lesbian don't hate boys. They're just not as attracted to males as they are to other females."

"But I've been with boys—sexually. As a matter of fact, Gretchen is my one and only gay . . . experience."

"Face it, Babs: you never got from a guy what you got from Gretchen."

"Maybe that's because they didn't know what they were doing. Maybe they just lacked the experience to bring me to orgasm. Maybe they were just interested in themselves."

Joyce smiled condescendingly. "Come on, Barbara, not one young man you've ever been with did everything right—mechanically, even passionately? Not one really tried to help you come?"

Barbara exhaled deeply. She studied the floor. "You're right. There have been times. I guess I just never faced up to it.

"Oh, Joyce . . ." She looked at her mentor, tears flowing. "How did this happen to me?"

Joyce shook her head. "You're beginning to sound as if you had leprosy—something terminal and communicable." She chuckled. "I've got it too, you know."

Barbara felt apologetic. "I'm sorry. You're right. But I can't help thinking that what we are is unnatural . . . or freaky."

"That's because that's how the rest of society wants us to think of ourselves. At best we're simply different from the majority. And that scares them. Now you're wondering how you got to be part of our minority."

Barbara nodded with great interest.

"Well . . . nobody's been able to pin down the cause for certain. It may be something genetic. It may be a chromosome. It may have something to do with early development. Take yours, for instance. How could anybody have had a much more screwed-up formation? A steady diet of incest resulting in pregnancy. The abortion. Your mother sleeping around. The fact that you're as well put together as you are is a testimony to something inside you that survives.

"Whatever, it's futile to fixate on the impossible. Anyone in this business who is honest will admit we don't have any incontrovertible indication of why some—the majority—are straight and others—the minority—are gay.

"You are what you are. You live with it. You play the hand you're dealt."

Barbara, lost in thought, was trying to digest all she'd just heard. "Okay," she said finally, "so you and I are lesbian. What I don't understand is your husband and your kid. Aren't they impossible for you?"

"Not really." Joyce went to the credenza and poured two cups of coffee. She gave Barbara one and placed the other on her desk as she began to pace between the desk and a bookshelf. "You see, Babs, there's this glass ceiling. You're familiar with the term?"

Barbara shook her head.

"Well, the glass ceiling is a metaphor and at the same time a very real barrier that blocks women and minorities from rising from middle to senior corporate management positions or to tenured professorships.

"About the only way a woman today can be top gun in her profession is when she creates—is the founding mother, if you will, of the business. But how many people, men or women, can bring that off successfully?

"You haven't been exposed to the glass ceiling yet. But you will be. You will be because you're smart and you're talented. There's no reason why you couldn't—shouldn't—rise to the top. What do you want to work at after you graduate?"

Barbara tapped a front tooth with her index finger. "I'm not sure . . . I think maybe advertising or public relations."

"Hmmm. There have been some moderate breakthroughs in those fields. Still . . . take a look at the larger firms in those fields and you'll find at the very top a white male or a bunch of the same. The opposition to a minority or a woman getting those top positions is enormous.

"The obstacles are significant. Just look at large corporations, law firms—all men, all white men, at the top.

"Now, maybe you're wondering why this system is called a glass ceiling."

Barbara sipped her coffee and nodded.

"Babs, it's because everybody, especially everybody on the top side of the ceiling, pretends it isn't there. 'There's no opposition to you women and minorities joining us up here. Why, you can see us clearly.' But try climbing up there with the big boys and you'll rap your head on that invisible barrier.

"Got that, Babs? You can't see it, but it's there: a glass ceiling."

Barbara nodded slowly. Yes, she did understand. She'd just never given it much thought. This was America. The Land of Opportunity, where anybody can become anything he or she wants.

But now that she thought about it, that wasn't the way it worked.

"There's something there even after the glass ceiling," Joyce continued. "Suppose a woman or a minority member does manage to break through the ceiling. The white males occupying that floor just put up a concrete wall.

"For years—lots of years—there were no minorities, let alone women, who managed major league sports teams. Even today there still are damn few. But a few African-Americans have made it through that glass ceiling only to find a concrete wall blocking the way to ownership.

"But why am I telling you all about the glass ceiling and brick wall when you asked about my husband and our child?" She gazed into a distance that wasn't there. "It happened after I discovered I was gay," she said finally. "With that came the realization that I was not what the straight world expected a woman to be. It was then I concluded that we—gay women—have two strikes against us. The first strike is the glass ceiling that I just talked about. The second strike is that we don't find men natural beasts of burden."

"Huh?"

"Lots of women—most women?—rise socially, economically, whatever, on the backs of their husbands. It's 'Doctor and Mrs.' or 'Mr. Ford and his socially active wife so-and-so.'

"See, it's not that women aren't intelligent enough or are incapable of the skills needed to climb to the top; it's that the male world prevents them from achieving the ultimate success.

"So lots of women—most women?—blocked from achieving all they're capable of, ride the coattails of their husbands. But what gay women do not need are husbands—"

"So," Barbara broke in, "you got married because it was the 'proper' thing to do. And you're going to accomplish more as his wife than you could by yourself."

"Let me put just a little different spin on that, Babs. I'm going to accomplish lots more because I am Joyce Hunter, wife and mother —and thus what the world wants me to be—than I ever would have as Joyce Matthews, lesbian."

Barbara thought about all this for several minutes. Joyce gave her time to absorb many facts that until now had been completely foreign to her concept of what life held in store for her.

At length, Barbara looked intensely at Joyce. "Your husband, your child: how do they react to your lesbianism?"

"They haven't a clue."

"What?!"

"It's true. No one would be more surprised than they if they were to find out."

"But . . . ?"

Joyce smiled broadly. "It's time for us to pity the poor boys."

"Huh?"

"They can't fake an orgasm. As even you very well know, the male orgasm is part and parcel of his ejaculation. As a matter of fact, his ejaculation *is* his orgasm. In other words, he has to put up or shut up. He has to get aroused enough to reach a climax. A very visible, discernible climax.

"Not so with us women. It is a standard part of our equipment that we ejaculate nothing. We lubricate, but if we don't we can use a cream or almost any sort of lubricant. After that, noises—a squeal, a moan, a scream or two—will convince the male that we've come. Maybe, if one wants to carry conviction, our noises, our body movements will convince our partners that we have come in a very big way."

Barbara was aware that her mouth was hanging open. She closed it. "You mean you've faked orgasm totally, throughout your marriage!"

"Well, maybe not totally. There've been times when we're together and I . . . well . . . fantasize. That's kind of common in any number of people who make love. How many women while they're having intercourse with their husbands may be envisioning Robert Redford, or Mel Gibson, or someone else? That's a fantasy.

"Sometimes, when I'm with Harry, I picture someone else in his place. I should admit that Harry is quite good in bed. So, when I'm not particularly turned on by him, I can respond to my fantasy."

"I see." Barbara hesitated, not knowing whether to try the question on her mind. But Joyce had been so open and frank . . . Babs decided to risk making herself vulnerable to rejection. "May I ask, Joyce: was I ever your fantasy?"

Joyce almost blushed. "You ask too many questions, gal." Then, seeing that she had hurt Barbara, she added, "Babs, you're a beautiful person, inside and outside. Sure you've been my fantasy. More often than not."

Silence for several long moments.

"But even if you have a fantasy partner," Barbara asked, "isn't it still like being raped?"

The word "rape" stung Joyce. "I hope I haven't given you the wrong impression. It's never even close to rape with Harry. He's very considerate. He would never insist on lovemaking if I were not in the mood or didn't feel well or something like that. It's just . . . my physical love object is going to be a woman. That's just the way it is . . . the way it has to be." After a few moments, Joyce asked, "Want some more coffee?"

"No, thanks." Pause. "You know, Joyce, it needn't be a fantasy."

"What?"

"Us . . . together . . . making love: it doesn't have to be a fantasy for you or for me."

Warning lights went on in Joyce's mind. "Wait a minute, young lady. You're a student in college. I'm an established psychologist."

"You're not hiding behind the difference in our ages!"

"Not that so much as the fact that you were—you are—my patient. It smacks of bad ethics to make love to one's patient. It's too dangerous. As inviting as it is, it's also fraught."

Barbara stood and walked over to Joyce. Face to face, they were only inches apart. "How about this: suppose we wait till I graduate. Suppose during this interval I'm not your patient. We sever our doctor-patient relationship. Supposing then we became lovers."

"I don't know. . . ." Joyce shook her head. "How do we know how we'll feel after this? How do we know we'll feel the same way then? Wait: there are no strings here . . . right?"

"None."

"Open-ended, then. Okay, we'll see what we will see."

They held each other's hands and looked penetratingly into each other's eyes.

Then Joyce leaned forward and kissed Barbara as she might embrace a friend. And thus they separated until Barbara could begin her assault on that glass ceiling.

Eighteen

Tʀᴜᴇ ᴛᴏ their agreement, Barbara Simpson and Joyce Hunter did not see each other, either professionally or socially, while Barbara remained a student at Western Michigan.

Gretchen offered to introduce Barbara to Kalamazoo's gay community. Barbara tactfully declined. She resumed dating boys, reasoning that once out of the closet there would be no getting back in.

After graduation, Barbara joined an ad agency. She was clever and successful, but it soon became obvious that though her ideas and her talent would advance her, there was no way she would get to the top; the glass ceiling was there—transparent, but rock solid. She could see through it—but she would not be able to rise through it.

She had talent, skill, brains, and her customer relations were excellent. But she was a woman.

Disgusted, she accepted an offer from one of the auto companies. The glass ceiling was still there, but the perks and the salary sweetened the status.

She began seeing Dr. Joyce Hunter again, ostensibly as a patient. In effect what was going on was not completely foreign to some doctor-patient relationships. They were conducting a love affair—clandestinely, but an affair nevertheless.

By appointment they met at Joyce's office monthly. They were able to get together more frequently at Barbara's apartment. And when Joyce reserved a post office box, they were even able to correspond. Things were going along as swimmingly as possible.

Until . . .

Until one day Barbara got a phone call from a man she had never met: Harry Hunter, Joyce's husband.

He knew.

He had found one of Barbara's letters. Joyce was supposed to destroy them after reading. Instead, she had kept one in a "safe" place.

Barbara had received angry phone calls, but none like this. He was so damn righteous. Unlike the biblical woman caught in adultery, in Barbara's case, there would be no defender to protect her. Harry Hunter had been betrayed and, by God, someone would pay for it. He was going to file for divorce and he damn well knew he would be granted custody of their teenage daughter. He called Barbara every foul name in his arsenal.

When he finally slammed down the phone she felt as if she'd been shot at close range with a shotgun. And that she'd never be able to pick out all the tiny fragments of pellets.

Her hands were shaking as she dialed Joyce's office. An answering machine offered to take a message. Barbara hesitated, then decided against that. She tried Joyce's home. No answer.

Barbara was close to panic. She desperately needed to talk to Joyce. But how to reach her? She didn't want to chance encountering Harry in her efforts to contact Joyce.

She decided there was nothing she could do now. Literally. She was so shaken there was no possibility of working further this day. She pleaded a sudden migraine. Her concerned boss, who prized her work, told her to take as much time as she needed.

Barbara went to her apartment and tried the two numbers again. No response.

She tried a bath. Inexplicably, she became claustrophobic in the water.

She tried to read. But her mind refused to focus on the printed words. Again and again she returned to a panic state. She paced endlessly. She could neither stay seated nor lie down. She was frightened for herself, but far more concerned for Joyce. This could mean not only the end of Joyce's marriage, but, quite possibly, her career as well.

Periodically, she dialed Joyce's office, hoping against hope that Joyce would have returned—if she had gone out. As the phone rang, Barbara would mutter, "Pick up! Damn it, Joyce, pick up!" But after several rings, the familiar if professional voice of Dr. Hunter would invite the caller to leave a message at the tone.

Why wasn't Joyce calling her? Was she being held captive by Harry? Had she been injured? Had there been some sort of accident? Anything was possible, but not probable.

If Joyce were free and able to call, why wasn't she calling?

Was it because Joyce was angry with her? Maybe. After all, it was one of Barbara's letters that was the proximate cause of this catastrophe. But dammit, Joyce was supposed to have destroyed those letters!

It was sweet but dumb of Joyce to save one. She must've thought she was keeping it in a "safe" place. She should have realized that as long as she kept even a single letter, it stood the chance of being found.

Certainly, both Barbara and Joyce were aware of the danger and the consequences if anyone—most of all Harry—learned of their affair. But it was possible that neither woman could have imagined just how cataclysmically Harry would react.

God, but she wanted a cigarette! Barbara hadn't smoked in many years. But then, she hadn't been hovering on the brink of a nervous breakdown either. Yet she dared not go out; at any moment Joyce might call.

It was almost 11 P.M. Barbara turned on the TV, convinced she would not pay attention to a word. If nothing else, she needed noise.

A local lawyer, himself a celebrity, had been found guilty of drunk driving as well as some legal improprieties, and disbarred. Barbara continued pacing. She paid no attention whatever to the story.

The Detroit Lions were in Miami to play the Dolphins. Some local teens had attempted to mug the Lions' middle linebacker. Several of the teens were under arrest and recovering in a Miami hospital. The linebacker, none the worse for the attack, would play this Sunday.

Barbara paced heedlessly.

The local health care community was shocked to learn that one of their number had committed suicide. Dr. Joyce Hunter had apparently taken her own life. A colleague found the body late this afternoon. She had died instantly after a single shot to the head from a handgun. No suicide note had been found. An autopsy had been ordered. There were no funeral plans at this time. Neither her husband nor their daughter was available for comment.

Several therapists expressed astonishment at the news. None could think of any reason for her action.

More details would be reported as they were forthcoming.

Barbara shuddered as she shook her head and wept.

*   *   *

"I really do believe that the people of Detroit will remember Al Ulrich. He didn't die for them. But he lived for them. In accepting his assignment, he placed himself in harm's way in order to serve people unaccustomed to wholehearted service."

Barbara Ulrich shuddered, shaking her head as one does when reliving a nightmare.

She had no idea how long Father Tully had been speaking nor what he had said. She was wrapped in her private memories.

She wondered if anyone at this wake service had noticed her brief spasm. If they had, she hoped her tremor would be ascribed to grief over her husband's death.

Slowly, she sank back into the past.

*   *   *

The manager of the apartment complex found her the day after Joyce's suicide. Her employer, concerned, had tried to contact her to ask how she was feeling. The last he'd seen of her she was complaining of a horrible headache. He wanted to assure her that she needn't return to work until she felt better. When there was no answer to repeated phone calls, he called and asked the manager to look in on her.

She was curled in a fetal position and comatose.

She spent a brief period in the intensive care unit of St. John's Hospital on Detroit's east side. From there she was transferred to the psychiatric ward of the same hospital. For over a week she was fed intravenously and permitted no visitors. No one knew the cause of her anxiety reaction. It took some time before she was able to join in the battle to return her to normalcy.

Among those waiting during the doctor's ban on visitors was Harriet Hunter, daughter of Harry and the late Joyce Hunter. When Harriet was finally allowed to visit, she had to introduce herself to her mother's lover. Barbara had never met Harriet and knew only what Joyce had told her about her child.

At first Barbara was apprehensive. She was tempted to call the nurse to usher Harriet out. There could be little doubt that Harriet knew the truth. How many others knew the whole story Barbara could only guess. Since her breakdown, she hadn't seen a newspaper, listened to or watched the news. The few visitors she'd had hadn't mentioned anything concerning Joyce. And Barbara hadn't asked.

But Harriet wore a genuine smile. It faded when she saw the fear in Barbara's eyes. "How are you feeling?" Harriet pulled a chair close to Barbara's bed and sat down.

"A little numb." Barbara tried to smile. "My, you're a pretty young lady. I can see Joyce, especially in your eyes."

Harriet's open smile returned. "And I'm glad to meet you at last."

Barbara looked uneasy. "How long have you known . . . I mean, about your mother and me?"

Harriet seemed puzzled. "You mean because I said 'at last' I'm getting to meet you?"

Barbara nodded.

"I didn't. I didn't know. Not till Dad found your letter, and all hell broke loose. I wish I had known. But Mother didn't want that. She was very discreet. Well . . . up until she kept your letter."

"I'm sorry, Harriet. I'm so very sorry."

Tears welled in Harriet's eyes. She blinked them back. "It wasn't your fault."

"If I hadn't entered into that relationship with your mother . . ."

"If you hadn't, it might've been someone else. Someone not so caring. Or maybe Mother would've lived a dreary, loveless life with Dad. And no one besides her would have known."

Tears spilled over as Barbara for the first time was able to express her sorrow and loss. Both women wept, embracing each other.

When the tears subsided, Harriet said, "Do you have any idea what's happened since Mother . . . since Mother died?"

Barbara shook her head. "No. No idea at all. I've been . . . afraid to ask. Afraid to know."

"After the investigation—the police and the autopsy—Mother's death was officially declared a suicide. Dad was furious. He should have been heartbroken. But he was too angry to recognize his loss."

Barbara nodded. "Before Joyce . . . before your mother's death, your father called me. I'm sure it was just after he found my letter."

"Was he a bastard?"

"I'm afraid so. That and more."

Harriet sighed. "He blames you for Mother's suicide. Even after her death he was going to go public."

Barbara swallowed nervously. This was the moment she dreaded even though it was inevitable. Was their secret a secret no more? She waited, unable to ask.

"I talked him out of it," Harriet said. "It got down to the last

moment almost. After all, Mother took her life as a direct conse-
quence of what Dad threatened to do. She didn't commit suicide because of you. She loved you. She couldn't bear to see you
embarrassed. Just as she couldn't stand the humiliation she would
have suffered.

"I promised my father that if he breathed your secret to a soul, I
would never speak to him the rest of his life. And I told him I would
let everyone know that he and his threats were the cause of Mother's
death.

"I'm convinced he'll keep quiet. That's really the main reason I
wanted to see you as soon as I could. I told your apartment manager I was a friend. He told me you were in the hospital. I called
around till I found you. I was sure knowing all this would help your
recovery. It's been a hard fight getting past the doctor. I can't blame
him, I guess. He didn't know why I wanted to see you so badly.
And I couldn't tell him, of course.

"As far as the police and other officials are concerned, Mother's
death was a suicide. And since there was no note, and since Dad kept
his mouth shut, there is no official reason or record.

"There's one last thing, Barbara. I'm straight, but I understand
you and Mother . . . at least I think I do. And I think it's a wonderful thing the two of you had."

Barbara nodded wordlessly, her eyes again filling with tears. What
a beautiful job Joyce had done raising such a daughter. Harriet was
only a teenager, but she had a maturity far beyond her years.

Harriet patted her hand, then, after a long, heartfelt hug, she left.

After this visit, Barbara's health and outlook improved steadily
and remarkably. She soon returned to work. When it became clear
she wasn't going to talk about what had happened, her co-workers
and those involved in her social life gradually stopped asking.

It was difficult to adjust to the absence of Joyce, the total absence of Joyce.

Life goes on.

She took a page from Joyce's formula. Barbara determined to take a husband as her launching pad to *la dolce vita*. Someone with lots of promise. Someone who would make it big. Not someone who was already standing on that glass ceiling. No, she wanted to build and mold carefully so that when her husband made it, she wouldn't be that out-of-place newcomer. She would be a person in her own right.

Enter Al Ulrich.

Handsome, young, unmarried, a banker; definitely on the rise, he seemed to be sent from central casting.

With her looks, style, and personality, she would've had no problem whatever attracting anyone she chose. She chose Al Ulrich and cultivated him till harvesttime. They were sexually active, each bringing their special experience to their union.

Occasionally she might have been awarded an Oscar for her feigned frenzied orgasms. But then, sometimes her climaxes were very real. Those were the times of her fantasies. Usually, the fantasy was of her beloved Joyce.

Babs and Al took great care to avoid a pregnancy. Al did not want people counting to corroborate their suspicion. She definitely did not want a child.

In due course they were married.

Al quite naturally took it for granted that the barriers against pregnancy would fall once the nuptial niceties had been observed. He was wrong—very wrong.

Fortunately for tender-souled retiring neighbors in adjoining apartments the insulation was thick enough to muffle nearly any outcry. And outcry there was. For once it became painfully clear that while Barbara's playpen would be open, her nursery was closed, all hell broke loose. *Virginia Woolf*'s George and Martha couldn't hold a candle to Al and Barbara.

In time, Al became convinced he was not going to father a child —at any rate not by Barbara. Their marriage then settled prematurely into loveless cohabitation.

One of the considerations about which they were in total agreement was divorce.

For one, Al did not want to publicly admit that he had failed in making a success of his life with this gorgeous, desirable woman. For those who might have assumed that they would be able to control this vivacious creature, Al would have had two words: *try it.*

For another, Al had a secret hope. He was determined to climb the ladder at Adams Bank and Trust. And when he was seated at the right hand of Tom Adams, Barbara would come around. He was convinced that was her ultimate aim: to be the wife of a singularly successful man. When this happened—and happen it would—he would take counsel with himself. At that point, like Henry Higgins, Al could be a most forgiving man. Or, he could throw the baggage out.

For Barbara, short of having Joyce, things could scarcely have worked out more smoothly. The only fly in the ointment was the fact that Al's rocket remained on the launching pad.

She complained to him—and to just about anyone who would listen—that he had sold his soul to the company. But in her heart of hearts, that was precisely what should be happening.

If and when Al made it to the big leagues—which meant nothing less than an executive vice presidency—she might even entertain thoughts of a child.

In this, Joyce Hunter had marked a path. From all Barbara could tell in one meeting, Joyce's daughter had turned out ideally. Not only was she a loyal daughter—to both her parents—she had stopped her father from making public something that would hurt everyone concerned.

No, Barbara would not be averse to having a daughter like Harriet.

But that could not happen till Al made his mark and Barbara's biological clock was far enough advanced that she would deign to compromise her fabulous figure.

And no talk of abortion under any circumstances.

Sadly, Al was in sight of the magical goal when he was cut down.

Part of Barbara's present plan was to test the water in four directions to ascertain if any of the present three VPs—or their CEO—might have had a hand in Al's murder.

She also planned to convince four individuals that each was the father of her unborn child.

Finally, to insure the most comfortable settlement for her, she hoped to uncover some financial hanky-panky perpetrated by any or all of the VPs.

Blackmail, like greed, could be good.

And that is how Barbara Simpson Ulrich grew from an innocent little girl into a scheming, blackmailing widow.

*   *   *

Father Tully seemed to be winding up his eulogy.

Barbara had no idea how long he'd been speaking, how long she'd been lost in thought. She glanced at her watch. She had only a vague notion of when he had begun. Her best guess was approximately fifteen minutes ago. Acceptable timing.

Evidently, Father Tully was drawing some sort of analogy between Al's involvement in the bank's new branch and a pair of mountain climbers.

"They were nearly three quarters of the way up," said Father Tully, "when the storm hit. It was as powerful as it was sudden. The blizzard effectively cut off any chance of further progress or retreat. One climber took refuge in a small natural overhang. The other tried to go on.

"When the storm finally lifted and rescuers were able to find the pair, the climber who had tried to go on was found frozen to death. He was leaning against the wind and died with his knee bent, as if he was taking another step when he passed on.

"One of the rescue party looked at the man and his bent knee, and said, 'at least he died trying.'

"And that, finally, is what we can say, with some pride, of Al Ulrich: at least he died trying."

Father Tully paused, then took his seat.

The room was quiet. His eulogy had been effective. Some whose presence at this wake was pro forma were actually thinking serious eschatological thoughts.

At length, Tom Adams stood, thanked Father Tully, and pronounced an end to the proceedings.

There followed a good bit of milling about as people paid their final respects to the widow and to the body of the deceased.

Those who offered Barbara words of consolation did not mind that she did not meet their eyes. Today they were willing to excuse her nearly anything.

And as the mourners left the funeral home, they spoke to each other of how well Barbara was holding up. What a shock it must be to have one's life partner taken so suddenly and out of due time. "Isn't she brave!"

Even those who ordinarily bad-mouthed her—and there were more than a few in this gathering—even they were in sympathy with her. Exceptions were two of the VP wives—Marilyn Fradet being a latter-day convert to Barbara's corner.

Barbara of the absent gaze actually was trying to lock eyes with four men. She succeeded with three, but Tom Adams was concentrating on those who offered *him* condolences.

It didn't matter. Later this day she would begin her own investigation and interrogation to find who actually was responsible for her husband's murder. For murder it was, she was certain. Who would accept responsibility for her unborn child. And whose hand might be in the company till.

And her manner of inquiry, as ever, would be unique.

Nineteen

THE CASUAL OBSERVER might be prone to say something like: the apple doesn't fall far from the tree; or, like mother, like daughter.

Claire Simpson had discarded a husband while juggling four lovers. Claire's daughter first discarded, then lost forever a husband while juggling four paramours.

As Barbara long ago took note of her mother's sexual athletics, the girl had vowed not to follow Claire's track record. Yet, numerically at least, she had. But by now she had forgotten the comparison. Particularly since, unsettled by the pressures triggered by one or another of her lovers, Claire had committed suicide.

Though devastated by her mother's tragic act, Barbara drew no parallel when Joyce Hunter chose the same violent end. Barbara had a selective memory. She chose to remember the more rosy incidents in her life. She did not dwell on tragic events—particularly those that portended any sort of evil. She was the embodiment of the phrase, Those who do not learn from the past are doomed to repeat it. However, her attitude toward her past and future appeared to be an effective defense mechanism.

*   *   *

At this moment, several hours after the funeral service for her late husband, Barbara was in her apartment preparing to greet a man who quite possibly might have been involved in her husband's death, and who also might be the father of her unborn child.

After her shower, she was careful to break routine and do nothing to enhance the natural allure of her body. No powder, no perfume or cologne, no lipstick. Everything must be natural because his wife was the suspicious sort. A foreign fragrance, a dusting of powder, a smudge of lipstick could lead to an ugly scene.

She selected one of his favorite dresses—if it could be described as a dress. It was a series of leather straps overlapping at strategic areas, definitely meant to be worn, if ever, over a shielding slip. The dress was held together at several side points by Velcro. She wore no undergarment.

As if she had a repertoire of many plays, musicals, or operas and was about to appear in one of them, she now conducted for herself a quick refresher. She would have to mentally run through the work before taking the stage.

This would be repeatedly so for the next twenty-four hours, during which, according to her plan, she would be visited by all four of her lovers.

First, due in less than half an hour, was Martin Whitston, vice president in charge of commercial lending.

Over the years she had grown familiar with the background of "her" men. Their peculiar history is what made them what they were today. As such, it was important to Barbara.

Marty sprang from a financially modest, middle-class background. He was the oldest of five brothers, no sisters. His father was a roughhouse character who was a "pal" to his boys. But he took no nonsense from them. It was fortunate that Marty's mother lived throughout her sons' formative years or there would have been little or no softening influence at all on the growing boys.

Marty's father was a Detroit policeman. The archetype of the bygone-age beat cop who knew that rattling a nightstick on a crook's head more often than not was more effective than taking the hood to the precinct and booking him. The cops who went by the book climbed the ladder more quickly. But they didn't earn the respect Patrolman Whitston had both from his peers and from the bad guys.

Marty's mother died when he was eighteen and a senior in high school. In the following year, his father was shot and killed trying to stop an armed robbery at a liquor store. He was off duty and out of uniform and, as it turned out, at the wrong place at the wrong time. It would have been a matter of pride for Patrolman Whitston to know that his final action in life was the killing of the two thieves.

Marty, taking an accounting course at Wayne State, by default became head of his family. He was in charge of his four younger brothers. He accepted this responsibility and did well with it.

In an effort to leave home in an honorable manner, as well as to bequeath responsibility for his siblings to the next in line, Marty enlisted in the Marines.

He was a Marine in training just long enough to be shipped to Vietnam in the early days of that conflict. He was quickly promoted to sergeant.

In Vietnam, Marty learned many things. Unlike his father, who was free to be a maverick cop, acting on his own, Marty was part of a team—his platoon. If he was to survive Vietnam, it would be as part of his outfit. Even then there was no guarantee that he would leave that green country alive. But the odds were better that way.

He learned that the moral standards that had been inculcated, principally by his mother, might be applicable stateside, but not in the jungle. So he went along with fraudulent body counts, fragging officers, whoring, stealing, and cheating.

He also learned to kill. It was his most distasteful and difficult lesson. His father might have cracked a few ribs, banged a few heads, but though he carried a loaded gun at all times, he had never fired it at anyone until his final action. Indeed, both Marty's father and mother had lectured him on the sacredness of human life.

'Nam was a distinct reversal of priorities.

He killed the enemy, sometimes with gunfire, sometimes with grenades, sometimes in hand-to-hand combat. He torched villages and their inhabitants. He killed women and children because frequently women and children were the enemy. And if you didn't kill them, they would kill you.

Of course, sometimes the women and children were not the enemy. But who could tell?

Barbara knew all this. She and Marty did not roll in the hay constantly. They talked. Mostly Barbara squeezed information and detail out of Marty. He reminisced reluctantly and slowly. Little by little Barbara had a working profile on him.

She was not at all clear on how she would use all this information, but she had stored it for future contingency. And this was that contingency.

She had concluded that under pressure Marty could revert to his alter persona of the jungle. And she now judged that her Al, his dedication to the bank, his volunteering, his likely reward of an executive vice presidency, his possible bumping of Marty out of a job—all of that could have provided sufficient pressure to impel Marty to revert to savage behavior.

And what might Marty do if he perceived he was again trapped in a kill-or-be-killed situation?

He might make some hasty moves to salt away some of the bank's money. He might feather a nest that was in danger of falling from the bank that was his tree. He might arrange for the final solution as far as Al Ulrich was concerned. For someone who had killed so prodigally in the past, paying someone to do the job would be simplicity itself.

The doorbell rang. The moment of truth.

Barbara checked the peephole. It was the big guy. She opened the door.

His mouth dropped. He quickly stepped from the subtly lit hallway into the apartment. With one uninterrupted gesture he pulled apart the Velcroed straps. The dress fell to the floor.

He scooped her into his arms and practically charged into the bedroom. He dropped her the short distance onto the bed. In record time, his clothes were also dropped and lying where they landed.

She welcomed him. But she was not quite ready for him. That had not stopped him before and it did not now. She was uncomfortable. He was rougher than usual.

He tried to hold back to enhance his pleasure. But even after all these years, he could not. Not when it was Barbara.

Mercifully for her, it was over shortly. He rolled over, panting lightly. His arm was under her head, but he did not hold her. She did not expect more.

They lay silently for some moments. He had no words. She was trying to find a way to begin. "This is the first time, isn't it, Marty?"

"Huh? First time? What . . . ?"

"The first time we can really relax, is what I mean. No motel room, a different one every time. No cramped car. No secret meeting on vacation. No sneaking off together when Al or Lois is out of town. This is the first time we don't have to worry. You didn't even have to be concerned about a rubber. And I didn't have to worry about the jelly or the diaphragm."

Martin smiled and breathed deeply. "You mean because you're pregnant."

"Uh-huh."

He thought about that for a few moments. Then he chuckled. "You're right. I didn't even think of that."

"You didn't?" She was surprised.

"I didn't intend to screw you either."

She turned toward him and raised herself on one elbow. She regarded him appraisingly. "For someone who didn't intend to get under the sheets you damn near set a world's record."

"I wouldn't be here at all if you hadn't practically summoned me at the funeral home." He glanced at his watch. "Good God, that was only a few hours ago. The body isn't even cold yet." He looked down at both of them, in indication of their nakedness.

"The body's not cold, Marty; it's hot. He's being cremated."

"A figure of speech."

She reached for a robe.

"No. Don't put anything on. I like to look at you."

She smiled. Compliments flowed from Martin like water from frozen pipes. Besides, she was proud of her figure. She liked to exhibit it under appropriate situations. This was such a situation. She and Marty had few anatomical secrets from each other.

She leaned back on the pillow, her head turned toward him.

"We wouldn't be doing this if Al weren't . . . gone."

"Dead," Marty corrected. "Al is *dead*. Get used to the word, Babs. Al is dead."

She reminded herself that Marty had an occupational familiarity with that word. Vietnam. "That's right, Marty: dead. If Al were alive, he'd be at the opening day celebration. You'd be at work, probably looking at the handwriting on the wall."

"What handwriting?"

"Well, you know the bank gossip as well as or better than I. According to the scenario, Al was supposed to be rewarded if he made the new branch a success."

"So?"

"The reward . . . being made an executive vice president."

Martin guffawed. "Just like that, eh?"

"In time. In time." For the first time in this affair Barbara lost a tad of her confidence.

"In lots and lots of time . . . if ever."

"Well, not according to the scuttlebutt. Sooner than later."

"I wouldn't put my last buck on that," Martin cautioned. "Al wasn't equipped to be a VP. He didn't have the patience for the job. And there's lots of other caveats that would make that kind of reward unlikely."

"If not VP, then what?"

"Oh, I don't know. Haven't given it much thought. His pick among the branches? Something like that."

Barbara pulled the quilt up. She hoped Martin wouldn't make a fuss; she was chilly. "Then I suppose you'll deny the rumors about you."

He sat upright and looked down at her. "Rumors?"

Barbara nodded. "One of them has it that you set Al up."

"What!?"

"That this was a contract killing and that you paid for it."

He could've gone either way. He might have been furious or he could've been amused. Fortunately for Barbara, he laughed uproariously. "Me? A contract killing? The morning of opening day? How could you believe a pile of crap like that?"

"I didn't say I believed it. Just that there were rumors."

"And what else did these rumors say?"

By this time, Barbara had lost a larger measure of self-confidence. But she plowed on. "That failing to kill Al you were already feathering your nest . . . something like building yourself a golden parachute."

He ground his teeth and flushed from the neck upward. "And how was I supposed to do that?"

"I don't know. Make some sweet deals with commercial customers. Make some overly generous loans. In return for their taking good care of you if you were bounced."

"Listen here, little lady . . ." He stood up and reached for his clothes. "If I wanted Al—or anybody for that matter—dead, I certainly wouldn't hire someone to do it. I like to think I know enough about killing to do it myself and not rely on some crackheaded piece of shit who'd lead the cops right to me.

"That's for one. And for two, it's true we made a few loans that didn't pan out the way we wanted. But those were inner-city businesses in the neighborhood of the new branch. And we absorbed those losses and made up for them—and more—with other investments. You could check with Jack Fradet about that. He knows."

He had wasted no time; he was buttoning his shirt.

"Okay, okay," Barbara said. "I told you they were only gossip. I

didn't say I believed them. But before you go, what about my baby
. . . our child?"

He was putting on a shoe. He stopped and looked at her. There
was an odd embarrassment in his expression. "That's something I've
got a problem with."

"What do you mean, 'problem'?" Barbara sat up. The quilt fell.

"I mean it's a problem. Look, you say you're pregnant. I know
how much you didn't want to get pregnant. So, I suppose you're
telling the truth. Why would you lie?"

She was about to object. But Martin raised a silencing hand. "Listen to me. This'll be hard enough without interrruptions. If Al had
lived, and if it's true that he couldn't possibly be the father, then he'd
be mad as hell and telling the world about it. And when you gave
me that note at the party, Al was alive with no prospects of dying
soon. So that's probably true too—that Al would know for certain
he couldn't be the father.

"Now we come to the hard part."

He paused. Barbara couldn't imagine what was to come next.

"Babs, I don't know who the father is, but it isn't me."

"W . . . what?"

"For years, Lois and I tried to have a family. We couldn't. I've got
rock bottom motility. In other words, I'm sterile. As you well know,
I'm as potent as a guy can be. But I can't father kids. If you've got
a baby inside you, I wish it was mine. But it's not. I didn't want
anybody but Lois and the doc to know. If your pregnancy hadn't
happened, you wouldn't know. I'd never have told you. All that protection we used . . . we didn't need any."

Neither spoke nor moved.

At length, Barbara said. "You lie! How contemptible can you be!"

Martin smiled sadly. "No. I have no reason to lie. No more than
you do when you say you're pregnant. I know how you feel about
abortion. So if everything goes well, you'll have a child. There's no
reason for you to lie about it.

"Same with me. I can get my doctor to share his findings with you. Or I can go to the doctor of your choice. Whoever does the exam, he's going to find the same thing: a bunch of sperm turned over on their backs floating when they should be swimming like hell."

He stood up.

"You knew it was going to end this way." Barbara held back tears. "From the time I gave you the note you knew we'd come to this moment when you would claim you're sterile. Why did you play it out? Why did you have sex with me?"

He shrugged. "I didn't intend to. Then you opened the door, and there you were, wearing that dress that never fails to turn me on. What did you expect me to do, Babs: ask if you wanted to buy some Girl Scout cookies?"

She drew a robe about her as she followed him to the door.

He turned. "Babs, I believed you then and I believe you now when you say Al, for years, hasn't screwed you or even fooled around with you . . . although I can't understand how he could've kept his hands off you.

"I thought I was the only one you were having an affair with. That was until you let me in on your little secret. You're pregnant. Then I knew you had to be seeing somebody else. Thing is, I haven't the slightest idea how many 'somebody elses' you're laying. The bottom line is you're a whore. And that's that.

"We may have to meet again. Maybe at a company get-together. Tom Adams is the kind of guy who would see to it you're included in the company doings. That's about it for us. I won't be seeing you on any other basis—ever.

"And one last thing: if you intend on making this public . . . if you reveal my secret in any way so that anyone besides Lois or my doctor—or another doctor, if you insist—finds out that I'm sterile, I'll show you what I learned in 'Nam. I'll show you how to kill and leave no clue."

He closed the door behind him, leaving Barbara standing there trying to absorb and comprehend what had just happened.

William X. Kienzle

This very definitely had not gone as she had planned.

Still, it wasn't time to panic. She was only a quarter of the way through her very flexible scenario. She had allowed for a setback, just not so soon.

Clearly she hadn't been prepared for that naked threat. That had sent a chill up her spine.

She had known he could do it. Now she knew he would.

Twenty

BARBARA hadn't even considered a death threat.

And a palpable threat it was. He had killed before, prodigally in Vietnam. He made no secret of that.

The threat had its desired effect: Barbara would not reveal Martin's secret. She only hoped that neither of the other two who were in on the secret might let it slip, leading him to suspect her.

No doubt about it, Martin could be dangerous.

It was just possible that Marty was lying. Should she go ahead and request his physician's report? But if she did go to his doctor, she'd have to be extremely cautious. No need to roil those waters.

So, pending checking a couple of his statements, she had struck out with Martin. She was now pretty well convinced that he'd had no part in Al's death. On the surface at least there appeared to be nothing improper in his management of commercial loans. And if he was honest about his reproductive system, he couldn't have gotten her with child.

There was time to kill before her next guest arrived. She had allowed for a generous space between visitors. That gave her flexibility in grilling them, as well as insuring that none would meet in the revolving door that was her apartment.

She heated some soup, more because it was dinnertime than due to hunger. Nervousness had destroyed her appetite.

As she awaited the arrival of Jack Fradet, she went over what she knew of the comptroller of Adams Bank and Trust.

If one word could describe his early years, it probably would be "sickly." If there were any germs around, they would attach themselves to Jack like zebra mussels.

Being of a practical nature, the lad made no plans to excel in sports or any other type of strenuous activity. He didn't star on the field or in the gym. But in the classroom, he was a whiz.

Though he was attracted to the study of almost everything, his forte was math. When Jack landed a job with Adams Bank and Trust, it was a marriage blessed by the god of matchmakers. He could've taken and kept a vow of stability. He was there for life.

Rather rapidly he rose to what in effect was the number-two position in the bank. He had no desire to go higher and supplant Tom Adams.

Adams did what his job required, and he did it well. He was visible, a hail-fellow-well-met. Jack Fradet was not suited to that role in any way. He would have been awkward and ineffective, to say the least. He was most content to stay in the shadows and take care of the money. For in that, he was taking care of the bank.

Those who knew him at all well—and there were few—wondered that he had married Marilyn—or anyone, for that matter. It was difficult to imagine him in bed with a woman unless he was asleep. Marilyn seemed genuinely bewildered that she was mated to this math machine with flesh.

But they had three children, all now adults with families of their own, so something must have happened besides refreshing slumber in preparation for the next day's adventures in the bank.

Almost from the time Al began to work at the bank, Barbara knew who Jack Fradet was. After all, he was an executive vice president. But if she thought of him at all, it was as the little man who counted money.

Yet over the past several years, Jack and Barbara had been paramours. People who were astonished at the mating of Jack and Marilyn would've been struck dumb by Jack and Barbara.

How had this happened?

Al has been assistant manager of one of the Adams branches. There was an annual picnic for ranking employees down to Al's level—and their spouses. Barbara had gone along hoping to steal some time with Martin Whitston, the first of her four conquests. That was the day she bumped into Jack. She thought it was an accident. For Jack, it was no accident.

It began simply enough. She'd had no opportunity to be alone with Martin. His wife, Lois, had seen to that. For Barbara, the picnic grew deadly dull. She was peripherally alert to her husband's whereabouts. She didn't care what he did, she just didn't want him spying on her.

Keeping an eye out for Martin, on the one hand, and Al, on the other, she was totally unaware of Jack Fradet.

But he was acutely aware of her. Oh, not in any obvious manner. He stayed on the fringe of groups of guests. He had long had an eye for her—as did lots of men. The difference between them and him was that, over the long haul, Jack Fradet usually got what he went after. Barbara was one of the most desirable goals he had set for himself.

His opportunity occurred this day when Barbara found an unoccupied bench under a corner tree. With a bored look, she sighed deeply and settled herself in the middle of the bench, hoping to discourage anyone else from sitting down alongside.

Jack waited a few minutes, then approached, leisurely, with no indication that he had anything particular in mind. He paused when he reached her. She looked up and gave him a perfunctory smile.

Still standing and making no move to sit down, he introduced himself and began talking. He didn't direct his words at her specifically—or toward anyone in particular, for that matter.

He began explaining the cloud formations of this day: cumulus—piled high, but granting shade and little chance of precipitation.

At first she paid no attention. But several general topics later in his monologue, it occurred to her that he seemed to have a great interest in and knowledge about a great number of things. His knowledge attracted her.

She couldn't believe it: by the time Al came to collect her that evening, the time had passed so quickly while she conversed with Jack Fradet that the two had missed dinner.

Slowly, that's the way it started, and grew. Jack and Barbara met infrequently in parks or out-of-the-way restaurants. Except for the fact that each had a spouse, there was nothing sinful, illegal, or even fattening about their interest in each other.

Then they turned a corner.

When they'd first met several weeks before, Barbara would have covered any odds that they would at any time become physically involved. Freud had said it all for Barbara: anatomy is destiny. And Jack Fradet's anatomy did not destine him to capture her favors.

What Freud left out of the picture was what he himself asked with significant frustration: "What does woman want?"

Manners, deference, tenderness, and, up near the top of the list for at least some women, power.

Jack Fradet definitely was unimpressive physically, but he possessed, or could fake possession of, some tender virtues. And at one remove from the top of an established banking firm, he did have power—a significant amount of power. As Henry Kissinger said, power is an aphrodisiac. And then of course women generally seem able to look beyond mere physical appearance much more so than men.

It was a banking convention in Florida that transformed the relationship of Jack and Barbara. Jack Fradet was empowered to select Adams delegates for this convention. Among those selected was Al Ulrich. Jack went no further than that. He also did not go to the convention.

It worked. Barbara invited Jack to dinner in the Ulrich condo apartment. He enjoyed dinner and again went no further than that.

Eventually she seduced him according to the plan he had cleverly composed.

Of all the men who had romanced her, the best lover of all was

Jack Fradet. No one, including Marilyn Fradet, would have believed that. His services during foreplay made it virtually impossible for Barbara not to reach climax. Afterward, all he required was a brief, releasing orgasm for himself.

Now, with this in mind, she felt somewhat callous in summoning him here tonight, to the very apartment where it had all begun for them. But this was the hand dealt her by fate; she had drawn cards and she would play that hand.

A knock at the door. He never rang the bell. She didn't have to check the time; it would be precisely seven o'clock. That's the way Jack was.

She wore a modest housecoat. She could no more envision Jack ripping off her clothing than she could imagine Marty Whitston turning away from a lovely, near naked woman.

Barbara opened the door. There he was, wearing that slight, enigmatic smile. She ushered him in and took his coat and hat. It wasn't cold, or even chill outside—but Jack always protected himself and his health. Jack could quote statistics on catching cold in early autumn.

They sat facing each other, neither speaking.

"Thanks for coming," Barbara said finally. "This is about my note—at the party."

The smile didn't change. "Things have changed since then."

"What do you mean?"

"Al. You feared he would blow the roof off. He's gone. If we were in a novel, I'd say Al's death was a deus ex machina and highly unrealistic. But since we're in real life, I have to look at it as a major coincidence."

Barbara rose and got two cups of coffee. She didn't need to ask: Jack nearly lived on coffee. She wondered that he ever slept. "Maybe a coincidence, maybe not," she said as she placed their cups on the small table that separated them.

"'Maybe not'?" He took a sip and compressed his lips in appreciation. It was out of character for one so gorgeous, but Barbara was a marvelous cook.

"Doesn't it strike you as odd that as careful a person as Al was, that he would be killed by a kid who needed money for dope?"

"This is excellent coffee, Barbara. What's so odd about that? It happens all the time. We live on the downtown riverfront. Things here are about as safe as anywhere.

"As far as that goes, the branch Al left was in comparably safe territory. He volunteered for the new branch. He stepped from the safety of a pantry shelf to a heated frying pan, as it were. Which is not to say that anyone anywhere in this country is really safe.

"But, Barbara dear, all of those people, as Al did, have just begun working in a risky area of this city. What if there were a residency restriction? What if someone in authority required the people who work in that neighborhood to live there too? Like they do the police and firefighters. You think we'd be able to even plan on opening a branch in a neighborhood like that?

"No, my dear, Al's death certainly is tragic, but not a complete surprise. Nor do I think it at all odd that a dope addict would kill to feed his habit. It would be nice if all addicts had jobs so they could afford to buy the drug of their choice. But eventually and inevitably, drugs incapacitate the user to the degree where he can't hold down a job. But he has to have dope and he'll do anything to get it—even commit murder.

"So, no, dear, I do not think it odd that our addict goes to a bank to get some money for his addiction. After all, banks are all about money. That he was not thinking all that clearly fits nicely in the whole picture. The error may very well be in our decision to open there."

Barbara's eyes widened. "You mean you think that branch never should have been planned, let alone opened?"

"Tom and I had words on the subject." All hint of a smile had vanished. "But . . ." He shrugged. "It was not my place to make that final decision. Actually, I think we're moving away from serving our faithful and long-standing customers. As I say, we've had words. We know each other's thinking in the matter. But Tom is still the boss.

"However, just between the two of us, I think Al was a fool to accept, let alone volunteer, for the job."

It was Barbara's turn to smile. "You don't think he did it from some altruistic motive, do you, Jack?"

"Not for a moment." Jack shook his head vigorously.

"Then why?"

"I suppose he knew there'd have to be some sort of reward at the end of the stick."

"What do you suppose that would be?"

"A choice of the next assignment, I suppose. Maybe a choice of a prime branch. There are lots of things working here. Leave Al where he is and, in time, when the right manager retires or dies, Al moves up. But that's all guesswork. That's up on Tom's level. He created the monster; he'll have to deal with it."

"But why do you ask? You have an idea?"

"How about an executive vice presidency?"

Jack paused with his cup half raised. Then he began to laugh. He laughed so hard he had to set the cup down again. "There are only three, you know, Barbara," he said when he could control his laughter.

"Then one of you would have to leave, wouldn't you?"

"Al an executive VP? That's rich. None of us is anyplace close to retirement. And even if it happened, *I* certainly wouldn't be the one to be replaced. Not in this world of business." A curious look of amusement appeared on his face. "Wait a minute . . . wait a minute. You couldn't . . . oh, this is rich! I'll bet you were figuring that one of us . . . me?" He began to chuckle. "You think that I hired that young man to kill Al so my job would be safe. Good lord, what an active imagination you have, my dear."

While he enjoyed what he seemed to think was a hilarious notion, Barbara fumed.

Practically the same reaction as Martin's. Either both men were completely innocent of complicity in the murder of her husband, or they deserved some sort of award for their performances.

However, even if Jack had had nothing to do with murder, still there could be something unsavory in his vice presidential dealings. Perhaps Jack was involved in some hanky-panky that would lend itself to a little blackmail.

She waited until he stopped chortling. "That idea didn't originate with me, you know." Actually, to her knowledge, the only other person who shared the suspicion that one of the vice presidents could be behind the death of Al Ulrich was Father Zachary Tully. And the priest was nowhere near as convinced as she.

"Oh?"

"No. But it got me to thinking. . . ."

Jack shook his head, condescendingly. Suddenly she was furious. Why in hell did he have to be so damned smug? Well, she'd fix his wagon!

"Yes. I did. I did think a lot. Oh, not about you and me. No, Jack, I thought about you and the bank. That precious bank that you're all so crazy about. And I started digging, and I asked some questions—" For the first time she seemed to have his undivided attention. Good! Let Mr. Smartypants Knowitall stew in his own smug juice. "Oh, don't worry; I was very careful; nobody could possibly connect you with any of my questions. But you know, Al has always talked about his work . . . and believe it or not, I've always listened. And I can put two and two together. And guess what, Jack: it came up four!"

He just looked at her, waiting.

"Yes, sweetie, I know what you've been doing." Actually, she didn't know a thing, but she was so teed off at his supercilious attitude that she plowed on. "You've been building yourself one helluva golden parachute, haven't you? So that if or when you were bounced out of your position—replaced by Al—you'd land softly and sweetly and have a pile for as many rainy days as might come along. And just imagine what would happen if Tom Adams found out—"

Suddenly, his entire demeanor changed. His expression became feral. She'd seen this look before. Animals, especially small animals, when literally cornered, fix their adversary with such a gaze, seeming to say, "Okay, you've put me in an inescapable situation. Now it's you or I—and I'm going to do everything I can to make sure you are not the winner."

A shiver passed through Barbara's body. Had her trial balloon touched reality? For the first time she had reason to question this inquisition.

Had she hit paydirt? What if Jack really was playing fast and loose with the bank's finances? What might he do to silence her—or anyone who might guess at the truth?

With evident resolve, Jack once more pulled a veil over his expression. He was his erstwhile enigmatic self. "Barbara," he said at length, "that's a pretty serious charge. But because there's no truth to it whatever, I know this allegation is your brainchild and yours alone. You're bluffing—why, I don't know—but"—he smiled sardonically—"you'd make a rotten poker player, my dear. And"—he leaned toward her—"just in case you've a mind to try to make trouble, let me tell you: this cockamamie accusation had better not leave this apartment."

Barbara stared at him, speechless.

"Besides"—he sat back, relaxed—"there wasn't the slightest possibility of my being let go. Al had little or no chance of supplanting any of us. And in the unlikely—extremely unlikely—event that it might have happened, *I* would most certainly not be the one displaced. Not now. Not ever."

She had, it seemed, struck out again. Both Jack and Martin had been convincing in their innocence of any involvement in Al's death.

As for bank misconduct, Jack's mask had slipped—momentarily, but a slip nonetheless. Despite his words, her bluff had hit home: something was highly questionable about his dealings with Adams Bank. Yet she seemed somehow to have missed the target. Was she on the mark with her guess about the facts, but wrong about the motive? No way of knowing.

However, for all practical purposes, she could prove no charge against either Martin or Jack. She shrugged mentally. Two down. Two to go.

But first the little matter of paternity, and a generous support through the distant future for mother and child. She might not be able to pin Jack to the wall as far as his bank dealings were concerned, but he wasn't going to weasel out of his paternal responsibility. Composing her thoughts and her face, she affected a sort of wry, little-girl sweetness, as if he had defeated her in a tennis match that she had known in advance she would lose because of course he was so much better at everything than she. "Care for more coffee, Jack?" she asked, every inch the gracious loser.

"Please."

She poured for him. No more for herself. "We have only one more outstanding matter to be taken care of."

"If this is what I think it is, I'm just surprised it wasn't the primary, if not the only concern."

"A matter of paternity, Jack. Al's gone, so he won't be kicking up a stink—and he certainly would have. But if everything comes out okay, in about seven or so months I'll have a baby and you'll have a son or a daughter. What do you intend to do about it? I don't think either of us wants to go public with this. We don't want a mess . . . at least I certainly don't."

She didn't know what to make of his lively smile. "Well?"

"No. No, my dear, we do not want to go public and get into a mess."

Why was he making such a production of this?

"I have taken the trouble of photostating the bill for a doctor's services rendered a little more than three years ago." He reached across the table and handed her a rectangular piece of paper.

It was an itemized bill for outpatient surgery.

She was flabbergasted. "A vasectomy!"

"That's what it says. And that's what it was."

"I don't understand." And she did not. "You had a vasectomy before we ever got together! You were sterile before we—! Why did you bother going along with my insistence on using birth control? Why, for God's sake, would you bother wearing a condom?"

He held out his cup. "Just one more cup, please, Barbara? One for the road." The smile became a smirk. For that and his cocky attitude as he defeated her every effort to entangle him in any facet of this affair, she hated him. But she held any external manifestation in check.

She poured another cup of coffee and handed it to him. He sipped it and smiled a bit more genuinely.

"Why?" she repeated.

He tipped his head to one side as if considering how to phrase his response. "Why? No one does anything for one reason alone. Let's see: why would I go along with your demand that we be super protected: you with spermicide, a diaphragm—maybe an IUD, for all I know; me with a condom; just about everything but rhythm—and, of course, the Pill?

"Well, it was amusing, that's one. It enabled me to play a trump that you never knew I held—as I just did. That's two. And it provided protection for me from any venereal disease if you were sexually active with anyone else.

"You see, Barbara, I bought your story that you and Al were not participating in conjugal life. It was just too bizarre not to be true.

"And, as it turns out, your sleeping around was exactly what was going on. That was borne out by your note. You are pregnant. That I believe. The father is not your husband. That I believe.

"But the father is not I. That I know for an indisputable fact."

Barbara's head hung. She seemed to be studying the floor. "Vasectomies aren't always foolproof," she said in a small voice.

He looked at her almost pityingly. "Mine is, I guarantee you. I have a semen test as part of my regular six-month checkup." He shook his head. "No, my dear, that dog won't hunt."

He stood, and picked up his coat and hat. "I'll just let myself out. Out of your apartment, and out of your life very probably."

She didn't move. She continued to stare at the floor as the door closed.

If she had looked at Jack as he departed, she would have seen that his smug demeanor had been replaced by one of dark determination.

What rotten luck! Her first two candidates hadn't panned out at all. And all this time she'd thought she was in a win-win situation. She couldn't lose; none of her candidates could have passed all three tests. But the first two, indeed, had.

The other two she had scheduled for tomorrow. They would not fail her. She had a premonition. Her intuition was very strong on this.

Still, she wasn't as confident as she had been. Perhaps she would never again be that confident.

*   *   *

"How'd it go this morning?" Lieutenant Tully sipped from a cold beer can.

"Not bad." His brother slowly swirled the ice cubes in a glass containing a rough blend of gin and tonic. "Not bad at all, considering."

"Considering," Anne Marie observed, "that you didn't even know the deceased outside of meeting him briefly at dinner."

"True," Father Tully acknowledged. "But I think I could sense correctly the feeling of those who truly came to mourn at Al Ulrich's funeral."

"'Truly'?" Lieutenant Tully raised an eyebrow. "Who truly came to mourn?"

"I think I know what Zachary means," Anne Marie said as she worked over the pasta salad. She was preparing dinner as the two men sat at the kitchen table. "We've seen it often enough ourselves, Zoo. For lots of the people—maybe most—who attend a given funeral it's an obligation. They're friends of the deceased, or of the deceased's relatives, or maybe business partners. But they're dry-eyed and present only because they feel an obligation."

Zoo nodded in agreement. Although he attended few funerals, generally, they were those of fellow police officers. Such occasions affected him deeply. He always felt a sense of pride in the solidarity that drew together an otherwise disparate group of law enforcement officers. Contrasting uniforms of police from other jurisdictions as well as those of state police and, of course, the Detroit police were evident.

It was, as well, a somber reminder of his own mortality and the innate danger of his work.

Father Tully sipped his drink. "I didn't get the impression that many there this morning were truly grieving. The person who seemed most moved was Al Ulrich's boss, Thomas Adams."

"Not the widow?" the lieutenant asked.

"I don't know for sure. She may just have been numb. Actually, she just didn't seem to really be there."

"Not there?" Anne Marie had almost finished the dinner preparations.

"I don't know; she just seemed to be in her own little world. Maybe it'll hit her later on. Sometimes it works that way—especially when it's a spouse. When the other partner is gone, the tendency is to expect him to show up for supper. Or for her to be the first one up in the morning. There's just a huge hole in a person's life when someone whose presence is really important isn't there as he or she always was. Maybe that will happen with Mrs. Ulrich."

"So," Anne Marie said, "there weren't many real mourners at your wake service."

"Not as such, no. Mr. Adams, as I said. But there seemed to be a pretty general kindred feeling." Father Tully set his glass on the table. He didn't want too much alcohol on an empty stomach.

"What I sensed was a feeling of bitter defeat. Most of those at the wake appeared to be discouraged that a much needed program had gotten off to such a tragic start. I mean, just about everyone at least wishes the city good luck. And branching into the inner city is a tangible step toward redevelopment. I think a lot of people were counting on this move by Adams Bank and Trust to be a success. Instead, they end up with a murdered bank manager.

"It hurt the city as well as the city's image. I think most of the people at this morning's wake shared that feeling."

"Here it comes, boys." Anne Marie brought serving dishes to the table. Neither brother needed to move; they were already at their dining places.

Father Tully led them in a preprandial prayer—a formality his brother thought would not outlive the priest's visit.

Anne Marie began to fill their plates. "Did you have a chance to talk much with the widow?"

Father Tully hardly knew where to begin. All the food looked so appetizing. "Yes, I did. I thought I'd at least try to console her. But she just seemed to want to talk about her husband's death and what caused it."

Anne Marie looked at her brother-in-law inquiringly. "I thought that was open and shut—what Zoo calls a platter case."

Before Father Tully could reply, Zoo, smiling, said, "It's something like the Kennedy assassination. There's the school of thought that Lee Oswald alone killed the President: one shooter, one killer. Then there are the conspiracy theories: it was a CIA plot. Or maybe FBI. Or maybe Cuban. Or maybe a mob hit. Two shooters. More than two shooters. An army!"

"Come on!" The priest winced.

"Okay," Zoo relented. "So this one doesn't have that many theories. But my brother here has been worrying over one like a dog with a bone."

"What's that?" Anne Marie was genuinely interested.

"It involves three executive vice presidents of the Adams Bank," Father Tully said.

"Why three?" Anne Marie pursued.

"The way I understand it," the priest explained, "there is no set ruling on the part of any governmental agency, state or federal, with regard to this. But most banks, especially small banks, segregate the hierarchical duties. And that usually spells out to business loans, mortgages, and financial control—in other words, a comptroller."

"The employee who gets to manage the new Detroit branch," Zoo said, "eventually gets rewarded for being so civic-minded. He—or she—gets to leapfrog to right next to the top: an executive vice presidency.

"By simple math, if there are only three VPs at the top, one of them gets displaced. So—and this seems to be the bottom line—find the present VP who is most likely to get bounced and you find the man who took out a contract on Al Ulrich . . . that about it, bro?"

Zachary chuckled. "Every time you tell that story, it sounds more humorous. I could give it a far more serious delivery. But I gotta admit: that's the essence."

The two men laughed. Anne Marie didn't. "If that theory were true, what about whoever was appointed to take Ulrich's place as manager?"

"Yes," Father Tully said, "the new manager—and the only other candidate who was considered for the job—is Nancy Groggins."

"Well, if there's any substance to your theory, Zachary, then wouldn't the same reward system apply for her?" Anne Marie pressed. "And in that case, wouldn't she be the target for another contract killing?"

"Now, wait a minute," Zoo said. "The next thing you'll be saying is that the manager of that bank needs round-the-clock protection!"

"I'll tell you the same thing that Al Smith is supposed to have cabled the Pope after losing the election: unpack." Father Tully was chuckling.

"What's that supposed to mean?" Zoo asked.

"Two things really," Father Tully replied. "First, I was surprised to find that the widow, Barbara Ulrich, is maybe the only one in the world who agrees with my theory about a contract murder.

"And second, she feels very strongly that none of the executives would bother with a contract on Nancy Groggins."

"Why's that?" Anne Marie asked.

"Because Nancy Groggins is a woman. And, according to Mrs. Ulrich, in Tom Adams's M.O., no women need apply."

"What!" Anne Marie exclaimed.

"I have that on Barbara Ulrich's testimony alone. I've got nothing to back it up. But she seemed convinced that her theory was incontrovertible. According to the widow, Mr. Adams believes there is a place for women—and that place is anywhere in his organization except near the upper echelon."

"So," Anne Marie clarified, "none of the executives would need to have her killed: she's no threat to their position because she's a woman."

"That's about the size of it."

"Seems to me," Anne Marie said, "you gave an award to a man unworthy of it!"

Father Tully shrugged and dug into the vegetables. "No one's perfect. Tom Adams has done a lot for our missions, there's no doubt of that. Besides, I have reason—plenty of good reason—to believe that Tom Adams lives his life closely patterned on the Bible. And remember: women do not fare all that well in Scripture."

"Not too badly though," Anne Marie pointed out.

Father Tully studied the ceiling for a moment. "True enough," he admitted. "There were some heroic women in the Old Testament: Esther, Ruth. . . ."

"And in the New Testament," Anne Marie added. "Mary Magdalene, Martha and Mary, the Blessed Mother, the women to whom Jesus appeared after His resurrection . . . and so on."

"Right you are, Anne," Father Tully said. "But, by and large, it *is* a man's story. And besides, Tom Adams is, or seems to be, an extremely faithful son of the Catholic Church. And we all know where women stand in the Church: absolute equality except where it counts—the priesthood . . . bishops. So he's got a lot of heavy example there."

"Conceded," Anne Marie said.

"I didn't know this wrinkle about women not being allowed in the upper echelon of Adams Bank," Zoo said. "Interesting, but a detour. So Nancy Groggins is not in danger as manager of the bank—not from any of the execs, that is. But you two are overlooking the point that neither was Al Ulrich in danger from the execs. He was in danger from his new neighbors. One of them, stoned on dope, killed him. End of case!"

"Easy, easy, brother." Father Tully laughed. "If my short-term memory serves, *you* were the one who brought up my theory a few minutes ago. But you see, I've abandoned that theory; I agree with you. In fact, when I talked to Barbara Ulrich about it, I went out of my way to try to convince her to let the police handle it. I told her *not* to meddle or get involved in something that is distinctly and exclusively police business.

"Now, I ask you, brother, have you ever heard that sentiment before?"

Zoo chuckled as he dug into some pasta. "My very own words. I wasn't sure you were paying me any mind."

"Case closed." Father Tully stabbed an asparagus spear, dabbed it in hollandaise sauce, and nibbled on it.

He noticed that Anne Marie seemed to be toying with her food rather than eating it. "Something wrong, Anne?"

She smiled briefly. "Oh, I was just thinking . . . your visit with us is almost over. That makes me sad. We've had so much fun together. Isn't there some way you can extend your visit? Maybe you could get a Detroit parish? They seem to be short of priests around here. . . ."

"Hey," Zoo said, "that's a great idea. How much longer can you stay?"

"Until Bob Koesler returns. That's open-ended, sort of. He could be gone a month. But I'm betting he'll show up any day now. And I don't know about getting a Detroit parish. By the way, Anne, is the coffee done?"

She glanced at the counter. "I think so. Let me get you some."

She poured the coffee. He tasted it. Hot. And good. He had yet to divine Father Koesler's technique that turned out such unpotable brew. "The major problem with my staying in Detroit on a permanent basis is that I'm a Josephite—an order priest. The Josephites don't have any benefice in this part of the country. Not a parish, a seminary, or any other operation.

"So, as a Josephite, I've got no reason to be here full time. I guess when my time's up, I'll just have to return to Dallas."

"Wait a minute," Zoo said. "It seems to me we've been through this before. A couple of years ago there was this priest who belonged to some missionary outfit . . . can't think of the name just now . . ."

"Maryknoll," Anne Marie supplied.

"That's a foreign missionary order," Father Tully said.

"You know about them?" Zoo asked.

"Sure. They're distinctively an American order—as are we. Except that they aim at evangelizing in places like China and Africa and South America. What was a Maryknoller doing here? If he found a way to stay, maybe there's hope for a transient Josephite."

"I'm not sure how that worked," Zoo said. "You'd have to ask Father Koesler."

"Or me." Anne Marie smiled. "I remember the priest. He was on sort of a sick leave from his Latin American assignment. He got mixed up in a homicide case. He was cleared, of course, and then he decided to stay here. He went through some sort of Church process. He's still here, so I guess he was successful in becoming a regular fixture. Now he's pastor of a southwest Detroit parish."

Father Tully had emptied his plate. "He must've gone through excardination and incardination. I assume that when he came to Detroit, he still belonged to Maryknoll. He was incardinated in that religious order. Evidently he wanted to belong to Detroit, for whatever reason. In effect, he had to belong to *some*body—in this case, either Maryknoll or the Detroit archdiocese.

"It's something like passing the baton from one runner to the next in a relay race. Only in this case it's a priest who's being passed from one organization to a diocese. Maryknoll agrees to free up this priest—and excardinates him. The Archdiocese of Detroit agrees to take him and authorizes him to function as a priest here—incardination. That must be what happened in the Maryknoller's case."

"So," Zoo said, "what's stopping you? Get on the stick and start the process going."

"There's only one problem with that, Zoo: I like being a Josephite."

Silence.

Clearly, neither Anne Marie nor her husband had considered that there could be a contest between keeping this newly formed family together and their brother's religious order. "You mean you'd rather belong to your order than stay with us? At least within visiting distance of us?" Zoo asked.

Father Tully compressed his lips in concentration. "That's a tough one. I've been wrestling with this the whole time I've been here.

"It was one thing to learn about your existence from Aunt May. That was exciting. And I couldn't wait to meet you. But the reality of being with you has been so much more than this. In no time at all, I've come to love you—twice as much because we've missed so much of each other's life.

"All I can tell you is . . . I've been thinking and praying about this. I haven't reached a decision yet. But I'm trying to. And it's not that I don't love you . . . or even that I love you more—or less. It's that I loved my order before you came along.

"But when I do decide you'll be the first to know."

"We appreciate that." Anne Marie wiped away a tear.

Father Tully grinned. "But I still think there's something fishy about those three execs. . . ."

"Leave it, brother," Zoo said. "Intuition fits better on the womenfolk."

They laughed and started stacking dishes.

Twenty-One

I⊤ WAS just after ten Tuesday morning—time to start the day.

Barbara Ulrich groaned inwardly. She looked several times at the clock on the nightstand. She never slept in. But then she also never had as much to drink as she'd had last night.

Simply, she had tried to drown a disastrous day.

The funeral had taken much more out of her than she'd bargained for. That was followed by two consecutive strikeouts: Martin Whitston and Jack Fradet.

Definitely a bad news day. Today had a lot of catching up to do.

Lou Durocher was expected at eleven, less than an hour from now.

She sat up and quickly clutched her temple. *Uhhhh!*

Coffee might help. Slowly she made her way into the kitchen, where she started things percolating.

Next, a shower. She padded back into the bedroom. She let her nightgown slip to the floor and turned to study her body in the full-length mirror. Flawless. But one of these days . . . one of these days the new one would begin to show. Long before that, this would all have to be straightened out.

The shower seemed to help. She absorbed its pulsation and forced herself to think about good old Lou Durocher.

He wasn't really all that "old." Somewhere in his early fifties, she guessed. Although she and Lou had been intimate, they'd never gotten personal. While she was familiar with the others' backgrounds, she'd never delved into Lou's. She had always assumed it wouldn't prove to be fascinating—after all, *he* wasn't. Hell, she could probably get him to admit he was her baby's father even if she'd never had intercourse with him! She laughed and blew water away from her face.

She began to take stock: what did she know about Lou and what could she speculate about with reasonable certainty?

Lou Durocher was walking proof of the Peter Principle: He had risen to the level of his incompetence. He would have made a good . . . what? Golf pro—though not under tournament pressure. No, just about competent to instruct men and women who wanted to improve enough to qualify as duffers.

He was good at glad-handing, acquaintances and strangers alike. He was good at meetings, as long as he didn't have to chair them. He was trim and fit, blond and usually bland. He was enthusiastic once he knew that was the appropriate response. Hell, he even looked like Dan Quayle.

But most of all, Lou was Catholic. She was convinced that was what had triggered "the grand experiment." At first, Tom Adams had been willing to let nature take its course. Greed, ambition, backbiting, backstabbing, dirty dealing—the natural selection of those who were aggressively proficient at these enterprises composed most of the hierarchy of Adams Bank and Trust.

For no rationally sound reason—was it that so few Catholics were really good at these capitalistic, winner-take-all games?—Adams set out to place a fellow Catholic into a position of power.

Why he had selected Lou Durocher as the guinea pig was unclear. But select him and stick with him Adams had. Adams also took the blue ribbon for bullheadedness in believing—as no one else did—that Durocher one day would make it.

Of course Barbara saw through all this from the beginning. Except that Lou Durocher was one of the three execs, Barbara would never have given him a second look. She needed him to fill out her hand.

The doorbell! He must be more nervous than usual; he was almost half an hour early.

It wouldn't do to go the door nude. Lou became confused too easily as it was. She threw on an opaque white robe. With that, she could go in any number of directions.

She opened the door to a visibly shaken Lou Durocher. "Barbara! Barbara!" he exclaimed before even entering the apartment.

"Get in here," she said in a peevish tone.

He did, depositing his hat and coat on a nearby chair.

"Sit down," Barbara commanded, "and get hold of yourself. This isn't the end of the world."

"It could be the end of *my* world." It was an overstatement to be expected from this emotionally slight man. "Are you sure . . . I mean, are you certain you're pregnant?"

"Yes. The doctor and I are certain I'm pregnant. Not just a little pregnant—completely pregnant, and a bit more than seven months till delivery."

"That's all the time we've got!" He was breathing heavily and perspiring profusely.

"What do you want? The most you can have is nine months for gestation. Given that, we've got about as much time as we could possibly have."

He slumped into a chair and began wringing his hands.

This not unexpected behavior she could handle coming from Lou. Now that she was dealing with a distraught weakling, she contrasted his reaction with that of Martin Whitston and Jack Fradet.

Both the latter had been cool from the outset. And why not? Each knew he could not be the father. Now near to hyperventilating, Lou certainly hadn't even considered that he might not be the father.

She decided not to wait any longer to settle this matter. Her recent experience with Martin and Jack had taught her not to waste time on secondary issues. Cut to the chase: somebody was the goddamn father of her baby! It wasn't Martin or Jack. And it wasn't the presently deceased Al. It had to be either Lou or Tom.

My God, she thought, what a lineup! Could she have overstocked her pool of lovers?

No pussyfooting! "Okay: How did you do it?"

"What?"

"You heard me: How did you do it?"

"Do what?"

"Get me pregnant. I'm not the Virgin Mary. God didn't do it and I didn't do it all by myself. So don't stand there and tell me you're sterile or something. How did you do it?"

"Sterile!" He was indignant. "Of course not! How can you, of all people, say a thing like that? When have I not been ready for you? Why it's all I can do to hold on without premature ejaculation! I'd rip that thing off you and take you on the floor right now if we weren't talking about a really serious matter."

Sure, sure, she thought. If he tried the floor bit, he'd probably trip and fall through a window.

She had to admit he had no trouble with erection. But that, of course, wasn't the question. "I'm not talking about getting a hard-on. I'm talking about getting a baby. Your baby. From your sperm." She shook her head. "You must have one helluva sperm count."

He smirked. "Yeah . . . how 'bout that? I've got 'em, I can tell you that. The sperm count is part of my annual checkup. I insist on it. And you know, babe: I'm all man!"

Her reaction was a silent but heartfelt, *Ha*!

"Okay then," she said, "we know you're always hot to trot. That's not the point. The point is: how did I get pregnant?"

"I don't know. God, I don't know. You took every precaution. We both did. What more could either of us have done? Even with everything we did, something must've gone wrong. "Yeah, that's it." He nodded vigorously. "Something went wrong."

It *was* a puzzle, she had to admit. Not unheard of, but most rare, given the amount of protection she and her partners always used.

Of course this didn't prove that Lou actually was the father of her child, just that there was no cogent argument against that possibility. But what a relief after yesterday's shutout!

It was such a relief that Barbara almost was willing to forgo the other two areas of inquiry. But what the hell; she'd gone this far, might as well go the distance.

She stretched out on the sofa. He didn't stir from the chair he occupied, his head drooping as if he were a boy about to be lectured.

"Well, Lou, look at it this way: it could be worse."

"'Worse.'" He raised his head and looked at her incredulously. "How could it get worse than this?"

"Al really should've lived. And if he had, pretty soon he'd be nailing your hide to the wall. You'd be the other man in a divorce complaint. He would've seen that you paid not only child support, but with your reputation too."

"Yeah, I guess you're right."

"Al's death"—she paused for effect—"appears to be more than a coincidence. It's downright convenient!"

"Huh?"

"Convenient that he's not here to point his finger at you."

Lou didn't respond.

"Not only is he not here to accuse you, he's also not here to displace you."

"What?"

"You must have heard it, Lou." She sat upright on the sofa. "There's been a lot of talk about the pot of gold at the end of the rainbow."

"What?"

"The way the talk went, if Al had made a success of the new bank venture—and he would have—he would have been promoted. He would have been given an exec's position."

Lou smiled nervously. "There's only three executive positions. And they're all filled."

Barbara smiled in return. "Then one of them would have to be vacated."

His perspiration increased. "What are you saying?"

What, indeed, she thought. Left to his own devices, Lou would never figure out all the ramifications. He needed help. And that, she thought, might be the understatement of the day. "This is how the talk is going, Lou. . . ." She leaned forward to heighten the almost palpable tension. "Some are saying you were involved in Al's murder. . . ."

"Me—! But I . . . but that's . . . that's ridiculous. The police killed the man who shot Al. The police said he was the guy! I mean, that's over. How could anyone say . . ." The uncompleted statement hung in the air.

"They call it taking out a contract. Don't you ever watch TV or go to a movie?"

"A contract! Wha—I wouldn't have the slightest idea of how to go about a thing like that. That's as bad as pulling the trigger itself. That's . . . that's monstrous!"

"I'm just telling you there's been talk."

"But . . . but why would I do a thing like that?"

"Well, according to the talk—and mind you, I'm just relaying what I've heard—you knew that, one, Al would make a success of his venture. Two, that he would get the reward—a seat as an executive vice president. And the seat he would take would be yours."

"Why mine?" It was the whine of a querulous child. "Why mine?"

"Because you're the most vulnerable. Some of the loans you make . . . ! Well, they're as good as down the drain. How long do you figure you can continue like this? Even Tom Adams's patience is at an end . . . or so I'm told."

"No! It's not true! Not anymore, anyway. You can ask Jack Fradet. He says I'm doing much better. He's even suggested some areas that escaped my attention. Maybe I did make some mistakes in the past. But that's over. You can ask. Not the troublemakers who're spreading gossip and rumors. Ask people who know."

"Well, all right, Lou." Barbara switched to a consoling tone. "Take it easy. Don't get mad at the messenger. I'm just telling you what's on the grapevine.

"And you're right: we shouldn't pay any attention to the petty people who don't really know what they're talking about. Just relax. Take it easy."

Lou shifted in his chair. Suddenly a silly smile took over. "Whatcha got under the robe?"

Damn! Why hadn't she gotten fully dressed for Lou Durocher? They'd had relations numerous times. But she felt as if she'd just played a maternal role with her frightened little boy. She didn't want to add incest to their relationship. She didn't respond.

"You wearing anything, babe?" he persisted. "It just came to me: we don't have to be safe anymore. You're already pregnant. What say we visit the bedroom? Nobody to hide from now. Whaddya say?" He stood. Plainly he was ready.

Not quite so plainly, she was not. "Really, Lou! Don't you think we ought to wait a decent period of time? I mean, Al's funeral was just yesterday."

Later—too late to do anything about it—Durocher would consider Barbara's reasoning intentionally specious. At this moment, and with his confused mind, somehow it made sense. "Well . . ." he stammered, "if you think so. . . ."

"I think so." She rose to see him out. "One last thing: does Pat know about us?"

"About us?" He pulled on his lower lip. "I don't think so," he said finally. "No, I don't think she had a clue—at least till now."

"'Till now'?" Her brow knit. "What's that supposed to mean?"

"Just that since I got your note, I've been pretty nervous. I think it showed at home. Pat's been asking me what's wrong maybe a million times. I keep putting her off. What I mean is I'm pretty sure Pat knows *something* is wrong; I don't think she knows exactly what."

"Let's keep it that way. Until we figure out what to do."

"About what?"

"The baby, Lou. About the baby. We're going to have to make some arrangements."

"Huh?"

"Support. Child support. The baby and me. You're going to have to support us of course."

Perspiration flooded forth again. "Support? How can I afford that and not involve Pat? And how can I involve Pat without her finding out about us? Oh my God!"

"Something you should have thought about when we began this affair. Don't gamble unless you can afford to lose.

"Anyway"—she brightened—"let's leave that for another day. Enough for now. Go on home—or back to work—wherever you're supposed to be. Don't call me. I'll call you—and you can put your last dollar on that."

Having experienced only a moment or two of relief during their tête-à-tête, Lou Durocher left as nervous and disturbed as he'd been when he arrived, if not more so.

*   *   *

Barbara closed the door behind him and leaned against it.

She'd *never* wanted to have relations with Lou. She did it, as she did with all men, only to manipulate those who sought to exploit her.

But today especially she did not want intimate contact with Lou Durocher. Fortunately, he bought the bromide of observing some interval before restoring a happy hour.

In retrospect she had her doubts about what had transpired between her and Lou Durocher.

Almost on the face of it, she was willing to believe Lou had nothing to do with Al's death. He seemed totally incapable of such a conspiracy. If he had been a party to the deed, it almost certainly would not have been implemented as successfully as it was. Besides, it was against his religion—some of whose tenets he kept.

That would mean—if she gauged correctly—that none of the three execs was involved in Al's death. Of course Martin and Jack would be much more believable liars than Lou. In the end, though, she had no proof of any kind that one or another had taken out a contract on Al.

Nor on the surface of it did it seem that any of the three had any sort of scam going on at the bank. Like feathering their nests against being dismissed. Lou, the one who had most to fear on that score, seemed genuinely to feel that he had turned a corner and was on—for him—fairly solid ground.

Which led to the final consideration: paternity.

Impossible for Martin and Jack—if their claims bore out.

Entirely possible for Lou.

Unfortunate for Barbara: of her four candidates, the least qualified as Mr. Romantic was Lou Durocher.

One thing was certain: Pat Durocher, should she learn of her husband's infidelity, might well divorce him, but she certainly wouldn't need to as far as Barbara was concerned. Under no circumstances was she in the market to marry Lou Durocher. That would be a case of out-of-retirement into the hell of war. At least Al hadn't had anything physical to do with her. Lou would be all over her.

Just send money.

Yet the bottom line had not been written. All she really knew was that Lou *might* be the father of her child. He had no reason to reject the possibility.

Still, another county remained to be heard from. Tom Adams was to check in this afternoon. And until Tom spoke his piece, there was still a chance that Lou Durocher—and she herself, for that matter—would be off the hook.

There was more talking and thinking to be done. Until then, she would rest.

Twenty-Two

BARBARA sat at her kitchen table. She looked out the window at a parking lot where cars baked under a blazingly hot Dallas sun. A child's cry broke her despondent mood.

She turned to look into the living room where her baby girl fussed as she awakened from her afternoon nap. Debbie had thrown her toys from her playpen. Barbara walked by the pen, absently tossing the toys back into the enclosure.

She gazed out the living room window. Approximately twelve feet of parched, fissuring clay separated her apartment from an eight-foot-high brick wall.

Debbie had her prison. Barbara had hers.

The air conditioning pumped in its battle with the intolerable outside furnace. It was a Mexican standoff.

She went to the dining room table on which she'd dumped today's mail. All of it was addressed either to her husband, Lou Durocher, or to Barbara Durocher, or to both Mr. and Mrs.

Tom Adams had fired Lou after learning of his adulterous relationship with Babs and that Lou was the father of her baby. He offered Lou the opportunity to do the honorable thing. Having no sword to fall upon, Lou was given the chance to divorce his wife, Pat, and marry Barbara, the widow.

Lou refused. So he was fired. Pat divorced him and got a huge financial settlement plus all their property. And he ended up married to Barbara anyway. No one had ever accused Lou Durocher of being exceptionally intelligent.

In truth, they would have been on the dole had it not been for Lou's brother, who owned a used car franchise in Irving, Texas—a suburb of Dallas—where the Durochers now lived in a vast rabbit warren of an apartment complex.

On the rare occasion when Barbara ventured outside, she seldom saw anyone. Not a human, not a dog, not a cat. It seemed that Dallasites stayed inside their air-conditioned apartments, homes, offices, cars. While swimming pools bubbled in the simmering heat. Some more enterprising citizens dumped 500-pound blocks of ice in their pools to render them swimmable. And one woman's published letter to the editor claimed that she preferred to think of the Dallas temperature as a wind chill factor of 123 degrees.

Barbara turned the fan on the baby to maximize the a/c's cooling. Debbie first looked startled, then burst out crying. Barbara felt like screaming.

The doorbell rang.

Who would venture out on a day like this? The discomfort would discourage Jehovah's Witnesses. She opened the door—and staggered as if she'd been struck. "J . . . Joyce! It can't be! You're dead!"

Joyce Hunter smiled. "May I come in? Or would you rather watch me melt?"

Wordlessly, Barbara stepped aside to let her erstwhile lover enter. Joyce looked wonderful, just the way Barbara remembered her.

"What's going on? You committed suicide!"

"That's what we wanted everyone to think. I worked it out with Harry. In return for my 'disappearance,' he and I faked the suicide."

"But all this time! Why didn't you contact me? How could you not contact me?"

"It was part of the deal. Something like the Witness Protection Program where a person is given a new identity. The agreement I reached with Harry was that I would move far away and continue to practice psychotherapy. In return, Harry would not reveal that I was gay.

"But I couldn't tell anyone . . . especially not you. It was part of our agreement. Otherwise I would have been destroyed as a therapist."

"This . . . this is such a shock. I mean, you've come out of nowhere. What are you doing here? What about your agreement with Harry?"

"Harry's dead . . . a little while ago. Cancer. So now, all bets are off."

Barbara felt faint. "It's . . . it's going to take me a while to get used to this." She shook her head.

"I understand. After Harry died I began looking for you. You were hidden away almost as well as I was. Then, once I found you, I wasn't sure how to handle this. If I phoned you, you'd never believe it was I. I had to come in person. So . . . here I am."

"So here you are. And what are we going to do about this?"

"Why . . . take up where we left off."

"'Take up . . .'? Joyce, I'm married. Lou Durocher. You never met him. He came along after . . . after you died. What am I saying? You didn't die. Anyway, you didn't know him. And we—he and I—we've got a baby."

"So I see." Joyce walked over to the playpen, leaned over, and picked up the baby. "Boy or girl?"

"Girl?"

"Name?"

"Debbie."

"Pretty. I like it."

"Joyce! How are we going to pull this off?"

"Why, the same way we did before. Only now in reverse."

"Reverse?"

Joyce continued to bounce the baby gently. Debbie seemed to love it. "Sure. When we first became lovers, you had the freedom to get a room at a motel, or when the coast was clear, we met at your apartment. I had the husband and family. Now you've got the family and I've got the open house. See how simple it is?"

"It's not that simple, Joyce. What am I going to do with the baby?"

"Why . . . bring her along, of course."

"I don't know. . . ." Barbara tapped a tooth with her fingernail. "It could get complicated in a hurry. Lou is an idiot, but he comes home at unpredictable times. The chances of his finding out about us are too good."

"There's another, even better solution." Joyce smiled broadly.

Barbara raised a questioning eyebrow.

"Leave him."

"Leave him! You mean divorce Lou?"

"Sure. He means nothing to you. Dump him. If he had an offer like this, don't you think he'd dump you in a minute? You never should've married him in the first place."

"I know . . . I know." Barbara was filled with remorse. "I thought I had that all figured out when Al—he was my husband—"

"I know."

"Well, when Al died I had four guys on the string. Any one of them could've been Debbie's father."

"You wicked thing, you!" Joyce said with a smirk.

"I thought I could get all four of them to contribute to me and the baby. I thought I had it made. Then, one by one they proved they couldn't have been the father. Only one had no excuse. He had to be the father, and he knew it."

"Lou Durocher."

"Lou Durocher."

"Even so, Babs, you shouldn't have married the jerk."

"What was I to do? I was going to have Lou's baby. The only way I could get support from him was to marry him. He was virtually destroyed by the scandal. There was no alternative. I *had* to marry hi—" She looked up, startled. "What's that noise?"

"I don't know." Joyce held the baby aloft and, like a sword swallower, fed the baby into her mouth and down her throat. Somehow, Barbara did not find that odd.

*   *   *

The phone rang. It rang again. And again.

Barbara awakened. She was covered with perspiration. She was alone in her apartment. Instead of a parking lot and a brick wall, she looked out on the magnificence of Belle Isle and the Detroit River.

Struggling to return to the present, she sat up and reached for the phone. "Hullo . . ."

"Barbara? Is it you?"

"Yes, it's me, Tom."

"You don't sound yourself."

"I was resting. I fell asleep and had a ghastly nightmare."

"You're all right?"

"Yes, I'm okay."

"Listen, Barbara, I'm coming over now, a little early. I just wanted to call ahead. I'll be there in a little while."

"I'll be here."

"See you soon."

She replaced the phone in its cradle.

She had just had one of the most realistic dreams of her life. Where on earth had it come from? With a little thought, the answer was obvious.

Marriage to the father of her child had been among her tentative plans. Not a fait accompli but a possibility. That's where her dream got its manifest content. Her subconscious was drawing a worst-case scenario. Extremely worst-case.

There was nothing intrinsically wrong with Dallas. But it was terrifying to think of a parking lot or a brick wall as one's only vistas.

She had no reason to believe that marriage to Lou Durocher would be anywhere near as bleak as her dream portrayed it. Depressing it surely would be. No use even contemplating living with Martin or Jack; they were out of the game. The nightmare had excluded the possibility of Tom's being the father. It had no right to do that. But dreams followed their own illogic.

Well, then, what if Tom Adams did prove to be the daddy? At this stage, he could only claim it was impossible due to some physical impediment as had Martin and Jack.

If Tom were physically capable of fathering a child only a DNA test would indicate whether it was his or Lou's. If at all possible, she wanted to steer clear of the DNA thing. Messy! Plus indicating to all that there was more than one entry in the fatherhood stakes.

As things presently stood, if Tom were the father there could be a marriage. As for whether Pat would divorce Lou, that was beyond Barbara's control. But no marriage to Lou. Send the money.

But there could be no conclusion written yet. It all came down to Tom Adams. What if he proved to be the father? He was single—even in the eyes of his Church. So marriage was possible. Was it practicable?

She would move up several notches in the social register. There would be lots more money to spend. Tom was attractive, even if Barbara was not attracted. On the other hand, she found Jack Fradet the most romantic of the four, so what good was her taste in men?

All in all, marriage to Tom Adams didn't look bad.

Barbara began pacing in front of the window wall as she considered the ramifications.

There was Mickey Adams. Turned out to pasture because she'd objected to Tom's intense committed involvement with and considerable contribution to his church. That certainly wouldn't change. Did Barbara want to—could she—play a subordinate role to the Catholic Church?

One good thing about Tom's church: it would not condone abortion. So, for different reasons, she and Tom would be in total agreement on that matter.

However, sensitized by her recent nightmare, she would tread slowly and carefully here. For the time being, let's just pinpoint Daddy. Then, step by patient step, she would map the course for those involved.

It was like a gigantic game of chess. And she had the controlling move.

While waiting for Tom, she wouldn't try for a catnap; she didn't want to chance another nightmare. After she met with Tom, she'd be able to dream peacefully. Until his arrival, she would bury herself in a book. Maybe a murder mystery.

Twenty-Three

T HE BOOK she'd been trying to read lay on the end table. She just hadn't been able to concentrate.

The doorbell rang. She went to the door. As expected, it was Tom Adams. He entered without a word.

He was stooped, and seemed drained. In spite of her self-appointed role as grand inquisitor, she felt sorry for him. She took his coat. He wore no hat. "Something bothering you, Tom?" She was all too aware that the bother might well be herself.

He sat down near the window wall and lingered over the view of the city at the height of its midafternoon bustle. "Oh . . . some trouble at the bank." After a moment, he added, "Actually, we're better off than I expected."

She laughed. "That's a reason for depression?"

"No. No, of course not. Still, I'd feel better if I completely understood why we're where we are."

Was this a poor-mouth rationale for not giving her the generous settlement she was aiming for?

"But we're not here to talk about banking." He turned from the window to her. "How are you feeling, Babs?"

None of the others had expressed any concern for her condition.

"Physically, I'm okay. After all, I'm barely into this pregnancy. And this is my first so I'm not even sure how I'm supposed to feel. But I don't feel much different than I did before I was pregnant. So I guess all goes well."

Outside of her doctor, her father and mother, and Joyce, no one had known of her prior pregnancy when she herself was little more than a child. Now all those who had known were dead. So, as far as anyone but her obstetrician now knew, the present pregnancy was her first.

"You're under a doctor's care?"

"Yes, of course."

"He's good, is he? Top-notch?"

"I've got an ob-gyn recommended by my GP. So far, I've got no negative vibes." She tilted her head sideways questioningly. "Why this interest in my doctor?"

"I want the best. Give me your doctor's name so I can check him out."

"Again: why?"

He seemed surprised. "Why? Because you're carrying our child. I want you—and the baby—to have the best of care. Why would you wonder about it?"

"It's just . . . I didn't expect . . ."

"I should've told you when it happened." Adams turned and looked again out the window as if unwilling to face her. "It happened about a little over a month ago . . . when we were together in my apartment. After you left to go home . . . well, I had a feeling something was wrong. I was going to dispose of the condom. Just before I wrapped it to throw in the trash I looked at it more closely. There was a substance on the outside that looked like it might be semen. I experimented: I filled the condom with water and watched as a thin stream slowly escaped. Somehow the condom had been perforated."

Barbara was almost rapturous. At last something that made sense —a credible explanation of how she had become pregnant!

"I debated at the time whether to tell you. It seemed to make little difference. The harm was done; you very probably were carrying my sperm in your vagina. If you were going to get pregnant, you were going to get pregnant.

"Later, I thought that was a stupid decision. You could've douched. Not a lot of chance that would've made any difference—but it represented the only remaining protection you might have.

"Still, in light of all the protection we always took—the spermicide, the diaphragm . . . the condom, for that matter . . . and this was such an infinitesimal perforation . . . plus it could easily have been a safe time in your cycle.

"With all those considerations I couldn't think of anything better than to let fate take its course. And"—he turned and gestured in the general direction of her abdomen—"it has."

Barbara couldn't get over it. After all this maneuvering with the other three, the execs! The last person she'd expected to readily accept responsibility, the last person on her chronological list of candidates, Tom Adams, admitted to being the father of her child. Who'd a thunk it!

Her initial reaction was relief. And immediately she felt power returning to her grasp.

The failures on Monday with Marty and Jack had taken a lot of wind from her sails. At that point, to relieve her angst, she'd begun to entertain the concept of a virgin birth. Returning to reality, she realized that one of the two on Tuesday's list had to be the one. Still, she had been shaken.

She hadn't felt all that ecstatic after this morning's session with Lou Durocher. And the nightmare concerning marriage to him hadn't helped. But now that she considered the matter in light of what Tom Adams had just told her, Lou would've had to have had an experience similar to Tom's in order to be in this paternity sweepstakes.

No doubt about it, something, or some*things*, had to have gone very, very wrong for her to conceive. There simply were too many precautions taken for this to happen.

Tom Adams had just confessed that his condom had failed. Not much of a failure but, theoretically, enough. Even so, his sperm had to negotiate a diaphragm that was supposed to block them and a spermicide that was supposed to kill them.

On the face of it, Tom Adams, while not a leadpipe cinch, was a most likely candidate. At this point, only a DNA test would confirm paternity. But not now. Maybe never.

She rubbed her abdomen absentmindedly.

Adams chuckled. "Yes, there's a new life in you. We want to protect it. I do. And I know you do too."

"It's getting clearer and clearer: you really are the father of this baby."

He half turned in the chair to face her. "I'm the father? How could it be otherwise?"

Suddenly she felt weak and abruptly sat down. She had forgotten for a moment: Tom Adams didn't know about the other three, his executive vice presidents. "I meant Al, of course. Everyone will think it's Al's baby. But we know it's not."

Adams smiled. "I'd be a great character witness for that argument, my dear. If anybody would believe that you and Al broke off intimate relations long ago, I'm the one. I saw his dedication to work. It went beyond dedication: it was a total immersion in the business. And I could sense his estrangement from you. You told me about it. But I would have sensed it anyway."

She breathed a sigh of relief.

"And," he continued, "we can use that when the baby is born."

She was confused. "What are you talking about?"

"Why, when you have the child—after its birth. The gestation process will obviously be less than the nine months from our wedding—considerably less depending on when we marry.

"But we don't have to worry about any scandal. Everyone will assume you're having Al's baby. All we have to do is let that assumption stand. Let them think it's Al's baby; that will assure us ample time without our hurrying anything. It's made to order."

He seemed so complacent. As if their marriage had been made to order. Strength returning, she stood. "Wait a minute: who said anything about marriage?"

"Marriage! You and I! It goes without saying."

"That's a quantum leap from where I am now. I didn't know how you would react to my pregnancy. I was reasonably sure you wouldn't want an abortion. And you know my feelings on the subject. But, other than that, I had to wait until this minute to know if you would accept the child."

He stood and faced her, challengingly. "But of course I would—and do. What kind of man do you think I am? The child is my responsibility, and I intend to see this through."

She began to pace, not going far in either direction. She seemed unable to stand still. "Tom, if all this hadn't happened . . . if we hadn't had an affair . . . if I hadn't gotten pregnant . . . if Al hadn't been killed: would you have given a single thought to marrying me?"

He turned and walked to the window. "That's a lot of 'ifs,' Babs. But if ever there was a time when we ought to be honest, open, and frank with each other, now is that time. To be extremely candid, I'm not proud of our love affair."

She started to remonstrate, but he silenced her with a gesture. "I can make excuses for what I did. No, make that, I *have* made excuses for our affair. I was alone and lonely. You are just about the most desirable woman I've ever met. Gradually it became clear that you were in an extremely unhappy marriage.

"So much for excuses."

"Not so much excuses," she managed to break in, "but *reasons*. You were divorced. So it wasn't as if you'd chosen a celibate life like some priest. You didn't get married to be alone. But you were alone and lonely.

"I was married. But the marriage was a virtual prison. I was alone and lonely in the special sense of living with someone without love. There isn't any loneliness more oppressive than living with the wrong person."

He shook his head impatiently. "Call it excuses, call it reasons; it doesn't alter the fact that it was adulterous."

"According to the rigid laws of your church!"

"According to the law of God."

"According to how you define marriage!"

He jammed his hands deeply in his pockets as if to restrain himself from an angry gesture. "What do you mean by that!"

"I mean the rules and regulations of society and your church define what marriage is. And then they come along and tell you that the marriage is over—or that it never existed. Because now you have 'irreconcilable differences.' Or because you didn't have a priest around. No one can tell me I was living a 'married life' with Al. And your church told you you were never actually married to Mickey—that what existed between you and Mickey was never a marriage.

"It all depends on who's defining marriage—just like it all depends on whose ox is being gored."

"All right! All right!" Adams threw up his arms in a gesture of vexation. "Let's get to your other 'ifs.' Would I be talking marriage to you if you weren't pregnant. Or if Al were still alive.

"That supposes a return to how things were before you discovered you were pregnant. And the answer is . . . probably not. We're being candid. And, being candid, I had a good thing going. I wouldn't want to lose that."

"A *good thing*?" Barbara's lip curled. "Was using a condom a 'good thing'? Your church doesn't even let gays use condoms to protect against AIDS. You used them all the time with me. That was a 'good thing'?" In her fury, she overlooked the fact that it had been she who had insisted on his using the condoms.

"That's the point!" Tom pounded his knee for emphasis. "Our relationship was sinful. It was adulterous—even though there were extenuating circumstances. And it was sinful to use all these precautions—even though there were extenuating circumstances. I am a sinner. I never claimed not to be. But these were personal, private sins, if you will. I would *never* place myself outside my church by attempting an invalid marriage. Never!

"So, suppose you divorced Al. Would I ask you to marry me then? That brings us back to 'my church,' and who is defining marriage. I make no apologies: I would act in conformity with my church. But if the Church ruled you were free to marry, I certainly would have asked you."

"And now . . . ?"

"And now, of course, there is no need to seek a ruling from the Church. You are a widow. In anyone's eyes you are free to marry. And I've already been granted a declaration of nullity." He lowered himself into a chair and sat at its edge, eager. "Now, this is what I propose: after a little while we announce our engagement. We also announce that you are carrying your former husband's child. At that point, the date of our wedding is immaterial—sometime after your delivery, or before; whatever suits you.

"The ceremony will be a Catholic one of any size and detail you wish. At that point it doesn't matter: anything you want."

He grew testy. "What is wrong, Babs? I've outlined a perfect scenario. What more do you want?"

She shook her head. "I'm not sure. And I can't tell you anything you want to hear right away. There are things I can't explain just now.

"I'm not sure about our child. I'm not sure I want the child—and everyone else—to think he or she belongs to Al Ulrich when *you* are the father. And even more basic than that, I'm not sure I want to marry you."

Clearly, he was angry. "Send the money and shut up, is it? I'm not so sure *I* favor *that* solution! Think about this, missy—and think about it hard: I can't wait forever for you to see the light. Just damn well let me know when you see that light!"

He snatched his coat from the chair and stormed out.

*　　*　　*

Just as well he'd left: she had run out of things to say to him.

This whole thing had played out completely differently than she had planned.

At the very worst she'd expected four financially endowed men, each unaware of the others' involvement, to contribute generously to the poor widow and her star-crossed child.

The actual circumstance was far from that. Two men—each physically incapable of fertilizing an ovum—were cut from the herd at the outset. The third could be the father. The prospect of marriage to him was akin to volunteering for life in prison. Even accepting money from him was fraught with complexities.

Then along comes the perfect arrangement.

Tom Adams, CEO of a bank, presents a well-thought-out solution. She asks him if, without the present pressures, he would have proposed marriage. Probably not. But the bottom line? Now, he would.

However, she was just beginning to ask herself the question: would she marry *him*?

Some women live only for marriage. Perhaps no woman today exemplifies this more than Elizabeth Taylor. No matter how many times events seem to demonstrate beyond all doubt that the single life is her true destiny, she keeps on getting married.

Barbara Ulrich was beginning to think fate was giving her the same message.

Why, after all, did she need marriage? She was not heterosexual. She happened to be gorgeous, the physical answer to nearly every heterosexual male's dream. She had no problem attracting men, even to the point of having them propose marriage. They wanted what she had on a full-time basis forever. Or so they thought.

Marriage with Tom Adams . . .

She sat at the large window and inattentively watched the endless flow of the river.

He was a good man. He would care for her. He would provide for her on a level she had never experienced. Her social life would be glamorous.

Could she endure his absolute unquestioning fidelity to his church? Maybe wife number one had had a point. On the other hand, what difference could it make that her husband was preoccupied with Catholicism?

From firsthand, Barbara knew that Tom's sexual appetite was voracious. While that could be a problem, particularly after her delivery when she would again be fertile, it was a situation she thought she could handle.

For one thing, she was beginning to believe that while she definitely was not heterosexual, she might very well be bisexual. Jack Fradet had brought that possibility to the surface. Upon reflection, she thought she might lead Tom Adams to the same techniques perfected by Fradet.

All in all, life with Tom Adams was looking more and more attractive. Perhaps even compelling.

By this time she was sure of herself. At least as sure as she could be. She had, as Tom put it, seen the light: she would accept his proposal.

How to tell him?

He had left in a huff only minutes ago. Bad timing to pick up the phone. No, give him a little time to cool off.

A note. A letter. Yes, that would be perfect.

She'd have to word this carefully.

And besides enthusiastically accepting his proposal, she would add an item that she had picked up on when she had screened the other three. It was a tipoff Tom ought to be aware of. She would present this as gossip overheard during the award dinner. Telling him what she'd heard would create a new image for herself: not only a wife, but a collaborator. He would appreciate her interest and her help with the business.

She completed the letter, addressed, stamped, and sealed the envelope. There was just time for the last mail pickup. With any luck, it would be delivered by tomorrow afternoon. She could hardly wait for him to get this letter.

She began to anticipate her coming marriage with delight.

Twenty-Four

H E DID SEEM a bit sheepish about it. And I don't blame him." Father Tully had checked things out with his brother and had been invited to visit police headquarters. The topic of conversation was the vacationing pastor of St. Joe's.

Lieutenant Tully shook his head, chuckling. "How long's he been gone now?"

"Just a week today. For the love of Pete, he could've stayed a month if he wanted to! But he's been visiting his classmate up there in Canada. He says there's just so many stories of the Good Old Days he can relive and retell."

Zoo grew serious. "What does this do to your stay here?"

"I don't know. Father Koesler's decision came out of the blue. He called first thing this morning—must've been about seven. When I heard his voice, my immediate thought was, It's way too early to take the pulse of this parish just to see if I'm tending it all right. But all he said was that he was packed and ready to come back. There was no way I could talk him into staying a little longer."

One of the Tully's squad members handed him a phone message—a death the Homicide Division had to check out. Zoo scanned the message and nodded an okay. "So Father Koesler will be back later today?"

"I guess it'll take him four or five hours. He said he'd probably stop for lunch. So he should be pulling in sometime early to mid-afternoon. But yeah, the essence of his message was that he'd be back today."

"Does that mean you have to vacate today?"

The priest laughed. "You mean like a relay team: I pass the baton to him and he takes it from there?"

"Look, little brother, all I want to know is what to tell Anne Marie. 'There'll be an overnight guest . . . oh, and by the way, he'll be staying several overnights.'"

"Sorry, Zoo. I know there's a common sense side to all this."

"It's just that it didn't take long for us to fall in love with you. We don't want to see you leave. If it means putting you up at our place, fine. We want to do everything we can to keep you here as long as possible."

"The feeling is the same, Zoo. But I don't know what to tell you—except don't have Anne Marie fix up the guest room. I'll probably stay at St. Joe's until I leave—whenever that is.

"As far as that goes, I could stay at almost any parish in the diocese: the resident pastors would think they went to heaven without having to die. The rectories have plenty of room for priests; they just haven't got enough priests to fill the rooms.

"Take St. Joe's, for instance. There's plenty of room for three resident priests. Bob Koesler and I make only two.

"So, no difficulty staying over. I even made sure before leaving Texas that my substitute's availability was open-ended. There's no immediate hurry. But for the long run . . . well, I've got some more thinking and praying to do."

As Father Tully was speaking, the bulk of Sergeant Phil Mangiapane loomed. Zoo noticed him but waited till his brother had finished, then beckoned.

"'Scuse, Father. Zoo, a precinct cop just called this in."

"Yes?"

"Apparent suicide."

"Okay. You and"—Tully scanned the roster—"Angie take it."

"Uh . . . Zoo: you might want to take a look at this one. . . ."

"Oh?" Zoo read the message, then whistled softly. He turned to his brother. "Father, you may want to come with us."

The priest's unspoken reaction was, Yes, of course. He wanted to stay in contact with his brother and sister-in-law. His eyes widened as he read the message his brother handed him.

"That's right: Barbara Ulrich's dead. An apparent suicide."

"Let's go," Father Tully said. En route to the Ulrich apartment, the priest did little more than shake his head and murmur over and over, "I don't think so."

By the time Zoo and his party arrived, the police technicians with their plastic gloves were busy at their professional duties.

Barbara's body lay next to her desk. The phone, receiver off its cradle, was on the floor, where it apparently had fallen after being knocked off the desk as she fell.

Barbara was wearing a frilly nightgown. She seemed so fragile. Not unlike the doll her daddy had broken when he was doing bad things to her ... or the "broken doll" the doctors had wrenched from her body. Of course those who were investigating her death would have no knowledge of those incidents.

Father Tully found an out-of-the-way spot that held no interest for either technicians or detectives. The priest scrunched into the empty corner and quietly observed, his attention focused mainly on his brother, who was in charge.

Without touching it, Zoo squatted near the weapon. "Thirty-eight caliber." The dead woman's hand cradled the revolver, handle in her palm, index finger against the trigger.

Tully stood. "Who found the body?"

"The manager." The patrolman who had responded to the original call opened his notepad. "A Mrs. Marilyn Fradet tried to call the deceased this morning. She was concerned about the deceased—" He looked down at his notes. "A Barbara Ulrich—"

"I know."

"Well, Mrs. Fradet was worried because Mrs. Ulrich is a recent widow. She"—he inclined his head toward the body—"just buried her husband a couple of days ago." Zoo nodded, almost impatiently.

"Anyway, she called several times and didn't get any answer. So she asked the manager to check on the Ulrich woman. Which he did. This"—he gestured to include the living room and its contents—"is the way he found it. No one touched anything until the techs got here."

"Thanks."

Zoo slowly walked around the room scrutinizing the area and the furnishings. He stopped at the desk where a photographer was snapping pictures with near reckless abandon. "Was there a note?"

"None that we've found so far," one of the technicians said. "We've been over the top layer of the desk and the floor. No note. I don't think we're gonna find one. It'd be a first in my experience that somebody writes a note explaining everything or saying good-bye and then hides the note before committing suicide. If there's a note, the writer wants it found and read."

"Uh-huh." Zoo returned to the body, looked at it searchingly, then squatted again. From that position, he beckoned his brother.

Father Tully joined him near the dead woman's head.

Not for the first time the priest found it difficult to associate the finality of death with someone so young, so vital, and with so much of her life before her.

"You know that mantra you've been whispering over and over—the one that's been driving me nuts?"

"You mean about I didn't think this was a suicide? Sorry, I didn't mean to bug you."

"You didn't. Not all that much anyway—not really. But why, sight unseen, did you think this wasn't a suicide? I mean, it wouldn't be the first time a widow threw herself on the funeral pyre."

"Not this widow. Not from what I've heard and seen. Not unless the pyre wasn't going to be lit . . . not unless this widow could walk away anytime she wanted."

"Oh?"

"I'm not saying that she wanted her husband dead, or even that she was glad he was killed. But . . . I do think that both parties to that marriage would have felt better apart. As it was, they managed to live apart as much as possible without actually breaking their union publicly. I don't know why—and I doubt that anyone else knows either—they didn't just get a divorce.

"That's why I don't think it was suicide. Her life and her future must've looked pretty rosy once Al Ulrich was out of the picture permanently."

"Well, brother, I tend to agree with you."

"You do?" The priest was surprised that his brother would agree with any conclusion respecting police business.

"Not for the same reason you gave—though that *is* supportive. But look at that wound."

The priest looked, although he didn't know what he was supposed to be looking for.

"Notice anything strange or odd?"

Father Tully studied the wound more carefully, trying to remain objectively detached. It was difficult. He was a priest; caring for and about people was in his marrow, even if most of the time that care was for their souls rather than their bodies. It was hard for him to try to look at the bloody head of the lifeless Barbara Ulrich as a mere technical puzzle to be solved, when all he could think of was the living, breathing woman—a woman with hopes, joys, and fears. "I don't notice anything," he said finally. "What am I supposed to be looking for—or at?"

"No powder burns around the hole."

"No powder burns! I remember now," the priest reflected. "I think it was on one of the episodes of 'Hill Street Blues.' A corpse was supposed to have powder burns and didn't. What's that all about, anyway?"

Zoo sighed softly. "The closer the gun is to the victim when the bullet is fired, the more likely it will leave a gunpowder residue. Look carefully. See anything like a powder burn?"

Father Tully tipped his head back to get a better view through his bifocals. "Just a few specks, I think."

"Exactly. Of course we'll have to wait till Doc Moellmann rules on it. But I'm tentatively classifying this as a homicide."

"Homicide!"

"Why so surprised? You said from the beginning you didn't think it was a suicide. . . ."

"Yes, but . . ."

"She didn't die of old age."

"But why call it murder just because of an absence of powder burns?"

"Brother, it's this way: when somebody is going to take his own life with a handgun, he doesn't want to miss. See, the suicide is nervous; his hand is probably shaking. Try it. Pretend you're holding a gun and you're going to shoot yourself. If you hold the gun a foot away from your head, you can't be certain you're going to hit dead on. You're not going to be able to control the weapon that well at that angle, or without a firm surface to steady it.

"Now, you don't want to blast your nose or your ear away or just give yourself a painful flesh wound. No, you want to kill yourself with one shot.

"Now, to do this, the suicide holds the gun right up against his head. That way he's got a good idea of just where the bullet is going. Or, he may stick the gun in his mouth and fire . . . another sure way he's going to accomplish what he set out to do.

"So, my tentative label is homicide . . . uh, excuse me a minute." He beckoned to Sergeant Moore. "Angie, work this case as a homicide for now. Make sure the techs dust everything—*everything*. Is the body ready to go?"

Moore nodded. "They were just waiting for you to finish with it."

"Okay. I'll call the morgue and see if I can get Moellmann on it. There's something here and I'm betting Doc will find it."

The priest and the detective left the room with Zoo's arm around his brother's shoulder.

"Where to?" Zoo asked, as they entered the unmarked police car. "I've got to get back to headquarters. This has all the marks of being an extra-busy day. You're welcome to come with me, but I don't think I'll be much company."

"Thanks. But I'd better head for the rectory. Bob should be getting in any time now. It'd be good if I were there with a hearty welcome."

"Okay." The lieutenant smiled broadly as he set course for St. Joe's. "Well, Sherlock, got any idea who done it?"

His brother smiled in return. "I've got no idea . . . unless it was Moriarty."

"Who?"

"The archvillain of the Sherlock Holmes series."

"Oh . . . yeah. But seriously: you've been a witness to what's been going on with the Adams Bank people. Have you noticed anything out of the ordinary? We thought we'd closed this book when we got the kid who killed Ulrich. Now, we're opening another chapter. We've got a murder one on the guy's widow—"

"Murder one?"

"Murder one," Zoo repeated, "because anybody who tries to make a murder look like a suicide didn't stumble onto the idea. It had to be carefully planned.

"Anyway, as I was saying, you've pretty well been in the thick of this thing . . . you've talked to just about everybody who's mixed up in this. So, brother, what do you think?"

The priest was silent for some moments. Then, "There are a couple of things that I wondered about at the time. They're probably nothing . . . they just seem a bit odd in the light of what's happened since. I'm a little reluctant to even tell you because they probably don't mean a thing, and they might throw you off the track."

"No . . . no." Zoo's tone was earnest. "This is exactly what we're looking for. Just tell me about it. Let me judge whether it's relevant."

"Okay. Well, the first incident was just before the award dinner. Right after Barbara Ulrich made her entrance, she sort of worked the room. I noticed something curious: she seemed to be slipping notes to four men—well, at least four that I saw; I didn't watch her all evening. Anyway, the four were Tom Adams and his three executive vice presidents—Jack Fradet, Lou Durocher, and Martin Whitston.

"That seemed peculiar. Then, at the wake service for her husband, she took extra time talking individually to each of those same four men. I have no idea what they talked about . . . only that it seemed something was going on between them.

"And," he concluded, "that's about it." He turned to Zoo. "That's probably not going to help you much."

Zoo shook his head. "It's a start. We'll be asking questions and we'll definitely include those guys." He pulled into the parking lot of St. Joe's. "Well, here we are." He didn't bother putting the car in park.

As he exited the car, Father Tully said, "I'll see you later, eh?"

"I'll keep you posted. I know you're interested."

"Great!"

*   *   *   *

Father Tully was conscious of being pressed for time. Just inside the rectory he encountered a concerned Mary O'Connor. "I was just about to try to find another priest for noon Mass," she said. "Did you get lost?"

"Too much to tell you now, Mary. After Mass. Father Koesler back yet?"

"Good Lord, is he coming back today?"

The priest chuckled. "He can't stay away from you, Mary."

The faithful few who frequented daily Mass were in their places. In the brief time he'd been offering daily as well as weekend Masses, Tully had gotten used to the same faces occupying the same pews in the vast church.

He was not surprised that his nagging distraction during this Mass was the image of Barbara Ulrich lying like a discarded doll. He recalled that neither she nor her husband had been affiliated with any church or religious body. He might well be asked to deliver another eulogy.

Meanwhile, he would pray that she had already entered the new life. He had no idea whether his prayers were needed or wanted. He offered them anyway.

After Mass, Father Tully returned to the rectory and lunch. He had barely wolfed a sandwich before Mary O'Connor caught up to him with two phone messages. One was from his brother, the other from Tom Adams. He decided to return his brother's call first for more reasons than chronological order.

Zoo picked up at the second ring. On hearing his brother's voice, he asked, "I haven't pulled you away from something?"

"No. I haven't done that to you?"

"Well . . . we're a bit pushed," Zoo admitted. "But I thought you'd want to know what's happened since I dropped you."

"Absolutely . . . and thanks."

"I've been on the horn to Doc Moellmann—the medical examiner. He put the final nail in the homicide premise."

"Congratulations . . . I guess. Exactly what was it you wanted him to discover?"

"The gunpowder . . . remember?"

"I remember."

"The Doc saw the same thing we did. There were only a few specks some inches away from the entrance wound. And no muzzle imprint on her skin. So, there was good reason to suspect this was highly doubtful as a suicide.

"But what I was concerned about was that maybe the residue—the black soot—might've been blown inside the head. That would argue for the gun's firing at point-blank range. In other words, instead of the powder showing up on the external skin around the wound, that the force of the shot had simply blown the soot inside her head.

"But Doc didn't find any powder or soot inside. His conclusion is that the gun was fired at a distance of at least ten to twelve inches from her head. For a suicide that's highly unlikely."

"So you were right," the priest said. "It was a homicide." Once again he was impressed with and proud of his brother the cop.

"That's not all, brother. Our victim, Barbara Ulrich, was pregnant."

"Pregnant!"

"Only a month or two. But very definitely pregnant."

"Oh! That would've been their first child," the priest said. "What a tragedy. Now all of them dead—Al, Barbara, and their child. What a tragedy!"

"Hold on," Zoo cautioned. "We don't know that her husband was the father of her child."

"Wha—!"

"You were the one who told me they got along like oil and water."

"That doesn't mean they couldn't have a baby—even if it were spousal rape."

"It isn't just your opinion, Zack. I talked to her ob/gyn."

"What about professional secrecy?"

"There's not much reticence when there's a homicide investigation going on. Anyway, her doctor also tends to think her husband was not the father. She didn't come right out and tell him she'd stopped having relations with Ulrich, but she clearly implied it.

"It was obvious to the doctor that she was sexually active. Right up until he determined she was pregnant, she was using lots of protection. How many partners she had, he couldn't say. But her efforts to avoid STD and her insistence on being tested for it gave the doc the hint that she had more than one partner.

"And it seems that no matter how many she had, Ulrich wasn't among them—or so consensus seems to have it.

"Besides, it makes sense in another direction. Before this, we had a homicide and no evident motive. This gives us a very good motive. I mean, the way things were between them, I wouldn't have been surprised if her husband would've killed her. But Ulrich was dead long before she was shot.

"Now we've got a lover who doesn't want to be a daddy. But he's gonna be. So he murders the mother and fakes it to look like suicide. That clears up a lot of blind alleys for us and makes a very believable case. And this particular daddy has a lot of precedent going for him. He's definitely not the first reluctant father-to-be who gets rid of the problem by getting rid of the mother.

"So that's where we are: find the father and we find Barbara Ulrich's murderer."

"It certainly sounds logical," Father Tully said.

"Just wanted to clue you in. Gotta get busy. For the first time we've got somebody to look for . . . even if we don't know who he is yet."

*   *   *

Father Tully's head was swimming with this latest development. *Barbara Ulrich pregnant.* She had to have known it, of course. But he firmly believed that her husband was unaware of her condition. The priest was also convinced, from all he'd heard and his own evaluation, that the Ulrichs had long ceased conjugal relations. He also believed that if Al Ulrich had known that his wife was pregnant, he would not only have renounced her, but also denounced her *and* her lover publicly.

Was it possible, he wondered, that this fact—the newly discovered pregnancy, was what Barbara was communicating when she slipped notes to those four men?

Four men!

What was he thinking! Could Barbara Ulrich have juggled *four* paramours? All executives from the same company? And—even if it was logistically possible—why would she attempt it? The challenge? A psychological need for living on the edge—brinkmanship? If so, evidently one of her four had gone over the brink.

The priest quickly reviewed his impressions of the four he had so recently met. What could she have seen in such a disparate collection of men?

If the father/murderer *was* one of these four, good luck to Lieutenant Zoo Tully and the Detroit Police Department.

Twenty-Five

FATHER TULLY continued to speculate on his brother's speculation.

The phone rang. He looked at the instrument. One light was on while another blinked. Mary O'Connor must be on line one. He pushed the button for line two. "St. . . . uh . . . uh, Joseph's." Rattled for a moment, he couldn't recall which parish he was representing.

"Father Tully?"

"Tom? Tom Adams? I'm sorry I haven't returned your call. I just finished Mass." He didn't bother to mention that he'd been on the phone with his brother. Why complicate matters? He had intended to return Adams's call.

"I apologize," Adams said. "I should have waited for your call. But I'm so worried. Have you heard anything about Mrs. Ulrich? Someone here at the office said there was a rumor that she'd been injured . . . shot! I've tried to get some information, but no one I've called seems to know anything solid. Or if they do, they're not telling me. And I thought that with your connection with the police . . ."

My connection with the police. Ordinarily my relationship with the police department plus seventy-five cents might get me a cup of coffee, thought Father Tully. However, this was one occasion when Tom Adams was in luck. In this instance, bad luck. "Yes, Tom. I was with my brother when he was called to the scene. I'm afraid it's bad news, Tom. The worst."

"She's . . . *dead*?"

"At first the police thought it was suicide."

"Suicide!" Adams seemed dumbstruck.

"That's what they thought initially. But now they think it was murder made up to appear suicide."

"She's dead then." Adams sounded despairing.

"Yes."

Tully waited patiently. No response. He waited longer. He thought he could hear sobbing, but very softly. "Tom? Mr. Adams? Are you there?"

Silence. Finally, "Yes, I'm here. There's"—hope against hope—"no doubt . . . no doubt at all?"

"None. I saw her." Another pause. "There's more to the story, Tom. Mrs. Ulrich was pregnant. It was very early. The baby was no more than a few weeks along."

Still no response.

"The police are presuming there's a connection between her pregnancy and her death. They say that when they find the father they'll have found the killer."

"What!?" Adams almost shouted. "*I'm* the father! She was carrying *my* child! But I didn't kill her. I wouldn't kill her. I couldn't kill her!"

Father Tully could think of nothing to say.

"We were going to be married . . . at least I asked her—just yesterday. How could you possibly believe that I would kill the woman I was going to marry, much less kill my own child!?"

"Mr. Adams . . ." Father Tully was near dumbfounded. "I didn't believe that. I had no way of knowing *you* were the father!"

Someone must've entered Adams's office or at least come to the doorway; Tully could faintly hear a female voice . . . something about the afternoon mail; there was a letter marked "personal."

She must've put the mail on his desk. Father Tully heard the sound of papers being shifted about.

"Oh, my God! It's from her—it's from Barbara! Father, I'll call you right back. It's from Barbara!" He hung up, none too gently.

Absently, Father Tully also hung up. Words swam in his mind: *"She was carrying my child. But I didn't kill her. I wouldn't kill her. I couldn't kill her!"* Adams's words were clogging Father Tully's brain. It was such an odd sensation.

Then the final piece of the puzzle fell into place. And it was as if Father Tully had been unaware he had even been engaged in the game.

He thought about it from this angle and that. He searched his memory for events, people, and what those people had said. At best he had not thought any of these elements might be significant clues that would eventually solve a mystery. But it was all taking shape.

Uneasy, he checked his watch. It was now ten minutes since Tom Adams had hung up, promising to call right back. Father Tully quite naturally assumed that Adams had hung up in order to read Barbara's letter—a message from the dead.

But reading a letter would not require ten minutes—especially since it was Adams who had desperately wanted to talk to the priest.

What could be the cause for Adams's not returning the call as promised? What was going on? Tully shuddered as he considered the possibilities. He dialed Adams's number.

"Adams Bank and Trust; office of Mr. Adams. This is Lucille; how may I help you?"

"This is Father Tully. I was just speaking with Mr. Adams. He said he would return my call right away. Is he there?"

She caught the agitation in the priest's voice. "No, Father." Her tone became perturbed. "No. He . . . he just left his office."

"Do you know where he went?"

"N . . . no. He didn't say. Would you like me to—"

There was no point in continuing this conversation. Time was of the essence. The priest didn't know what was going on at the bank, but he sensed danger and impending tragedy. He dialed homicide, identified himself, and asked for his brother.

"Lieutenant Tully is on the street."

"Whereabouts on the street?"

The officer chuckled. "He's in his car, Father—on the far east side."

Too far away. *He'll never be able to get downtown in time!* Another cop. He had to get another cop. But who? He knew so few. The bread eater—the priest's mnemonic for one of Zoo's cops. "How about Sergeant Mangiapane?"

"One second."

The line clicked; a phone was picked up. "Mangiapane," a preoccupied voice said.

"This is Father Tully. I need you right away."

"Oh, hi, Father. What's the problem?"

"I think it's a matter of life or death."

"You want Zoo?"

"He's too far away. It's gotta be you."

Mangiapane hesitated a millisecond. "Okay, Father: Shoot."

"You've got to get over to Adams Bank and Trust headquarters. Mr. Adams's office. I'll meet you there—"

"But what—?"

"No time to explain. There's no time. Just hurry, please—fast as you can!"

"I'm gone!" There was a click answered by the one from the priest's phone.

Father Tully raced his rented car down Jefferson toward Woodward and the skyscraper that housed the headquarters of Adams Bank. He left the car double-parked on the street amid honking horns and imprecations not ordinarily directed at a man of the cloth.

The elevator seemed to barely move. He struck the wall in frustration. *Hurry! Hurry! Hurry!* Should he have taken the stairs? Immediately the thought of a run up twelve flights made him realize he would have left his game on the stairway. When the car finally reached the twelfth floor, he almost hurled himself through the not yet fully opened doors, banging his shoulder in the process. He shook his head as if to shake the pain from his arm.

"Did he come back?" he asked as he hurtled past an astonished Lucille into Adams's office.

"No . . . no, he didn't," a startled Lucille said to the space recently occupied by the priest. "Father, you can't go in there!" She followed the priest into the inner office.

"Oh yes, I can." Tully rifled through papers near the phone on Adams' desk. "You can call . . . uh . . . Nancy Groggins. She was there when he invited me to visit anytime at home or work."

"Well, that may be—" Lucille was becoming huffy; even if he *was* a priest, he had no right. . . . "You have no right to bust in here. . . ." Her increasingly angry protestation gained steam.

No letter. There was no letter from Barbara . . . or at least he couldn't find it. Then he caught sight of a piece of paper obviously ripped from the desk calendar. It bore a single word, written in big, bold letters. JUDAS!

By now Father Tully was accustomed to Tom Adams's regular reference to biblical figures and features. Judas was the quintessential traitor. Judas was one of those chosen to be closest to Jesus.

Who would play Judas to Tom Adams? Someone closest to him —one of the executive vice presidents. What did Tom Adams hold most precious? Independence—that his bank remain independent. Who of the three executives would be in a position to sell out the bank? Who, by manipulating figures, could show false profits and losses . . . lull the president into thinking his bank was secure when it was not? *Jack Fradet!*

This conclusion was reached in only a few moments. "Where are the executives' offices?"

Lucille was still sputtering vehemently. "One floor down," she answered before she realized her upbraiding had been interrupted. But Father Tully was already gone, running toward the stairs. Again he led with his shoulder, pushing against the stairwell door. *Open, damn you!* Then he realized that he had to turn the knob and pull to open the door. He hurtled down the stairs, taking some two at a time while praying that he wouldn't trip and topple down the rest of the way.

This time the door did open outward. He burst through it. Another dash down another corridor. His chest heaved; his breath pounded in his ears. *There!* The nameplate he was seeking.

"You can't go in there—!" But he was past her and into the inner office.

He found just about what he had expected to see.

Tom Adams, jacketless and, for him, disheveled, held a gun pointed squarely at an obviously terrified Jack Fradet. Adams stole a quick glance at the priest and just as quickly returned total attention to the cowering Fradet.

"Tom!" The priest was almost shouting. "Put the gun down. Please! It's not worth it. He's just not worth it. There are better ways. You'll just ruin your life. Everything you've worked for will go down the drain. Please. Put down the gun!"

"Father's right," said a commanding voice from the office doorway. "There's a desk in front of you, Mr. Adams. Put the gun on the desk. Carefully please." The cavalry, in the person of Sergeant Mangiapane, weapon drawn, had arrived. Father Tully breathed a half sigh of relief.

"You don't understand. You don't understand what this traitor has done." Adams, still holding the gun, spoke in an imploring tone.

"I think I do," said Father Tully. "But the place to settle this is in the courtroom. Not here."

From the maelstrom of thoughts whirling through the priest's mind, one was suddenly uppermost: he knew what kind of a person Tom Adams was at his core. "Tom, what you're thinking of doing is a sin—a mortal sin. It's murder. You're going against one of God's commandments. God does not want you to do this, Tom. I'm a priest and I'm telling you: God wants you to put that gun down."

He did not turn his gaze from Fradet. But Adams moved slightly. Then, slowly, he lowered the gun and laid it on the desk.

"Now, Mr. Adams," Mangiapane said in a calm, steady tone, "I want you to step back from the desk."

Adams did as he was ordered. Mangiapane stepped forward, picked up the gun, then holstered his own. He patted down both

Adams and Fradet, the former in a seeming daze, the latter in a state of shock. Mangiapane turned to Father Tully. "What's going on here, Father?"

"Fraud, I think, at the very least," the priest said. "And maybe lots more. Sergeant, seeing as how I'm the one who called you in on this, would you humor me? I need a few favors."

Mangiapane's cocked eyebrow evidenced his uncertainty.

"Could you give me a little time alone with Mr. Adams, make sure that Mr. Fradet doesn't leave, and, finally, get my brother over here?"

Mangiapane deliberated. While such a procedure was in no police textbook he'd ever studied, he could find nothing substantially problematic in these requests. Neither Adams nor Fradet was armed. Adams was not likely to step out an eleventh-floor widow. Fradet could be detained in one of the other offices. And, in fact, Mangiapane himself dearly wanted his superior officer here as quickly as possible. "You got it, Father. But make it snappy. Zoo was heading in when I left. I'll call him now; he should be here in a couple of minutes."

Mangiapane left the office with Fradet literally in hand. As he made his way through the outer office, he ordered a host of spectators back to work.

"Tom," Father Tully asked, "what was in the letter?"

"Letter?"

"The letter you just got from Barbara . . . the letter you're holding."

Adams slumped into a chair. As he did so, the now crumpled letter fell from his left hand to the floor. The priest bent to pick it up. "Okay if I read it?"

Adams nodded.

Tully read the handwritten letter aloud.

Dearest Tom,

Of course I'll marry you. I wasn't quite prepared for all you said today. After I recovered from the surprise and shock, I realized what a generous and loving proposal you made. I'm flattered—and grateful.

But you may not want to marry me after I tell you something I want you to hear from me and from no one else.

Here the handwriting became somewhat less legible. As if she were reluctant to go on—or at least undecided as to whether to go on.

I told you there was no love or lovemaking between me and Al. That is the truth. But I created the impression that you were my one and only partner. That is not true.

While I was with you, I was having affairs with Jack, Lou, and Marty, your three execs. It pains me even to read this as I write it. I honestly didn't know which one of you four was my child's father. I notified each of you about my condition. At Al's wake I made a separate appointment with each of you.

I was desperate. I needed money for me and the child. It wasn't that Al had left me—us—penniless; I wanted enough so we'd never have to be concerned about financial security. The other three were married. What I wanted from them was financial support—not marriage.

As I talked to each of them I fabricated office scuttlebutt that hinted that they were guilty of some banking crime. It was sheer blackmail on my part.

Not only did I strike out on the crime charge, but I learned that two of them are incapable of fathering a child. And the third had no reason to think he was the father.

But one thing may be of immediate importance. In bluffing my way to blackmail, I accused Jack Fradet of financial skullduggery—to provide a golden parachute for himself if or when he was let go. That charge seemed to touch a raw nerve. He looked like he wanted to kill me on the spot. So I backed off, more in fear than anything else. Then he calmed down. Regardless, I think I got close to a major problem for the bank and for you.

I feel better now that I've told you; I know you'll be able to handle it—

"Of course . . ." Adams interrupted the priest's reading. "I couldn't understand why we were showing such a profit. But he wasn't building a golden parachute. No, more than likely he was creating a false sense of security: he was paving the way for a takeover."

Father Tully nodded, and returned to the letter.

> Any other secret I may have is mine alone. Just please trust that there is no other problem that will interfere with the happiness of our marriage—that is, if you still want me.
>
> None of you four knew about the others. There is always the possibility that they will learn. That's why I wanted you to hear it from me.
>
> I await your response.
>
> With love,
Barbara

Oh, my! Father Tully had suspected something was going on between Barbara and the executives, but—oh, my!

He puzzled over her statement, *Any other secret I may have is mine alone.* One would think that after the first momentous secret, there couldn't be too many more. Evidently, the final secret seemingly was not of a nature liable to disrupt an otherwise happy marriage.

Father Tully could not know what only Joyce Hunter's husband and daughter knew—that Barbara was a lesbian.

"Would you?" the priest asked. "Would you have married Barbara knowing what is in this letter?"

Adams blinked several times as if returning from profound abstraction. "Would I have married her? Of course. She was carrying my child. I am not without sin. Who is?"

Silence.

"I am grateful to you, Father," Adams said finally, wearily. "You and you alone stopped me from doing something foolish and wrong. How did you know . . . ? How did you know what I was about to do? How did you know where I was?"

Tully pondered the questions. All that was on his mind, all that had come to him in an extended blinding flash was not yet coordinated to the point where he could explain it logically.

But he would try to address Adams's questions. "The police were working on the theory that if they found the father of Barbara's child, they would also have her killer—the idea being that the father didn't want the baby, so he killed both mother and child.

"But when you claimed that you were the father and also claimed that you hadn't killed Barbara, I believed you were telling the truth. That destroyed the hypothesis that the father of the child had killed its mother. As good a theory as that was in providing a motive for the killing, since you are the father and you did not kill Barbara, there had to be another motive for her murder.

"Then you told me you had just received a letter from her. You said you'd call me right back. When you didn't, I called you. Your secretary said you'd left your office.

"Why would you have done that? Why hadn't you returned the call? It had to have something to do with that letter. Barbara had to have written something that greatly disturbed you—enough to force you to some sort of action. Maybe she guessed who her killer would be? Whatever, it was something cataclysmic, I was sure of that.

"I called Sergeant Mangiapane and then I got here as fast as I could."

The priest had Adams's attention. "But how did you know where to find me? If you had been a minute or two later, I would have done the most foolhardy thing in my entire life."

"That was more luck than anything. I was looking on your desk for Barbara's letter when I spotted the word you had written on a scrap of paper."

"'Judas'?"

"Yes—Judas. An odd word to scribble. But it told me you were after someone you felt had betrayed you. I recalled what you had told me at your banquet: how your bank was not one of the conglomerates, but that the big banks were always out looking for smaller banks to devour.

"You were dedicated to keeping the bank financially alive and well. Yours is a family bank and you are dedicated to keeping it that way. You even belong to the Independent Bankers Association to join with other independents who want to avoid forced mergers.

"I knew from talking to Jack Fradet and others at your dinner that his job as comptroller of this bank is, among other things, to gather information and to assess the financial status of the bank. If he gave you the wrong information, misinformed you, the bank could be weakened—a ready victim for a takeover.

"He's the one who could best play the traitor. You went looking for him. I went looking for you."

Adams nodded slowly. "When I read in Barbara's letter about Fradet's reaction to her bluff, everything fell into place. I had thought the bank was having some extraordinary good fortune. That misinformation led us into one mode of business while we should actually have been going in the opposite direction. He deliberately set us up for disaster.

"After I read her letter I immediately checked the books. Now that I was looking for it and knew what to look for, I saw what Jack had done. I could have killed him!" He shook his head sadly. "I almost did."

"And this gives the police a different motive for Barbara's murder," said Father Tully. "She died not because she was carrying the killer's child, but because the murderer believed—falsely—that Barbara Ulrich was onto his game."

"Now . . . if only they can prove it," Adams said.

"What's going on here?" A demanding Zoo Tully stood in the doorway.

His brother looked up brightly. "Have we got some stories to tell you!"

Twenty-Six

Mᴏʀᴇ ᴛʜᴀɴ ʜᴇ ᴄᴏᴜʟᴅ ᴇxᴘʀᴇss, Father Tully deeply appreciated this farewell dinner.

This was by no means his first send-off celebration. In his twenty years as, in effect, a missionary priest, he had periodically been transferred from parish to parish.

Such priestly passages could prove financially rewarding, as soon-to-be-former parishioners sponsored a party at which gifts were given. But congregations in parishes serviced by a Josephite priest usually could afford only gifts of prayer and affection—actually sufficient for just about any truly dedicated priest.

This evening's leave-taking was especially significant because the participants were those with whom Father Tully had bonded to varying degrees in his brief stay in Detroit.

There was Father Koesler, back from vacation and eager to get back to the helm of his parish. Inspector Koznicki and his wife, Wanda, were the hosts. Rounding out the company was Lieutenant Tully—the brother who had become a brother—and Anne Marie, who was all a real sister should be.

The dinner bore Wanda's hallmark: good plain food prepared and served with love. As the clambakers in *Carousel* sang, "The vittles we et were good, you bet/The company was the same." Throughout, all joined in the conversation, which was, by turns, warm, witty, thoughtful, and stimulating.

When eventually the plates were empty, still no one made a move to leave the table, which was being cleared by Wanda and Anne Marie, assisted by the lumbering Walt Koznicki. Dessert and coffee were coming up.

Father Koesler had been surprised, indeed amazed, that his stand-in had been involved in a murder investigation. Was such clerical assistance in police work, he wondered, endemic to St. Joe's? Or was it just to a Koesler pastorate?

It must, he decided, be the latter. For in succeeding parishes, Father Koesler had been involved in this sort of thing almost as an annual adventure. And here was Father Zachary Tully at a Koesler parish for only a few days and, *voilà!* in a mystery up to his collar.

So much had been going on with Tom Adams and Jack Fradet and the Adams Bank people, as well as with the police and the prosecutor's office, that Koesler had a lot of lingering questions. With the table clearing causing a temporary lull in the conversation, he was finally able to get a question in. "What puzzles me most about all this excitement that's been going on in my absence is this business of equating Mrs. Ulrich's killer with the father of the child. I thought that a pretty good motive—"

"And in the light of that—" Father Tully interrupted.

"Yes," Koesler plowed on, "in the light of that, why would you reject that theory simply because Mr. Adams admitted that he was the child's father, but claimed not to have killed the mother? Why in the world did you believe him? True, he acknowledged paternity . . . but wouldn't most criminals deny the major crimes they commit while admitting the minor ones? I know you were eventually proven correct. But what—a lucky guess? Blind trust in Mr. Adams?"

Father Tully looked as if he'd hit a home run in Tiger Stadium on his birthday. "Thank you for finally asking that question, Father Koesler. I've been dying to explain. But I'd like to explain it in the form of a game."

"Really!" Lieutenant Tully protested, all the while smiling at his brother.

"Humor me," Father Tully said. "I've got the perfect cast of characters for this game right here and now. Playing against each other will be Father Koesler and my brother.

"Now, I'm going to tell you a story. Neither of you may interrupt me. Hear me out and then tell me the identity of the rich man."

By this time the dessert and coffee had been served.

"Okay," Father Tully commenced, after first taking a sip of coffee. "The rich man in this story is also very powerful. What separates him from most other rich and powerful men is his love of God. He religiously kept the first half of the great commandment to love the Lord God with all his strength and with all his mind and heart. He wasn't always strong on the second part of the commandment—that being to love all others in like manner. But he was outstanding in his love of God. It was a love that could prove costly to him. But he would meet that cost to maintain, demonstrate, and prove this love of God."

Zoo was smiling. Koesler was not.

"In the course of giving himself generously to God, he angered his wife. Every chance she got she scolded him because he was, in her eyes, making a fool of himself for his God.

"The result was not pleasant for him—or for either of them, for that matter. The man was forced to choose between getting respect from his wife or giving to God. Loving God as he did, the man had no real choice—and his wife had no chance at all: she was cast aside.

"Now, enter into the rich man's life a woman of outstanding beauty. In addition, she was extremely effective in the art of seduction. After shedding his wife, the rich man had a definite gap in his life. He filled that gap with the very willing, beautiful woman.

"The fact that the woman was married to a man in the service of the rich man made no difference: passion was the undisputed winner. As a matter of fact, the married man himself was so dedicated to the rich man's service that he had no time for his own wife.

"Then the wife became pregnant. The rich man had to be the father. Her husband had not had relations with her for months.

"The rich man tried to get the married man and his wife back together. But the married man would have none of it."

Now Father Koesler was smiling. Good, thought Father Tully; both his brother and Koesler had solved the mystery at exactly the proper time for each.

"Now the rich man managed to place the married man in harm's way. And in that place of peril, the married man was killed."

"Now," Father Tully concluded, "who is the rich man?"

"David," said Father Koesler.

"David! Who the hell is David?" exclaimed Zoo. "The rich man is Tom Adams!"

"He's both," Father Tully said.

"Both!" Koesler and Zoo said simultaneously.

"Father Koesler is talking about King David—in the Old Testament," Father Tully explained, mostly for his brother's benefit. "He fits perfectly the description of the rich man in my story. He loves God totally. In a ceremony welcoming the Ark of the Covenant into Jerusalem, King David programs a massive celebration, during which, as the Bible says, David, nearly naked, 'dances with abandon before the Lord.'

"His wife, Michal, 'despised him in her heart.' When David gets home, Michal makes fun of his behavior in showing his love of God so completely. So David dumps Michal.

"Compare that to Tom Adams, whose generosity to the Church is his way of showing his love of God. His wife gets angry with him for giving away so much money. So he divorces his wife.

"Later, when Israel is at war, David is taking an evening stroll on the roof of his palace. On the roof of a nearby home, an outstandingly beautiful woman named Bathsheba is bathing. She doesn't seem to be a woman of much reserve.

"When her husband, Uriah, is off at war, Bathsheba and David get it on, as I believe they say nowadays. Bathsheba finds herself pregnant. Uriah can't be the father; he hasn't been home in months.

"David calls Uriah back from the battle lines, gets him drunk and tells him to go home, that his wife misses him. But keeping faith with his comrades in arms still in the trenches, Uriah instead spends the night on the cold, hard floor of David's palace.

"Since David cannot claim that Uriah sired the child his wife will give birth to, David tells his general to put Uriah in the forefront of the battle and leave him there to die.

"Which is exactly what happens.

"Now, back to Tom Adams. Tom is not a king, of course, but he *is* wealthy and powerful. And, like David, Tom loves God. And because of that love, he is very generous. David was exuberant in welcoming the ark into Jerusalem. In his place I think Tom would do the same. It's just that three millennia later it's a different era. Nowadays one doesn't dance before the Ark; one sends money. And Tom certainly sends money; the Josephites can testify to that.

"David's devotion is mocked by his wife, Michal. Tom's generosity is mocked by his wife, Mickey. Each man discards his wife.

"David is seduced by Bathsheba. Tom is seduced by Barbara. Both women are married to men each of whom is singularly devoted to his chief. Bathsheba and Barbara each become pregnant. The time factor makes it impossible for each husband to be the father.

"David tries to get Uriah drunk and send him home where his wife will seduce him and then claim he is the child's father. Nancy Groggins told me that Al Ulrich told her that Tom tried to get him and Barbara back together again. Al took that attempt as evidence of his idolized boss's effort to patch up the marriage. Whereas, in reality, Tom was trying the same trick that David tried. Both David and Tom failed.

"By the way, have you noticed the similarity of names? Barbara-Bathsheba; Ulrich-Uriah; Mickey-Michal. Purely a coincidence, I suppose.

"Anyway," Father Tully continued before anyone could reply, "David, being commander-in-chief as it were, then ordered that Uriah be placed in the front ranks of the battle and left there to be killed. In this, David was successful.

"The evening of the award dinner Tom told me he was leaning toward naming Nancy Groggins manager of the new branch in the risky neighborhood. Later that evening, Barbara passed notes to the foursome, announcing her pregnancy. The next day, Tom announced that Al would be the manager. Tom's intention was the same as David's.

"I'm sure that on the part of both Tom and King David there was remorse that their evil plot worked. Still, for their purposes, it had all been worthwhile.

"David married Bathsheba. Tom was about to marry Barbara. Bathsheba's child became desperately ill. David did all he could for the child, but it died as punishment for David's sin.

"And all this by way of explaining why I was certain, when Tom told me he was the father of Barbara's child but that he had not killed her, that he was telling the truth. The minute he said that, all the pieces fell into place: I saw the striking similarities between King David and Tom."

"Do you mean," asked Father Koesler, "that Tom Adams was consciously imitating David?"

"No, I don't think so. But with Tom Adams we are dealing with a person who makes the Bible his guide in life. Let me give you an example: Tom knew I was in the process of building a church for my people in Dallas. He wanted to make up what was lacking in our building fund. He gave me a blank check."

"A blank check!" Father Koesler had never seen one.

"You know why? Because he was identifying with the Good Samaritan," Father Tully explained.

"My God, he's right," Koesler reflected. "In effect, that's what the

Good Samaritan did: he promised to reimburse the innkeeper for whatever additional expense was needed to take care of the injured man. A blank check . . ."

"The man is amazing," said Father Tully. "I can't think of anyone who tries harder to live out what he's learned from his Bible.

"But I doubt that Tom was conscious of how closely he was paralleling the actions of King David. If he had been aware, I'm sure that, being the good man that he is, he would have pulled up short, confessed his sin, and tried to make amends. Even though those Bible stories are so real to Tom that he can fall into living them without even realizing what he's doing, had he recognized the parallel, he would have reflected on David's sin and thus, by extension, on his own.

"And that, finally, is why I believed Tom when he said he fathered the child but didn't murder the wife. He was ready to do everything King David did. David married the mother and did his best to care for the child.

"I believed Tom Adams when he said he had proposed to Barbara Ulrich. He was going to do more than just support her financially and provide for their child; he was going to take care of Barbara and help nurture their child. So . . . if Tom didn't murder Barbara Ulrich, someone else had to have done it. Enter the police." Father Tully made a sweeping "ta-da" gesture in the direction of his brother.

"It wasn't that hard," Zoo demurred. "By the time I got to Fradet's office, the case was almost on a platter. The technicians had already come up with some interesting prints and we wanted to try for a match. We were just getting to that phase when you came up with Adams and Fradet.

"We were going to check everybody's prints. Now, we had to book Adams on a charge of assault, and we wanted Fradet to sign a complaint. While we had them we wanted to print them both. Adams didn't make much fuss. By that time he was almost a zombie. Fradet objected. Then I told him we'd picked up some prints at the crime scene. I said that what we were doing was as much to eliminate suspects as to implicate anybody. With that, he agreed.

"The bottom line was, he matched."

"Then why did he agree?" Koesler asked.

"He was sure he hadn't left any incriminating prints. He knew he'd been in the apartment plenty of times and his prints were all over. But he wore gloves when he shot Mrs. Ulrich. So he knew he'd left no prints on the gun or anything else that could link him to her death. And of course he was hoping that everyone would take it for granted that she had committed suicide."

"But the match?" Koesler asked.

Zoo smiled. "He forgot what lots of killers forget: he wasn't wearing gloves when he loaded the gun."

Several of his listeners gasped.

"We were able to get a couple of well-formed prints on the casings that were a perfect match with Fradet."

"So," Father Tully said, "what I did was nice as far as a game goes, but it wasn't so terribly important." Again he pointed to his brother: "Good, sound police work solved the crime."

"Don't be so hard on yourself, brother," Zoo said. "You saved Fradet's life. And you probably saved Adams's life in the bargain. If he had pulled that trigger, he'd probably have kissed his freedom good-bye—for life."

"Which brings up: what about Adams?" Anne Marie asked.

"We have booked him on an assault charge," Koznicki said. "It is a misdemeanor. He is free on his own recognizance. He may be given probation. More than likely his attorney will ask that he be taken under deferred sentencing for one year. If he is clean for that period, the case is dismissed and he will not have a record."

"We can't have people walking around waving loaded guns," Zoo said. "But what Walt just explained is the next best thing to giving Adams a medal. Adams was just a hair from being charged with a felony. The prosecutor considered Adams's clean record and the murder Fradet is charged with."

"It's kind of interesting," Anne Marie mused. "It seems that Tom Adams was going to kill Jack Fradet, not because he'd had an affair with Barbara Ulrich, but because of his treachery to Adams Bank and Trust. I wonder if he had any inkling as he held that gun on Fradet that Fradet had murdered Mrs. Ulrich."

"I don't think Tom Adams was even thinking about her just then," said Father Tully. "But it is ironic. We have to assume that Fradet figured that normally everybody was too wrapped up in their own affairs to pay any real attention to company scuttle butt. So there was little or no chance that his treachery would be discovered before the situation reached the actual takeover point.

"But Barbara Ulrich was something else. We know from her letter to Mr. Adams that she taxed Fradet with the alleged rumors. Presumably, he figured she was not only capable of further digging, but that she was most apt to follow up. She and she alone, seemingly, had picked up on the rumors and was starting to put two and two together.

"Fradet didn't dare risk that. The bottom line was, Barbara Ulrich had to go . . . and as soon as possible. So he killed her," Father Tully summed up in the manner of a prosecuting attorney.

"What's going to happen to the bank?" Wanda walked around the table refilling coffee cups. "Has that horrid Fradet man ruined Adams's bank?"

"He came close," Father Tully said. "But all this publicity, especially about the sweetheart deals that were promised Fradet after the takeover, seems to be making the monster bank back off. That kind of notoriety they don't need. As hard as Tom Adams has been working to bail out his bank, it's a wonder he's been able to take such good care of Mrs. Fradet. At the end, she was about as good a friend as Barbara Ulrich had. And Mr. Adams is grateful to her as well as sorry for her—after all, it's not Marilyn Fradet's fault that her husband is such a selfish traitor."

"From all this," Koznicki said, "it looks as if Tom Adams may have to replace every one of his executive vice presidents."

"Well," Father Tully said, "Fradet is gone. Of the other two, Martin Whitston is the only one with even a slim chance of survival."

"Funny," Zoo said to his brother, "about your theory that one or all of the execs might've put out a contract on Al Ulrich: Nothing came of that, even though it was plausible as theories go. But they *were* involved: each of them was having an affair with the Ulrich woman and even though they weren't connected in any actual conspiracy, they unknowingly went along with Fradet's plot to undermine Adams Bank."

Father Tully pushed himself back from the table, a delighted smile playing about his lips. He turned to Father Koesler. "Is this how it is for you, Bob? You get drawn into an investigation and one thing after another falls into the religious arena until eventually it all gels in your mind . . . and you get emotionally high?"

Father Koesler smiled in return. Actually he almost laughed out loud. "That's about the way it is, Zack. I can only hope that you took my turn this year.

"But look: all we've talked about is the investigation. This is a farewell party for Father Tully, who now returns to a far-off land known as Dallas. Forgetting about the investigation for now, did you enjoy your time at Old St. Joe's? And are you coming back to stay, perhaps?"

"I enjoyed everything about this trip—the parish, Mary O'Connor, the Koznickis"—he bowed toward his hosts—"you, the thrill of the case—and very much mostly my new family—my brother and my sister. I've still got some thinking and praying to do. All I can tell you is that I'm close to a decision. But"—he smiled—"it would be premature to say which way I'm leaning."

"I can think of a parish here that would welcome you with open arms," said Koesler.

"Oh? Which one?"

"Mine. Old St. Joseph's. I retire next year."

The announcement caught all of them by surprise. The resultant gasps segued into a barrage of questions.

"It's my turn to take off the harness," Koesler said simply.

"But what will you do?" asked Walt Koznicki with genuine concern.

Koesler shrugged. "There are lots and lots of things to do. I haven't begun to discover all the possibilities. One thing for sure: I won't be involved in any murder investigations."

The inspector laughed. "You say that every year."

"Well then," Koesler said, "there's one more thing that is certain sure." He paused. "You—any of you—all of you, will always be welcome to visit me wherever I am and share a cup of coffee with me." His smile was as broad as it could be.

His listeners were in varying states of shock.

Zoo spoke for them all. "You don't suppose he's getting his own joke!"

But Father Koesler just kept on smiling.